BLACK JADE

A Daiyu Wu Mystery

Gloria Oliver

Black Jade

A Daiyu Wu Mystery - Book 1

All rights reserved.

Cover Art and Design © **Charles Bernard**

Editing by **Serenity Editing Services**

Dimension Palace Publishing

ISBN: 978-1-7339511-6-6 (Print/Trade)
ISBN: 978-1-7339511-7-3(Electronic/Multiple Formats)
ISBN: 978-1-739511-8-0 (Electronic/Epub)

Fan Icon by **Eucalup** from the Noun Project
Fonts Grado Gradoo NF and Ricks American NF by **Nick Curtis**

DEDICATION

This book is dedicated to Roxanne Longstreet Conrad, AKA Rachel Caine. Your passion and fertile imagination will be sorely missed. Thank you for all the marvelous adventures. You give us all something to aspire to.

Novels:
Alien Redemption (SF)
Cross-eyed Dragon Troubles (YA Fantasy)
In the Service of Samurai (YA Fantasy))
Inner Demons (Urban Fantasy)
Jewel of the Gods (Fantasy)
The Price of Mercy (Fantasy)
Vassal of El (Fantasy)
Willing Sacrifice (YA Fantasy)

Novelettes:
Charity and Sacrifice

Has Short Stories in the following Anthologies:
Tales From a Lone Star
A Lone Star in the Sky
Ladies of Trade Town
A Time To ... Volume 2
Ripple Effect
The Four Bubbas of the Apocalypse
Houston: We've Got Bubbas
The Best of the Bubbas of the Apocalypse
Flush Fiction

CHAPTER 1

"Jacques, I need you!"

My copy of the *Dallas Morning News* twirled to the floor as I jumped to my feet. The rare emotions in the summons made my pulse race. It wasn't often that my companion felt either surprise or excitement, and I'd just heard both. "What is it, Dai?"

"Can you smell it?"

Daiyu was the only child of the immigrant Wu family. She was also the principal reason for the continued success of White Laundry. My companion wasn't what anyone would expect. She was more of a 'doll' than most women called by the moniker could ever hope to be. A mere four foot eight, she was a tiny thing—but assuming that was *all* she was would be a grave mistake.

"Lye? Soap?" I had no idea how anyone could smell anything else in here.

Dai half-turned on her stool, her dainty gloved hands on her lap. "Garlic, Jacques. I smell *burned* garlic."

Her straight black hair fell to just above her shoulders. It was untouched by the finger waves currently in fashion, so there was nothing to detract from its silky fall around her heart-shaped face and almond eyes. Her skin was the color of

1

yellowed porcelain, but the bad lighting in the crowded work area made it seem darker, like transparent yellow amber. A line of perspiration trailed down her long neck, the only sign that she was bothered by the laundry's oppressive humidity. Her opaque teashade glasses sat ignored at their assigned spot on the worktable, along with the chemicals and powders she mixed for the family business. Her meticulous efforts and her enhanced sense of smell gave her family's company an edge over the few remaining Chinese laundries in town, and placed them at an even more significant advantage over the American ones. The glasses themselves were more to ease other people's discomfort than her own. She did not need them. Dai had been blind from birth, her unseeing eyes almost silver and possessing no pupils. Most thought the sight of them disturbing. To me, they were anything but.

"Do you see any garments colored bright green?" Dai's excitement rebounded in every word.

I was used to being her eyes. It was the main argument she'd used to win her parents' permission to keep my then seven-year-old self, whom she discovered following her at Dallas City Park. She'd been only eight, her mind already sharp and looking to the future.

"Yes. It's a ballgown by the looks of it. It's still hanging with the recent arrivals. Should I fetch it for you?"

"No, don't!" Dai shook her head. "Not without first donning gloves. No one should let that fabric touch their bare skin."

My eyebrow rose. What were we about to get into?

As commanded, I found a thick pair of workmen's gloves and fetched the gown. It was an old-fashioned evening dress, all gossamer and lace. Not something typically found in Texas—more like New York or London, and at least thirty years ago, at that. I hung it nearby, making sure it wouldn't accidentally touch Dai.

"That's the one. Surely you can smell it now, can't you, Jacques?"

"I'm sorry, Dai, I can't. You know my nose is nothing

compared to yours." I smelled no garlic and had no inkling why that would be a concern, or how it had led her to the conclusion that the gown's color would be green.

A sharp bark near Dai's feet drew our attention as her second companion left the comfort of his pillow. Another mongrel she'd picked up off the street, and as loyal as myself. At a guess, I figured him to be a Scottish Terrier and Pomeranian mix. His owner had abandoned him as a pup in the streets as money became scarce everywhere.

"No, Prince Razor, you mustn't get near it. Sit."

He did as she asked. Prince set his small paws neatly before him, and his expressive brown eyes watched her every move.

"Jacques, is there a ticket pinned to it?"

I checked. There was one, although... "It's blank, but stamped paid."

"Really? How curious." The timbre of excitement in her voice grew. "Here, run this swab over the dress. Hold your breath while you do it, just in case."

Still wondering what this could be about—and growing more nervous about it by the moment—I ran the swab down the length of the gown, then deposited it into the test tube she held. "What now?"

She gave me a teasing, coy smile. "Now we go to the *lab*." With a spring in her step, Dai grabbed her teashade glasses and led the way, knowing every nook and cranny of the establishment. Prince scouted ahead, in search of any errant mice who dared be in the vicinity. We passed several of the Chinese workers at the vats. They stared as we walked past, but as usual, said nothing. A superstitious lot, many carried charms with pictures of gourds, long believed to be capable of warding off or protecting the bearer against evil. The workers touched them whenever she drew near—despite the fact they owed her. If not for Dai, there might not be a business to employ them or homes purchased in their names so they could stay in the country. But she was both blind and female and had been allowed to live and thrive. Expectations and traditions practiced even in these modern times would have called for

Dai's death when she was born—particularly since she was female and the family had no male heir. Even though from the time of Confucius the blind were supported in court as musicians, her parent's social class would not allow them to keep a child with such reduced status. But Dai's *mŭqīn* had lost all her other children before they were born, and hadn't been able to stomach the thought of giving up the one who'd made it through.

Going against convention and escalating social pressure were two reasons her family had abandoned all they knew, including their property and lofty status, to come to the land of the free. It was a fact they never spoke of, but one Dai never forgot. Yet even those who came to America to seek freedom from the class restrictions in their country still viewed her continued existence with fear. That she would not be shackled by her blindness somehow made her an abomination and therefore evil.

Dai's "lab" was located in a small corner of the cellar, which housed the bottom section of the laundry's large vats and pipes. It was damp and dark—not that the latter made any difference to her. But it kept others out, giving her privacy for what most considered unladylike pursuits. A hanging bulb had been added for my benefit, along with a hatch to make the room light-proof.

Prince dived under the table to keep watch back the way we'd come.

"I believe I have everything we'll require." Her hands ran over the small shelves in the corner, grabbing beakers, an oil lamp, and glass tubing.

"Required for what?" I mopped at my sweating brow.

"Why, to test for arsenic. What else?"

Arsenic? She thought the dress had poison on it? "Why would you ever think such a thing, Dai?"

"Please, Jacques—you read me an article on this just last year. Don't you remember?" She set a stopper in a flask and attached a glass tube to a funnel, which she then placed through one of the two holes on the stopper.

"My memory is far inferior to yours. As you so often enjoy reminding me."

"Why, yes, you're right. I do rather like that." She flashed me an impish grin. "But we digress. You see, arsenic was used before the turn of the century to create the color green in fabrics. But manufacturers weren't always conscientious about the amounts used in their dyes. Fatal cases were rare, but many consumers suffered health issues because of long-term exposure. Workers dyeing the textiles at the factories even more so."

More tubing led to a U-shaped vessel, which continued to another lengthy stretch of glass pipe clamped over the oil container of the lantern. "What is all this for?"

"Depending on its current oxidation, arsenic is odorless and, at times, colorless. So detecting it proved difficult for many years, until a brilliant man came up with the Marsh test. An ingenious and effective method of determining the amount of arsenic in the flesh, body fluids, and more." She ran her hands gingerly over the apparatus she'd made, double-checking her work. "If you'll place the swab into the beaker, I'll add the zinc and acid. By heating the mixture, we will further oxidize the arsine in the arsenic.

"Once that happens, please hold the ceramic bowl over the ensuing vapor. Then we shall see what we shall see."

Dai added the ingredients to the waiting flask. As the chemicals reacted with one another, I held the bowl above it. After that, applying heat to the container caused a silvery-black stain to appear.

"Did it stain?" she asked.

"Most definitely." It was black, dark as death.

Dai nodded as if she had expected nothing else. "The color and density of the stain are used to pinpoint the concentration of arsenic present. Unfortunately, it's not something I've dabbled in, so I've no data to compare it against. The pathologist should have access to a copy of Marsh's guide."

Prince Razor barked in agreement. Dai's excitement was becoming contagious.

"We must find out which of our employees handled the dress and have them wash off any residue right away. Also, have them turn the fans on high. We'll want to cycle the air as much as possible. Arsenic can convert to a gas, and since I detected the scent of a reaction, it's likely some got released upstairs. We were lucky a bit of the arsenic wasn't fully oxidized, so it reacted to the heat and the humidity here. Otherwise, we would have never known something was amiss. Whoever left the gown didn't count on Texas temperatures."

She paused for a long moment. I said nothing, still trying to digest all she'd just told me. Then she added, "Before that, please bag the bowl and the dress, as we must bring them with us. We're going on a field trip!"

"A field trip? Where to?"

"Why, to see the justice of the peace, Jacques! Where else?"

CHAPTER 2

In a whirlwind, Dai cleaned up her space. She then scooped up Prince Razor and headed upstairs, leaving me with no straightforward explanation of what we were about to embark on. I took care to bag the bowl and the dress as instructed, and followed her.

After a few questions at the front of the store, I determined it had been Mei Ling who'd hung the gown in the new arrivals rack. She'd found it hanging on the front door, with a dollar bill pinned on the inside, out of sight, to pay for the service—a very odd way of leaving something to be laundered. I wondered what Dai would make of it.

Above the main floor of the laundry were the company offices, a break room with a compact kitchen for the employees, and restrooms. Evaporative air coolers brought the temperature down to more tolerable levels. There was also a private chamber where Dai or her mother might freshen up or change after delving into the heat and the humidity downstairs. Having carried a change of clothes and a hand towel, I was soon back to a more presentable state.

Dai exited wearing a silk afternoon dress in light blue, with puffed sleeves and a belted waist, as well as white day gloves trimmed with lace. A wide-brimmed white hat with blue trim would deflect notice of her silver eyes and foreign heritage, even as it got hinted at with a Chinese collar on the frock rather than the typical large ones popular at the moment. Prince's dog collar matched Dai's colors.

Unlike Prince, I wasn't made to coordinate; I was more than happy in my double-breasted light gray chauffeur's uniform.

With our wrapped parcels in hand, we descended to the back of the building where our car—a 1930 Ford Model A Town Sedan, in brown and black—waited for us. The car sat to the side, out of the way of the loading dock. I settled the packages in the trunk that was attached to the rear of the vehicle, then helped Dai into the back seat. I drew the curtains over the windows to afford her some privacy; sadly, the view of the city and the lovely drive from Oak Cliff were always lost to her.

"So, where are we headed?"

"The Old Red Courthouse, if you please. South Houston Street."

Did she really intend to contact the justice of the peace?

A soft chuckle echoed from the back. "I can hear the wheels in your head spinning, Jacques. Should I take pity on you? Or make you wait to find out what I'm up to?"

A glance in the angled side peep mirror showed her reclining, her expression a contented cat's. "Whichever you deem the most appropriate will be fine, Dai." The Ford rattled to life, its twenty-four-horsepower engine eager to roll out onto the street.

"Jacques, sometimes you aren't any fun at all." She pulled a small fan from her clutch and snapped it open with a flick of her wrist.

"As you say." I tried to hide a grin as we merged into traffic.

She tapped her window with her fan, vying for my attention. "We're going to see the justice in the hopes of finding a body."

"A body? Why would we be looking for a body? And why

would the justice have one?" What mad errand was she sending us on?

Dai ignored my first two questions, only answering the third. "In Texas, unlike most other states, the duties of the coroner are entrusted to the justice of the peace. With any luck, he called in a doctor to examine the deceased before making a pronouncement. Better still if the judge requested an autopsy."

My eyebrow rose, wondering where the devil she'd picked up that bit of information. She was like a sponge where facts were concerned. It always amazed me what details she could glean that I did not, despite my being ever at her side. Perhaps the fact that she was blind—and thus not distracted by visual input—was responsible, but I doubted it.

I did wonder why she decided not to enlighten me on the reason she thought there was a body involved. Still, I recalled how dark the stain from the Marsh test was. Might that be why she believed this was an indication of foul play?

Traffic lumbered along, heavy even in late mid-morning. Though you might still spot the occasional horse-drawn cart or carriage, it was steel horses that ruled the roads of Dallas. The smell of their exhaust thickened the sultry air. But it was the scent of progress, of the future—of a city thriving despite the financial hardships hitting harder elsewhere. Wildcat wells and "black gold" erupting from the ground had people and businesses descending on the town, and they brought jobs and money with them.

The downtown Dallas courthouse reigned over its corner like a medieval castle. Built in 1892, its gray base and red stone walls rose over the site of four previous courthouses. Unlike its predecessors, which had all burned to the ground, the magnificent building looked as if it might easily weather even the worst Texas tornadoes.

With a bit of luck, I was able to park near the primary entrance. I helped Dai from the back, and with my hand tucked at her elbow, steered her toward the building. Prince Razor watched from the rolled-down back window, keeping guard over the car. Using a code we'd come up with as children, I tapped the inside of Dai's arm to make her aware we were about to reach a small set of stairs. Another tap alerted her that we'd reached the first step, warning her to raise her foot to climb it.

In a quiet voice, I described what was before us. It was a duty I'd managed for many years, a way to make my eyes her own. It allowed her to create a mental image of what she couldn't see for herself.

The tall stone, the rounded archway, and the gloom within increased the fanciful impression that we were entering a castle. Once through the large wooden doors with the stained glass lunettes, however, the romantic notion vanished as if it had never been. We'd entered a world of chaos.

Men in business suits mingled with others wearing cowboy hats, jeans, and boots. Texas twangs clashed with genteel accents. Everyone had a purpose, a drive, and they all aimed to get their business done before anyone else.

We stepped into the throng, and I used my body to shield Dai from those too rude to watch where they were going.

After inquiring with a guide in the lobby, I discovered the place we sought was on the second floor. Searching for an elevator or a set of stairs, we followed the crowd looking to obtain or renew permits, lodge claims, or yell out complaints. I'd heard that the courthouse had once flaunted a large cast-iron staircase, but that it was removed years ago to create more office space. The stairs I found were narrow and zig-zagged upward. Still trying to shield Dai as much as possible, I led the way up. Throughout, she said nothing, and I had no time to even glance in her direction. There were too many elbows and arms moving every which way.

Once we were off the second-floor landing, the chaos eased a bit. There appeared to be courtrooms and offices on this level. I steered her to a bench nearby.

"Dai, are you all right?" I kneeled before her, looking for any sign that she'd been hurt. Her cheeks were flushed, but she seemed otherwise unharmed.

"Yes, I'm fine." Her teashade glasses had slipped during the hurried climb up the stairs, and she pushed them further up her nose to set them right. "Just a little more exciting than I was expecting, to be sure."

"Why don't you wait for me here? I can track down the correct office and make inquiries for you."

A hint of a smile came and went. "That's very sweet of you to suggest, but also highly impractical. While I have my proof of residency papers, it wouldn't do to leave a young lady unattended in such a public place."

I felt my neck heating in embarrassment. Of course—she couldn't be left here alone. If Prince Razor were with her, it might not be as worrisome, but I shouldn't forget this was a government office. Anyone here could question her presence once they realized she was a foreigner. The Geary Act had placed even more stringent restrictions on Chinese immigrants, a roundabout way of battling the increasing popularity of opium in several major cities. Illegal residents faced a year of hard labor before deportation, and there were plenty of unscrupulous men who were willing to use the law to destroy others. It was the reason I carried duplicate copies of her residency papers on my person. "My apologies. I should know better."

"Don't worry about it. I know your heart is in the correct place." She rose to her feet, her head tilted at a slight angle. "I think if we go this way, we're likely to find what we're looking for."

As usual, she was right. A corridor to the left led to a series of offices which were cut off from entry by a half door. The sign hanging from the ceiling designated the area as belonging to the justice of the peace.

"Pardon me, sir," Dai said. "We have something of a unique inquiry—I wonder if you might help us?"

The middle-aged man sitting at a desk just beyond the split door, as if guarding the offices beyond, glanced up in surprise. Between her tiny figure, dark glasses, and ribboned hat, I was certain she was a better sight than most of those who sought to talk to him. I filled the space behind her to be sure he was aware of my presence.

"Why, I suppose I could, depending on what it is you want to ask about, miss." He seemed intrigued, studying each of us.

"Thank you." She flashed him a smile. "In carrying out his duties, to whom would the justice turn for medical advice on the recently departed?"

The man's eyebrows rose. "Why in the world would you be wanting to know that?"

His reaction was pretty much what I expected. "Sir, it's a private matter," I said. "But my mistress would appreciate an answer all the same."

"Well, being as I'm the constable in this district, I'm thinking 'private' won't cut the mustard after a question like that one." He stepped closer to the half door, his gaze more piercing than before.

"You must be George Higgins, then. This is your third term as the precinct's constable, I believe?"

The man's jaw dropped. He moved up to the entry. "How would you be knowing that?"

"I have an interest in many things, Mr. Higgins. Being civic-minded is but one of them. It's hard to know whom to turn to if you don't know who your leaders are."

"You're a foreigner!" This close, he finally noticed the color of her skin and the slight tapering of her eyes behind the glasses.

"Yes, I'm afraid so. Despite the fact that I've lived here all but a few months of my twenty-one years. Unfortunately, Thomas J. Geary made sure we wouldn't have the choice, as so many other immigrants do, to become an American citizen."

To my amazement, the constable seemed taken aback by Dai's barrage of information.

"I meant no offense, miss." He held up his hands as if that would support his sincerity. "I just never seen a Chinaman before. It plumb took me by surprise. You don't even have an accent."

Dai tilted her head. "There are a lot fewer Chinese in Dallas than there used to be. Being called the 'Yellow Menace' tends to make us feel unwelcome." She gave him a dimpled smile. "Skin color means nothing to me. Blindness destroys certain barriers."

The constable's face crumpled in on itself. "Dang, girl! Not all of us believe that rot." He threw me a look as if asking for help. "Just give me a reason, and I'll tell you what you want to know."

I could sense Dai metaphorically circling to home in for the kill.

"I expect I have information that would assist in the investigation of a murder. Being a woman and part of the Yellow Peril, I am by law unable to bear witness in court. But as my intelligence is rather technical, I wished to share my findings with whomever the justice goes to for such matters, so they can bring up the scientific evidence we accidentally came across."

The poor man's jaw was hanging again. "Dang! I give. You win!" He shook his head. "Nobody will ever believe any of this, anyway. You'll want to talk to Dr. Aiden Campbell at Baylor Hospital." He shook his head again. "Now git. Go on!"

"Many thanks, Constable."

I sent the man a commiserating look, then steered Dai back the way we'd come.

"That was rather much, wasn't it?"

She barked a laugh. "He's an elected official. When else would I get a chance to give voice to the shackles that bind me and others? As if being blind weren't enough of a handicap."

"Still…"

She gave a small nod. "I'll try to behave myself. I promise. But you have to admit it did the trick, did it not?"

I said nothing, knowing that acknowledging it would only encourage her. Besides, we were almost at the bottom of the stairs. I needed to concentrate on getting her safely past the walls of men moving back and forth below.

CHAPTER 3

When we reached the relative safety of our Town Sedan, Dai brought out a laced fan to cool her face while Prince Razor licked her neck and nuzzled her shoulder. "I'm all right, Prince. Just too many people. The smells and sounds were a little overwhelming. You wouldn't have liked it at all."

Of that, I was sure. 'Razor' would have appeared and ankles and legs felt the bite of his sharp canines at every turn. That was the main reason we had left him behind.

Motoring through part of downtown and Deep Ellum to Junius Street, we reached Baylor Hospital in short order. A white, stately building in the form of an E, it was one of Dallas' progressive leaps regarding health care for the masses. We left the windows open and a small dish of food and water on the floorboards for Prince Razor, who remained in the car—a condition he protested until she gestured for him to be silent.

After carefully taking charge of our packages, I led Dai into the facility to search for Dr. Campbell. While the constable had been effortlessly overwhelmed, I wasn't sure Dai would achieve the same with the pathologist.

A query at reception sent us off to the hospital's laboratory area. Though small, the amount of equipment was impressive. It made Dai's homemade lab in the dark basement of the laundry look like the workings of a child playing pretend. I was glad she couldn't see it.

"Excuse me. We're looking for Dr. Campbell?"

Two of the three technicians working there ignored our presence. The third waved us down the hall without ever taking his attention from his microscope. "Basement. The morgue entry is in Room B301."

Dai took a deep breath as we walked away. "The smells coming from that lab are fascinating, Jacques. We must come back another time. Spend a while there."

Only she would find such a thing interesting. I'd preferred not to take the risk of catching whatever illnesses they might study there.

"Pathology started as the study of diseases, but it's been branching out to encompass a lot more. Since they examine organs, tissue samples, and cells, their objectives have extended to doing autopsies to determine the cause of death. It would be an enthralling line of research."

Dai could do an abundance of things, but even she wouldn't be able to manage either pathological work or performing autopsies, no matter how much she might want to. Not that she ever admitted to having limits.

The basement's hallways were spacious, allowing for multiple people to wheel through at a time. From the signs hanging over several doors, this level appeared to house equipment like x-ray machines or devices used for rehabilitation, and even some operating theaters. I wondered how many patients had been brought here, not realizing they were sharing the floor with the dead.

We entered Room B301 through an innocuous enough door. The tiny office area had a desk and several clipboards on hooks on the wall. Beyond was a set of double doors with small windows. A bit of mist escaped from the bottom of the new entryway. It swirled away as the escaping cooler air met the warmer, more humid atmosphere of the living. The office was empty, so we bravely walked forward into the realm of the recently deceased.

The room beyond was broad. White glared from the walls and the tiled floor at our feet. Metal tables and a wall of refrigerator-type doors with holders for small index cards sat in the back. The odors of strong cleanser and decay tainted the air. Dai removed a lace handkerchief from her clutch to place over her nose. If even *I* found the odors unpleasant, Dai's enhanced sense of smell would make them altogether repulsive.

Harsh lighting brought everything into sharp relief, including the fellow standing over the exposed body of an older woman. I averted my gaze even as I continued to describe what I saw to Dai.

"He's short, blocky, with a rugged face. Close-cropped brown hair." I dared another look, avoiding the cadaver on the table. "He's now frowning at me."

"A man, you say? Curious..." It wasn't a word she used often.

"Who are you? You shouldn't be in here." The person I assumed to be Dr. Campbell grabbed the folded sheet at one end of the autopsy table and threw it over the woman's corpse, hiding it from view. Campbell's frown deepened as he moved in front of the table as if to shield the body from us. I couldn't help but wonder what he thought we'd want it for.

"I'm sure you've heard that often, Dr. Campbell," Dai said. "Even in these modern times, so many are still prejudiced without substance."

The doctor's frown deepened even more, this time peppered with a flicker of confusion. "What do you mean?"

Dai tilted her head. "Oh, I think you know."

The fellow's scowl turned into a glare. "You need to leave. This area is for authorized medical personnel only."

"So, you'd allow a murderer to go free?" Dai's tone was that of an innocent babe's.

"Explain yourselves, or I will throw you out. Bodily, if I have to."

Unasked, I stepped forward and set the packages I'd brought on the nearest metal table. Once I'd unwrapped the gown and the burned bowl, I moved back to Dai's side, leaving the items for Campbell's inspection.

"I've been told you assist the justice of the peace with autopsies on unexplained deaths," Dai said. "After finding that dress and performing a Marsh test on it, it's my conclusion that it was recently used to murder someone by arsenic poisoning."

"The Marsh test... you?" The doctor glanced at the dress and the bowl but had yet to make a move toward them.

"Surely you, of all people, wouldn't form presumptions based purely on appearances."

Aiden Campbell's rugged face grew hard. "You're blind, so I'm basing my statements on facts."

Dai laughed with clear pleasure. "Blunt and to the point. I like that!" Then her expression turned serious. "I knew there was arsenic on that dress the same way I know you're a woman."

A loud gasp echoed through the room. A moment later, my neck grew hot as I realized the sound had come from me.

CHAPTER 4

Dai's elbow jabbed into my ribs, eliciting a different sort of gasp. "Really, Jacques. How rude."

Mortified, I stared at the tiled flooring and wished I were anywhere but here. Between the lab coat and butcher-shop-style apron, there were no curves to hint that Aiden Campbell was a woman rather than a man. Her rough-looking face and close-cropped hair didn't help either. She wasn't even wearing a dress or a skirt, but brown dress pants and flat-bottomed shoes. Nothing about her was feminine—not even her fierce ice-blue eyes.

"I don't keep my gender secret." Campbell was frowning again but for different a reason. "Why should I? It has nothing to do with how well I can or can't do my job."

Even I knew that's not how things work in our society. Though with Campbell's looks, she might have had it easier than women who appeared more girlish. In this field of study, anyway.

"The same applies to me," Dai said. "Please—examine what we've brought and then make your decision on whether we were right to intrude."

Campbell appeared to ponder the matter a moment longer before coming to a decision. "I will." The doctor donned a fresh pair of medical gloves and inspected the dress. Soon after, she took a sample, then turned back to us with an eyebrow raised high. "I'll run my own test, and then we can compare the samples against the burn chart." She frowned at us again. "But you can't stay here. Come out to the office section and wait there."

The only thing separating us from this room and the small office area was a set of double doors that didn't even lock. What difference did five feet make? But we were in her domain, and so would follow her rules. "As you wish, doctor."

Campbell didn't leave until I escorted Dai to the outer office. Even then, she hesitated at the door before finally exiting with the sample. I could feel her frown still pointed at us through the door. What an odd woman.

"Dai, how did you know?" I kept my question to a whisper, not wanting to offend the doctor again if she was still within hearing distance.

"That she is a woman?"

I squeezed her hand, indicating a 'yes.'

"I will admit I almost missed it. If the room had not been as chill or the decomposition more active, I would have never picked up on it. It's the doctor's time of the month."

I had to dig around in my head for a minute before I realized what she meant—the scent of blood. For the third time that day, my neck grew hot. "Oh."

"You did ask. Besides, it's a normal bodily function."

Not at the Wu household, it wasn't. Dai's mother, Lien, silenced any mention of the phenomenon, pretending it did not exist. They hadn't allowed me to see Dai when her womanhood came upon her. I'd been forbidden from her presence without an explanation. How frantic it had made me. I'd thought that first time that she was dying—that I'd be left alone again, set adrift. Her father took pity on me and told me Dai was all right, that she just needed a few days to herself.

Every month after that, they sequestered her in her rooms for several days. This new rule didn't stop Dai from sneaking out of her quarters late at night to make me read to her or come to visit. Finding books about the body and the menstrual cycle were at the top of the list of things to do after her first time. Since I needed to read them to her, I became as well-versed in the process as she was—a secret we kept under wraps better than they did the topic of menstruation.

"I know we just met her, but I have a great feeling about her."

It was unusual for Dai to show interest in anyone. "You do?"

"I do." Her mischievous smile was back.

We didn't have to wait long for the doctor's return. Her heavy, fast steps announced the results more clearly than a shout. Her square face was flushed, her eyes wide. "How? You?"

Campbell shook her head and tromped on to the next room, a bowl and a book in hand.

With an impish smile, Dai nodded for me to lead her onward.

Inside the working area of the morgue, Campbell compared her bowl to ours and then to pictures in the book she brought.

"I am assuming your tests confirmed my findings, Dr. Campbell?"

"Yes. I do not believe it, but yes. There is tetraarsenic hexaoxide in the dress. It would poison someone wearing it by both absorption and inhalation. The concentration here is not fatal, but is still higher than expected, and exposure over time would undoubtedly affect the wearer. Where did you say you found this?" Campbell's ice-blue eyes stared at us as if we'd suddenly grown horns.

"At my family's laundry business," Dai told her. "The garment was left there to erase the evidence. Luckily, I realized what was on it before more people handled it. I didn't know how much poison was there, so I figured it was better to be safe than sorry."

"Most definitely. Even diluted in the washing, it might have clung to other clothes and made people ill. Including your workers." Campbell nodded at us as much to herself, as if at last able to find the square hole for her square peg. "You are to be commended on that point. But what I don't understand is why you thought you should bring this to me, rather than the police?"

Dai frowned, as if she didn't altogether understand the doctor's confusion. "Are you saying you don't have someone here who's died recently? Who might have died of arsenic poisoning?"

Dr. Campbell's brow rose. "No. We do not."

CHAPTER 5

"That's... unexpected." Dai fidgeted with her gloves, her unseeing eyes moving back and forth as if reading an internal ledger. "Don't all bodies come here? Whether or not there'll be an autopsy?"

"No," Dr. Campbell said. "We only get the ones the justice thinks should be investigated further or patients who have died here in the hospital. Each justice has their own preference as to whom they like to consult from the pathologists available in their region and decide whether to even consider a consultation necessary. Otherwise, it is up to the deceased's family to decide which funeral parlor they wish to prepare the body for burial."

Dai sighed. "I'd assumed the case would belong to the justice from District One since my family's business is in that area. Even if he hadn't considered the death suspicious, I'd thought the body would be taken to the same location as those that are. Jacques, I hope you're taking notes. These types of details are hard enough to find."

I always kept a small notebook and pencil in one of my pockets, but why she'd want to remember this information was beyond me. Why would we ever require it?

"Dr. Campbell, may I leave this evidence with you? There's

every chance a body might yet turn up, and you'll require these. My line of inquiry will be aimed elsewhere, to make sure the death hasn't already occurred without anyone realizing it was foul play."

The doctor nodded. "Yes, of course. I'll speak to the head nurse and have her keep me apprised of any severe gastric problems, numbness, and other side effects of long-term exposure. If there are any, I'll test the patient for arsenic poisoning. Perhaps we might save them still."

"As you say." Dai dipped her head as if acknowledging the possibility, but not necessarily believing it. "Thank you for your help in this matter, Dr. Campbell. May I contact you again if we run across any more evidence?"

The doctor frowned for a moment then nodded. "I don't see why not. You seem capable and knowledgeable."

Dai gave her a huge smile. "My thoughts about you exactly!"

As I drew one of Dai's rarely used calling cards to give to the doctor, I studied the two women. So different in every way externally, yet their unexpected joy at crossing paths was precisely the same. Kindred spirits in the making, perhaps? It was a sight to behold.

"I do not have a card to give you; my apologies. I don't usually make social calls. But if I could borrow your notebook?" Red splotches dotted the doctor's cheeks as she held her hand out like a shy child. It was rather endearing.

"Please do."

She took the notebook, then turned her back to us as if embarrassed. She wouldn't meet my gaze when she returned it. Her handwriting was neat and tiny, yet another detail that didn't entirely fit.

"It was such a pleasure to meet you, Aiden. I'm looking forward to talking with you again soon."

The doctor blushed at Dai's use of her first name. "Yes, please, uhm…" She looked at the calling card. "Daiyu?"

"Dai, call me Dai. All my friends do."

I tried hard to keep my face from showing any expression,

afraid the doctor might misinterpret it. As far as I knew, aside from Prince and myself, Dai had no other friends. She'd never expressed a want for any. This was a momentous occasion.

"Your friends..." Campbell nodded, a bright smile transforming her bland countenance. "I will, Dai."

The telephone on the desk rang, its heavy tones destroying the amicable atmosphere.

"Excuse me." Dr. Campbell tromped to go answer it.

I touched Dai's elbow, indicating we should leave. With a small sigh, she placed her hand in the crook of my arm, and I led the way out of the morgue.

"What an unexpected find, don't you think, Jacques? We must make sure we don't allow her to slip away from us."

"She seemed as taken with you as you were with her." A smile tugged at my lips. "I doubt she'll let you go."

Dai shook her dainty head. "She's extremely focused. She won't mean to, but unless we make a concerted effort, we would lose her all the same. Medicine comes first."

"Gee, I wonder who else has that kind of determination?"

This earned me a well-placed jab to the ribs. For a blind person, she had impeccable aim.

"Speaking of determination, I know where we're going next." Dai's footsteps picked up speed.

"You do?"

"Yes. Our destination is the Carnegie Library downtown. Hopefully, they keep copies of recent newspapers." The impish smile was back. "It's how we will find our missing body."

CHAPTER 6

While the Old Red Courthouse had looked like a medieval castle, the Carnegie Library, the city's first free library, resembled something from the Roman Empire with its giant columns and squared-off shape. It was a temple of knowledge open to the public, where people could better themselves if they so chose, regardless of their race or social status.

"Prince, don't pout. It might be a public library, but they're still not educated enough to imagine dogs have a place there too." Dai ruffled the dog's fur then gave him a kiss. "You've been really patient, and I appreciate it. Plus, there's no one better to make sure nothing happens to the Ford."

Prince barked once, then lay on his back so she could rub his belly before she went. Dai was adept at twisting us both around her little finger. Not that we'd have it any other way.

I took us inside into a large foyer with arches on thin columns. Some were round, while others were rectangular and decorated with scrollwork. A card catalog sat against a wall, but there was also a counter area with the circulation desk for checking out books, renewing a book you wished to keep longer, or paying late fees. I was well acquainted with the premises and several of the ladies who worked there. Dai, however, had never been here.

"Mr. Haskin! You're early today." A young woman stood from behind the circulation desk, smiling.

"Miss Kuster." I tipped my chauffer's cap in her direction before removing it altogether and tucking it under my arm.

"Who's that with you? She's such a tiny, cute little thing!"

The warmth seemed to leech out of the air beside me. "This is my employer, Miss Daiyu Wu."

"Oh." She leaned forward to get a better look. "Oh!"

The space beside me was freezing. In a clipped tone, Dai said, "If you would direct us to the reservations desk, please? We're in something of a hurry." Icicles were likely to form at any moment.

"Yes. But you're… so why would you…? Um, yes!" Ever more flustered, the young librarian stopped talking and pointed, then realized her mistake and blushed a deep crimson.

"I'll take care of it, Miss Kuster. I know where it is. Thank you." I placed myself between them, turning Dai in the direction we needed to go. Slowly the cold defrosted beside me.

"Tiny. Cute. *Ugh*."

"But you *are*, Dai." Though I expected her response and moved, my side didn't escape unscathed. There would be a bruise there later.

"If it didn't make Mother and Father so happy, there would exist no lace anywhere near my person. Something loose and comfortable, without bits that catch on everything, would be more convenient. Aiden has the right idea there."

I shuddered at the thought. Dai might not see herself, but the rest of us could. Although I was sure she'd look good in almost anything, I loved this best. I would never mention it, though—not if I valued my life.

"Mrs. Lark, good afternoon."

The reservations desk sat toward the back of the library. The true keepers of the knowledge worked there. Mrs. Lark had assisted me many times when I'd been hunting for odd bits of information Dai wanted to know more about.

"It's nice to see you, Mr. Haskin. What puzzle might I help

you unravel today?" The small glasses hanging onto the tip of her nose made the light dance in her dark eyes.

"Something more mundane than usual, Mrs. Lark. My mistress is hoping you keep copies of newspapers?"

Mrs. Lark looked at Dai, but unlike Miss Kuster, didn't act as if there was anything unusual in seeing a blind Oriental girl in her library. "We try to preserve copies as space allows, though some of our patrons forget others might wish to read them and don't treat them as reverently as they should. Are you looking for something in particular?"

"Yes." Dai took a step forward. "I was hoping to see the obituaries printed in the last week or two, if possible."

Mrs. Lark nodded. "A more popular section of the news than one would expect. I should be able to get you what you need."

"That'd be most welcome. Jacques has often spoken of your keen ability to ferret out all manner of information." Dai smiled. "I'm grateful for your efforts."

"It's nice to have a challenge every once in a while. Plus, it's rewarding to know there are those actually seeking knowledge, and not just a copy of the latest romance novel." Mrs. Lark stood. "Our periodicals are in this direction."

Bookshelves served as partitions to separate the various areas of the library. The periodicals section held racks and poles with copies of the *Dallas Morning News* and the *Dallas Times Herald*, as well as copies of the *Washington Post* and *New York Times*. Other shelves held magazines, most of which looked well used. I settled Dai at a table in an out-of-the-way corner, then helped Mrs. Lark locate and bring over what we wanted.

After thanking her for her help, I chose a newspaper at random and flipped through the pages to the obituary section, skimming headlines as I went, in case a suspicious death was mentioned there. Listings covered two sheets, their length anywhere from a few sentences to multiple paragraphs. Some even included pictures of the deceased.

"Dai, there's a lot of entries here. Surely you don't mean for me to read you every one of them?"

"I don't imagine that will be necessary. We have a few clues which should help narrow our search." She tilted her head. "From the dress left at the laundry, we can assume we're looking for a woman. Though it was in an older style, from your description, the outfit sounded expensive—and handmade, unlike most fashions currently available. So we can, at present, also presume wealth is a factor. That'd mean a more prominent obituary, even if it has little to say. Those two things will hopefully make your search more manageable."

I nodded, agreeing with her logic.

"Don't assume she will be old. Despite the age of the dress, our victim could be young, old, or something in between."

I read the obituaries out to her in a soft voice so as not to bother any other patrons, knowing she'd have no trouble hearing me. Occasionally, Dai would make a comment, and I'd write the obituary's information in my notebook. Even using her criteria to narrow the search there were still a sizable number of entries each day. An hour later, I was thinking we might need to take a break to check on Prince and find some lunch when Dai stopped me in mid-sentence.

"That one—start that one again, Jacques." Dai sat forward excitedly.

Not sure what had caught her attention, I read the entry again from the beginning. "Laura Cooper, aged 23, died in the early hours of the 25th of natural causes.

"An entrancing flower plucked from the vine before she could truly bloom. Taken from the world just weeks before her nuptials to fiancé William Asquith, from London, England. A small gathering will be held in her honor. Miss Cooper has no living relatives."

I shook my head. "The wording is rather unique."

"Oh, it's more than that. Done by either someone extremely bereaved or someone looking to make a farce of it." She inched forward. "Did they make it stand out in any way?"

"Yes. There's a border around the notice with half-bloomed roses across it. Must have cost plenty of dough." I looked the entry over again. "You think this might be the one?"

"I do. Not only is the verbiage indicative, but it lists her death as resulting from natural causes. If there'd been anything suspicious about it, it would have made the news page. Everyone loves a juicy story, and no paper would just let it go unremarked upon. I don't recall you reading me any headlines of the sort recently, but we can double check that.

"The fact the fiancé is from London also points to this being the person we're looking for. The dress seems like the type of gown the gentry might wear to a ball or party. Something a girl who lived here in Dallas, without family, wouldn't be likely to own, especially in this day and age when most clothes are mass produced. Yet someone from overseas might well own something like that."

That didn't seem quite right. "Why would a man bring an old-fashioned gown with him abroad? Isn't that stretching things a bit?"

Dai waved my objections aside. "Jacques, it's a work in progress. Everything will line up eventually; we just need to gather additional facts. Plus, you must admit, this listing seems the most likely so far, don't you think?"

I wasn't sure what I thought. "What do we do next?"

"Is there any more information about the 'small gathering' mentioned in the notification? Or where and when the funeral is being held?"

"No. Nothing."

Dai nodded. "Some telephone calls will be in order then. Once we get back to the house."

"So you don't want to go through the rest of the notices?"

"We have the one we need. Besides, the intense staring is making me uncomfortable."

Startled by her words, my head jerked up. All the tables in the reading area were full, yet no one was reading. I'd been so busy looking for the correct entry I never noticed that we'd gathered an audience. Most of those seated kept throwing glances our way. We also had rubberneckers peering over the low bookshelves that cordoned off the reading area. Even Miss

Kuster had left the front desk to stare at Dai. Maybe coming here hadn't been the best of ideas. Dai wasn't some cheap exhibit at a carnival, and it made my temples throb to see the rudeness being visited upon her. She might be blind, but she still realized they were there. They seemed to think she'd never notice.

I stood up, glaring my displeasure at all of them. At least Miss Kuster had the decency to appear embarrassed. "Sorry, Dai. I should have noticed."

"You can only do so many things at once, Jacques."

It didn't mean I shouldn't try.

I gathered up the papers and left them on the table in a neat stack, rather than taking them back. I was afraid someone might accost her if I ventured from her side. I would apologize to Mrs. Lark next time I came.

CHAPTER 7

The ride home to Oak Cliff was uneventful. The bustle of the busy Dallas streets fell away, and family homes became more prevalent. Trees and grass replaced cars and smoke—a soothing ointment to my spirit, as my irritation at the people at the library had yet to abate.

Though she spoke little, I could feel the intensity of Dai's thoughts from the back seat. Prince lay on her lap, his small eyes closed and face content as she ran her fingers over his fur and occasionally scratched behind his ear.

The Wu home sat within the confines of Winnetka Heights. It was a two-story prairie-style house with covered porches most of the way around it. From the outside, it looked like a well-to-do American home in white and Texas-yellow-rose. Two flags—the American flag and that of the Lone Star State—flanked the porch steps to either side. A four-foot wall surrounded the quarter-acre lot, with eight-foot rose of Sharon shrubs for added privacy. It was a point of pride that the plant was native to China, especially as that fact wasn't well-known. The natural privacy screen was as much for the neighbors as for the Wus: If you can't see the Yellow Peril, then it must not be there. A back gate as well as a screened and covered carport ensured that the family would be seen by their neighbors as little as possible.

The first floor of the house was "as American as apple pie," the kitchen a marvel of the latest in stovetops and other cooking ware. But the second floor, where the family's bedrooms were located, was something else entirely.

Turning the corner midway on the stairs took you to another country. At the top of the stairs was a circular entry opening onto a hallway. At one end, a modest shrine to the family's ancestors took precedence, so the Wus could pay their respects and never forget where they came from or those who came before them. Lacquered furniture in the oriental style and tall vases with delicate flower arrangements decorated the rooms. Soft hues and minimalist simplicity transported one to a far-away land.

Yet even in China, certain things were the same.

"Daiyu! Where have you been? Mrs. Zhang informed me you left the laundry hours ago!" Dai's mother, Lien, stormed toward us like an angry dragon. Her accent was thick, but only when riled by emotion. She spoke better English than many who'd lived here all their lives. Having given up her old life, she embraced the customs of the new world for her daughter's sake.

I slid off my chauffer's hat and stared hard at the linoleum, trying my best not to attract attention. Prince scuttled to hide behind me, the coward. Dai prettily waited for her mother to reach us as if there were nothing to be concerned about. "*Mǔqīn*, I'm sorry." Dai bowed deeply. "I didn't intend to make you worry."

Like the black jade they'd named her for, Dai exuded a calming, grounding aura, diffusing the roiling torrent before us. "You've often told me I should try to enjoy more of the world, despite the state of my eyes. I guess I got a little carried away." She flashed her dimpled smile. "*Mǔqīn*, I made a friend today!"

The gale abruptly dissipated, taking the pressure in the room with it. Only then did I dare look up. The dragon had disappeared, leaving only a concerned parent before us. "A friend, truly?" One of Lien's brows rose high. "This is not another of your charity cases, is it?"

"Mother..." Dai shook her head in soft admonition. "I made a legitimate friend. A woman of character and one with a keen mind."

The dragon came out of hiding long enough to flash me a glance asking for confirmation. I was able to nod guilt-free, and just had to pray she wouldn't ask for more information later, like where the two had met. The word 'hospital'—or worse yet, 'morgue'—wouldn't buy me any goodwill.

"I'm so happy for you. But please, no more excursions without informing me first. While I want you to experience the world, I also don't want you unnecessarily exposed to it. Your life has been very sheltered. There are many ugly things about which you know nothing."

Lien thought she knew her daughter. She possessed no idea of the things Dai pursued information about, many of which would get my hide tanned for enabling her to research them.

Dai gave her mother another dimpled smile as if she would never care about such things. "Jacques will make sure I'm safe. You know that."

Lien moved closer, but didn't touch Dai. Overt exhibits of affection were not the Chinese way. "You are my one and only child. It is my right, if not my duty, to worry about you. Jacques is a trusted servant, but he cannot account for everything. He's been as sheltered as you."

That was an odd statement. Me, sheltered? How sheltered was I during the year I'd lived on the streets on my own? Little more than a feral dog, until the day fate showed me an angel. A blind angel who realized I was there and 'saw' me, despite all those others with eyes who pretended not to see. I'd experienced more of man's darkness than Dai's mother even realized existed. Which was, I supposed, as it should be.

"Yes, Mother. I understand."

Lien smiled at her daughter, her love an almost tangible thing. "My precious treasure." She caressed Dai's cheek with the backs of her fingers, then stepped back. "Try not to cause too much mischief before supper."

"I make no promises."

The dragon sent me a look, threatening dire things if I didn't do my part to keep Dai out of trouble. Maybe she knew her daughter better than I thought.

"Have you eaten?"

"Not yet. Time got away from us." Dai removed her hat and gloves as she spoke.

"Luckily for you, I figured as much. I have some chicken salad with grapes, just as you like, and wonton soup I can heat. Go freshen up while I get them ready."

"Wu *Fūrén*, I'd be happy to do that for you," I said. In addition to running the household and helping with the business, Mrs. Wu also kept herself busy with a couple of charitable organizations. So she was usually quite busy. There were those willing to ignore where she came from as long as there were timely donations made to the pot.

"I'm capable of making a few sandwiches and heating a bit of soup." Something I understood would have been scandalous in China for someone of her social standing. "You can feed his highness, however, if you would."

Though he'd been hiding behind me the entire time, Prince suddenly came round and sat on his hind legs, tongue lolling out the side of his mouth. One paw waved up and down, as he tried to look as cute as possible. I worked not to roll my eyes at this blatant attempt to curry favor with the mistress of the house. "Of course."

I hung my cap and jacket on the pegs close to the back door. My room was to the left of that, keeping me within easy access to the door for deliveries, any driving duties, and letting Prince out to do his business. It was also the farthest room from Dai's. Despite my lack of interest in Dai as a woman—to me, she was my sister and savior—the dragon thought it prudent to avoid any possible temptation. Plus, it'd been the most convenient location to keep me when Dai had first brought me home. A place where my transformation from a feral child to something more civilized could take place while making it less likely that I would destroy anything important in the rest of the home.

The novelty of having a dry place to sleep or be alone—a place that had a door, four walls, and kept out the weather—was still fresh even after all these years. They had gone to the extra effort of adding a bathroom for my private use, and including shelves for books in the room, making the compact space a palace in my eyes.

"Get your caboose outside, your magnificence, or no food for you."

Prince strutted out the door, well aware he had the women in the house on his side. Beside the sealed bin we used to keep his dog food dry, there was a paper sack holding a raw bone from the butchers'. Mangy mutt got treated better than I did.

I filled his bowl with kibble and placed the bone down beside it. A quick lick touched the back of my hand, then Prince was facedown in the dish, gobbling the contents down as if they might somehow disappear if left on their own for more than a second.

Hiding a grin, I went back inside.

Lien had the soup reheating on the stove and was spreading chicken salad over several thick slices of bread. I'd often wondered what those back in her country would have made of seeing her like this. From what knowledge I'd accumulated over the years from snatches of overheard conversations, the Wus' life back in China had differed vastly from the one they led here. They'd had wealth, position, power—much like the Rockefellers, except with an aristocratic lineage dating back two thousand years or more. They had given up everything to come here, a land where keeping a blind female child alive wouldn't be taken as an offense to society and tradition.

By saving Dai, they'd ended up rescuing me—a debt I wasn't sure I could ever repay.

I set the table in the kitchen, as the dining room was reserved for the evening meals when Mr. Wu would be present. Dai rejoined us just as Lien placed the food on the table.

Like me, Dai's mother was unbothered by her daughter's

silver-white eyes, so there was no need for Dai to wear her glasses. The conversation was light, sticking to people and things related to the laundry, the words switching back and forth between English and Mandarin without pause.

I just ate and listened, except for when they'd direct a question or comment in my direction. Prince barked at the back door to be let in, so I placed my dishes in the sink and moved to let him inside. By the time the two of us returned, the dishware had been gathered and was ready to be washed. Lien had gone.

Rolling up my sleeves, I washed everything, leaving it on the dish rack to dry and put away later. Dai kept me company while I worked.

"Jacques, if you're done, would you go into the study and look for the latest telephone directory for me? I had Father buy three of them, so we should have one here at the house. I'll meet you in Father's office in a minute." Dai got up from the table and left, showing no hesitation in her steps. She was intimately acquainted with each room and the location of every item in the house, and could navigate it flawlessly.

I should have known better than to expect her to let the matter drop.

CHAPTER 8

I found the telephone directory on the shelf closest to the door in the study. The 2,700-plus-page volume was hardbound and split into several sections, a few of which were in gold-colored paper. I found Dai sitting in one of the leather guest chairs in her father's office, with Prince curled up on her lap. On the spacious desk beside her, she had moved the telephone to the corner for easy reach from the front.

"Close the door, would you? It'll be best Mother doesn't hear what we're up to if she comes back downstairs."

I did as asked, then sat down and opened the telephone directory. The book was a font of public information. Local businesses were showcased in a special section, and their ads were seeded throughout the phone listings. "What am I looking for?"

"You really need to ask?" She waved the question away as irrelevant. "Find the listing for the *Dallas Times Herald*. Since they ran the notice, someone there should be privy to where and when they plan to hold the get-together. If not, they should at least have a contact number or name for whoever placed the obituary.

"If that gets us nowhere, we have the fiancé's name. Surely someone's heard of him. It's at times like these that I regret my lack of social connections." She pursed her lips, giving me the impression it would be the *only* reason she'd contemplate such a thing.

I turned to the index of the advertisements list near the front, thinking that might be the easiest way to find them. They had nothing under *Dallas Times Herald* but did under their old name, the *Times Herald*. I flipped to page 327, where the *Times Herald* had taken out a full-page ad showing a picture of their new building on Pacific Avenue. To my annoyance, the ad didn't list their number. Looked like someone had forgotten that tiny detail while expounding on being Dallas' Greatest Newspaper.

Flipping back to the front, to the 'Facts and Figures' pages, they were listed there as the *Daily Times Herald*. Going back to the detail listings, I finally found them on page 778. The telephone number was 2-3261.

I handed Dai the telephone receiver, then dialed the number for her. For the next few minutes, she asked questions and was transferred several times to other departments.

"Yes, I am looking for information on an obituary posted recently in the paper. Yes, Laura Cooper. The young lady engaged to Willy—I mean, William Asquith." Dai paused, listening. "I know, but it's essential that I contact him, so I was trying to find out where the funeral is to be held, or the location of the small gathering in Miss Cooper's honor.

"Yes. Yes, I understand. But I must insist. I would welcome any information at all. Willy and I—well, we didn't leave things on the best of terms." Her voice lowered a little. "Now that he has suffered such a shock, I think it's beyond time I mended fences, don't you agree? Ah, yes, the Adolphus. I should have guessed—that's so like him. Yes, thank you, thank you very much." Dai handed me the receiver with a smug look on her face.

"I take it they had what you wanted?"

"Sort of. The information was sent to the newspaper by courier—a rather unusual means to request and pay for an obituary. However, the request was written on stationery from the Adolphus Hotel, which gives us a place to start."

Finding the telephone number for the hotel proved to be even more involved than finding the number for the *Dallas Times Herald* had been. It seemed to be standard practice not to put your telephone number in your advertisements, which I felt defeated the entire purpose of having one. But perhaps I was too uneducated to understand. I finally tracked it down, and we followed the same process as before.

"Yes, I'm looking for a guest at your hotel, a William Asquith? Might he still be in residence?" Dai listened attentively to the voice on the other end. "Oh, I see. Yes, thank you very much. Do you know if the gathering for Laura Cooper will be held at the hotel? This afternoon, is it? Yes, thank you. You've been extremely helpful. Have a delightful day."

"Success?"

"Yes, indeed, Jacques. But we must hurry. The gathering is set for three o'clock today at the hotel."

I almost said nothing, but I had to at least attempt to stop her from following this path. "Dai, might you reconsider? We could give this information to Dr. Campbell. She could contact the justice of the peace and have him follow through on it."

Dai sat entirely still, considering my words. "I don't think that would work, Jacques. Despite having the dress and now a potential victim, there isn't enough evidence linking the two for the police to act on... yet. To get what is needed, we will need to continue to investigate."

"Your parents won't approve."

She barked a laugh. "What they don't know won't hurt them. Besides, I'm not a child anymore. I can make my own decisions about where to go and what to do."

Her words didn't surprise me. She was like a dog with a bone, loath to give it up and willing to fight to keep it. I just hoped it wouldn't get us sent to the pound.

CHAPTER 9

The Adolphus Hotel was located on Commerce Street in downtown Dallas. Built in 1912 at twenty-two stories, it was the tallest building in the city until 1922. It was designed specifically to be the grandest hotel in Dallas, and was constructed in the Beaux-Arts style. This gave the hotel an appearance that was a mixture of Imperial Rome, Italian Renaissance, and French Baroque. Red and trimmed in white, it became ever more impressive the closer we approached. Cherubs, shields, faces, columns, and armament façades were sculpted near rounded window frames. White iron rod screens gave a bit of color to the hotel windows. The entrance was extravagant, featuring columns and polished marble, while dark wood paneling covered the vast guest reception area. The check-in desk was inviting and fully manned, the back wall filled with rows of golden hooks on which hung the brass keys for the rooms. Several young porters in smart uniforms and pillbox hats stood ready to render assistance at a moment's notice.

Dai held Prince in her arms as I guided her forward with a light touch at her elbow. The front desk manager spied us crossing the lavishly carpeted room and came out from behind the check-in area to intercept us.

It surprised me when the pencil-mustached manager made eye contact with me rather than Dai. Her glasses were in place, so there was no way for him to realize she was blind—at least not yet.

"I'm very sorry, but you can't bring that in here."

Dai held Prince higher, and he raised his front paws to show he was all about obeying the rules. "I assure you, Prince is a well-behaved canine."

The manager ignored Dai completely and continued to look and talk only to me. "Sir, I wasn't talking about the *dog*."

Heat rushed up my neck and into my face as the meaning of his words crystalized in my brain.

"We can make arrangements, sir, *if* we must. But not here, not in public. We have a reputation to maintain and the sensibilities of our guests to consider. If you depart then come round the back, I will see what can be done."

Dai was blind, not deaf! How dare he say such things in front of her? Who was he to make such judgments? My hands curled into fists, my rage building by the second. His expectant and solicitous expression only made it burn hotter. I would show this cur what I thought of his misguided opinions!

"Jacques, don't." Dai grabbed my sleeve. "It's all right."

It wasn't all right. It was far from *all right*. I shook where I stood. It would be worth a night in jail to show this bastard some proper manners.

"Alphonse, my good man!"

A gentleman in his mid-twenties came toward us, trying to catch the front desk manager's eye. Clean-shaven with slicked-back sandy blond hair, he wore a black suit with thin gold stripes, a gold vest with black stripes, a black shirt and gold tie. With a knowing look in his blue eyes, he flashed a brilliant, pearly-white smile. I felt an instant and irrational dislike for him.

"So glad I caught you. I meant to let you know I was expecting a special guest today." His gaze roamed Dai's length and breadth, then focused solely on Alphonse. He lowered his voice to a bare whisper. "This is the daughter of Dr. C. C. Wu, the minister of China's legation in Washington, D.C."

Alphonse's face paled, and he darted a glance in Dai's direction.

"She's here incognito, you see—no limousines or fanfare. My father is very keen to get mineral rights in China. He invited the minister and his family to visit, to show them our famous Texas hospitality. I'm sure you wouldn't want to put the kibosh on Father's plans, now, would you?"

By this point, Alphonse was looking a little green. "No. Of course not, Mr. Pierce. I'm very sorry. If I'd known—"

Before I could think about what I was doing, I took a menacing step forward. "He's not the one you should *apologize* to."

The manager almost tripped in his haste to step back from my aggressively looming presence. "Yes, yes, of course." He half-turned and looked at Dai directly for the first time. "I'm very sorry, madam. Please forgive me for any offense I might have caused. Let me know if there's anything we can do to make your visit more agreeable." He swallowed hard. "Welcome to the Adolphus Hotel."

He bowed low, his entire posture stiff and awkward.

Our 'savior' chuckled softly to himself as the manager scampered away to the safety of the front desk. "I shouldn't say so, but that was a total gas." He flashed Dai a big devilish grin. "Alphonse gets a little too full of himself on occasion."

I was sure Alphonse wasn't the only one.

"Thank you for your help—Mr. Pierce, was it?" Dai set Prince down, keeping hold of the short leash she'd attached to his collar. The strap was more for the comfort of others than something Prince needed. Much like Dai's teashade glasses.

"Oh, forgive me, dollface."

Before I could intervene, he took Dai's hand in his and kissed it. "Truman Pierce at your service."

He lingered over her hand until a warning growl made him release it and step back. Luckily Prince's loud rumble drowned out my own. I liked this fellow less and less by the moment. The fact that Dai's cheeks had gained a bit of color at his attention didn't help matters.

"Prince Razor, quiet, please. We mustn't be rude."

The dog quieted but didn't move from between them. If I could have found a way to wedge myself in there without attracting even more unwanted attention than we had already, I would have.

"That's a unique name for a dog." Pierce flashed another devilish smile. "I rather like it."

If the fool didn't watch himself, there was a good chance he'd find out exactly why Prince's second name was Razor.

"And what might your name be, China Doll?"

With an entirely straight face, Dai answered him. "Daiyu Wu."

Pierce looked taken aback for a second then laughed. "For real?"

"Yes. But I'm not the minister's daughter or a relative. The matching last name is purely coincidental."

"But a gas all the same."

I'd had my fill of this. "Yes, well, thank you. Nice of you to help us out, but we have to be going. We have a meeting to attend. So if you don't mind…"

Pierce arched a brow in my direction. "You do realize Alphonse is watching our every move, don't you? If I don't at least pretend to go with you, he'll realize something is up, and you're likely to be accosted again."

Glancing toward the front desk, I saw that the manager was still frowning in our direction. I very much doubted he'd approach us again, despite Pierce's warning. Still, there might be more staff or even guests with outmoded views hanging around who might decide to take advantage of the opportunity.

"Jacques, we also don't know the exact location of the gathering," Dai pointed out. "Perhaps Mr. Pierce, with his knowledge of the establishment and the staff, will be able to assist in this as well."

I didn't like it. She might be right, but I didn't like it one bit. I wanted her far away from this cretin as soon as possible.

"I would be delighted to help." More flashing teeth.

"Nothing would please me more."

Yes, he was too keen, indeed. The sooner we parted ways with this playboy, the better.

The day, as I would find out to my chagrin, had other plans.

"So how can I help?" Pierce asked.

I gently guided Dai as we moved past the reception desk toward the elevators and stairs, and out of most people's immediate view.

"We're looking for a private gathering being held at three. A wake of sorts for a Miss Laura Cooper."

Pierce stopped in his tracks. "Oh, this proves it." He laughed out loud. "This more than proves it! It wasn't a mere coincidence that we met each other today, China Doll. It's *fate*!"

He stepped forward, looking as if he was going to sweep Dai off her feet and swing her around the room. In a panic, I dived to get between them, and we collided. This pushed me backward, and I bumped into Dai. Prince barked as she lost her balance and fell.

"Jacques! What in the world is the matter with you!" Dai smacked her small purse on the carpet in indignation. She had no way of knowing the embarrassment I'd just saved her from—though falling flat on her bum probably wasn't much better than being swung through the air like a child.

"Dai, I'm so sorry!" I reached to help her up, while Prince bounced behind her to keep any unseen threats from coming near her. I quickly made sure her dress fell correctly and that her hair hadn't gone into disarray. It was only then that I noticed her teashades were gone.

"China Doll, your eyes…"

Dai turned her head in the direction of Pierce's voice, her silver-white, blind eyes almost shining in the hotel's inner lighting. "Ah, you've caught me. Yes, I'm quite blind, as you can see." She gave him a dimpled smile. "I hope you won't hold it against me."

Though I hated how some people looked at or treated Dai once they discovered she was blind, this once I would have welcomed it. I hoped the sight would dissuade this popinjay from wanting to hang around us any longer.

Pierce gave an involuntary laugh for the third time that day. "For such a little package, you sure are full of surprises."

A bump at my leg made me look down. Prince was looking up at me, Dai's glasses dangling from his mouth. I took them from him, and after cleaning them, touched Dai's hand so she could take them and put them on.

Out of nowhere, Pierce slapped me on the back as if we were comrades. "I bet she keeps you plenty busy, Jackie. Not a dull moment in sight."

My back throbbed where he had touched me. "My name is *Jacques*, buster, not Jackie."

"Jacques, Jackie, what's the difference? Lighten up!" With that said, he turned from me, giving one hundred percent of his attention to Dai. "As I said before, fate brought us together today. I was meant to meet you, without a doubt."

Did he actually expect any woman to believe this drivel? Maybe his apparent wealth made a believer of the women he encountered at the speakeasies, but it wouldn't carry any weight with Dai.

"I'm curious. What makes you say that, exactly?" Dai asked him.

"Because I was just on my way over to William's gathering when I spotted Alphonse giving you a hard time."

Dai tilted her face up as if she could, by will alone, make her blind eyes see his expression. "You know Asquith?"

"Know him? Without me, he would have never met Laura in the first place."

Dai's expression brightened with delight.

Damn the man.

CHAPTER 10

"We're gathering in one of the meeting rooms in the mezzanine level. Nothing too outrageous, I assure you. Otherwise, we would have rented the French Room." He sent me a wink. "Or the much more exciting place in the hotel that can't be named."

That was something of a surprise. We were still in the throes of "the Noble Experiment" of Prohibition. Had the hotel created a place for those not believing themselves to be part of the overworked masses those laws had been put in place to protect? That Pierce might know the whereabouts of local dens of vice didn't surprise me in the least. Neither would finding out that his family had collected a private stash before the law went into effect. The actual *drinking* of alcohol was not part of the law; one could imbibe whatever liquor one had owned before the regulation took effect. A lovely loophole for those able to afford to keep a stock of it on the premises.

Moving past the grand marble staircase and the elevators leading to the rooms, Pierce took a side hallway deeper into the hotel. On a tripod outside one of the doors, they had placed a simple sign with the words "Cooper Gathering."

The room was mid-sized with four elegant chandeliers hanging from the ceiling. Padded chairs in autumn colors were set around long tables laden with platters of finger foods and jugs of iced tea and ice water.

On the wall, in a beautiful and heavy frame, was an enlarged photograph of Laura Cooper. She was young and attractive, her hair parted in the middle with waves of curls framing her roundish face. But it was her brilliant smile that gave the photo life, as if she might shift her gaze to you at any moment. A blooming flower, indeed.

I felt Dai hesitate, the tension palpable in the room as we entered. Pierce went on in. "I bumped into a couple of interested parties on my way in, Will, so I brought them along. Hope you don't mind."

I identified Asquith immediately. He was the only one in the room looking miserable, and had sizeable bags beneath his eyes. He waved Pierce's words aside and tried to rally a half-welcoming look for the two of us. "Please, join us. Did you know Laura?"

It was the first time either of us had heard a British accent in person. It was lofty, like what you might expect royalty to sound like—in every way quite different from the local Texas twang or the elongated sounds of English-speaking Chinese.

"We know *of* her. We came hoping to learn more."

I worried Dai's bluntness might seem insulting, but couldn't think of a better way she could have answered the question without making it an outright lie. To my surprise, Asquith brightened at her words, though not all in the room took it in a good way.

"I am so happy to hear that. Laura was a wonderful person. She made a great impact in my life, and I know she would have enriched the lives of many more people if she'd been given a chance. I'd be happy to tell you anything you'd like to know about her. Celebrating her life, reliving memories of her—it's the least I can do after all she did for me."

A young woman, her black hair glistening in the current waved fashion, rolled her eyes, then grabbed Asquith's arm and clung to him, her face changing into an adoring expression. "You're so right, William! You are so *very* right."

Looks of disgust flashed from the other three people already in attendance. From the woman's accent, I could tell she was a local. The others appeared better dressed but not in current American styles, so I assumed they were also foreigners. Two looked to be a couple and seemed to be a few years older than Asquith. The last member of the group was an elderly woman with the air of a matron about her. She stood a little apart from the others, a pleasant yet neutral expression on her face.

"Let me make the introductions." Pierce bounded forward, pulling Asquith from the black-haired lady's clutches. "As you've already guessed, this is William Asquith, fifth son of the second Earl of Oxford and Asquith." He grinned. "Quite a mouthful, to be sure."

We shook hands. Despite his grief, Asquith's grip was steady.

"You did insist on learning the full proper title, Truman." This came from the second woman. Her features were similar to William's, and her accent was definitely British.

"Too true, Lizzie. It adds an air of the Old World to things, doesn't it? Great for impressing the local yokels."

Did the cad take nothing seriously?

"Lady and Lord Domberry, also known as Lizzie and Paul. The clingy gal is Shannon Daugherty, a friend of Laura's. And last but not least is Mrs. Amelia Grey, nanny, chaperone, and moral compass of the Asquith clan."

I could do nothing but approve of the discontented glower the matron flashed in the popinjay's direction.

Pierce continued, "This here is Jackie."

"*Jacques* Haskin. Pleased to meet you." The arrogant twit had to be doing it on purpose.

"And this," Pierce said, sweeping his arm in a grand gesture, "is the captivating and irresistible Daiyu Wu."

All eyes locked on Dai.

"He exaggerates, I assure you. I am no one of import. But I am very pleased to meet you." She flashed them an adorable smile.

"Wu? What kind of last name is that?" Shannon tried to clamp herself once more to Asquith's arm.

Pierce leaned forward, his voice low as if about to impart a juicy bit of gossip. "It's Chinese."

The girl jerked back as if slapped. The others looked more confused at her reaction than at the imparted information.

"Does Dallas also have a Chinatown? The one in London used to be quite the place to go to experience exotic things." Domberry looked interested for the first time since we had entered the room.

"Paul, don't be vulgar." Lizzie's disapproving look was a mirror image of Mrs. Grey's earlier.

Dai shook her head. "I'm afraid not. Our numbers have dwindled dramatically in recent years, so there are only a few handfuls of us remaining in Dallas." She shrugged. "We're not especially wanted here."

William frowned. "Aren't the United States supposed to be the land of opportunity, a country of liberty and justice for all?"

"It would seem that 'for all' has a different meaning to those in Congress than to the rest of us."

Pierce barked a laugh. "Isn't she a hoot?"

"American politics are not relevant to today's event, surely." Mrs. Grey's voice was soft but laced with command, and it carried across the room.

William's face fell, the comment reminding him of his grief. "Laura. Yes."

Dai turned toward him. "Why don't you tell us about her? How did the two of you meet?"

Pained pleasure flashed across his face at the question. "It wasn't planned. I came to the States for a long holiday. I was hoping to travel to several American cities to look for opportunities, for ideas." He sighed. "To be honest, I've been looking for something to dedicate myself to. I'm not the family's heir, so I wanted to find something of my own, something with which to make my way in the world. I thought seeing another country, one where a person is less hampered by who his ancestors were, might show me more options, give me a direction to strive toward."

Domberry scoffed. "Poppycock. Lineage *is* everything," He took a caviar canape from the nearest tray and popped it in his mouth. "Making a fortune or being given a title in the last hundred years doesn't change where you come from."

"Paul!" Lizzie stared at her husband in shock.

Shannon took charge of William's arm again. "Don't listen to him, Will. He doesn't know what he's talking about. He's just an old *snob*."

The feeling of tension I'd felt in the room when we first entered was back again. I brought a chair over for Dai and stood behind her. Prince sat at her feet, alert. Truman Pierce, however, draped himself over another chair as if readying himself to watch a much-anticipated comedy performance.

"Why, you impudent, uneducated, American *peasant*." Domberry spat the words out like a curse.

Lizzie's face turned crimson. "P-Paul, you mustn't say such things! Certainly not in public!"

Pierce started chuckling at the implication of her statement. What kind of nuts were these?

Domberry pulled a metal flask from his vest, pointedly ignoring his wife as he took a long swig. Mrs. Grey quietly moved around the table and closed the door leading out into the hall.

Slyly, Shannon swept closer to Domberry, grabbing one of the caviar canapes for herself. "Better a peasant than a penniless, worthless royal."

Domberry spluttered, his face growing several shades darker.

"Enough!" William pounded his fist on the table, tipping over a glass of iced tea. Mrs. Grey produced napkins seemingly from the air and quickly mopped up the mess, making it seem in mere moments as if the incident had never happened.

"We're not here about you, or your opinions, or anything else related to *you*. We're here for Laura!"

Domberry cleared his throat and looked away. As William

turned back toward Dai, I saw Shannon shoot Domberry a dagger-filled glare.

"I'm very sorry. We're not typically like this." William wouldn't look at us directly. From the smothered snort that came from Pierce's direction, I got the feeling that they were always this way.

"Anyway, about how I met Laura." William grabbed a chair and set it close to Dai's, shutting the others out behind him.

Shannon didn't look pleased by this one bit, but didn't force the issue. Lizzie had moved closer to Mrs. Grey, the two talking in soft whispers. Paul continued to sample hors d'oeuvres and take sips from his flask.

"I met Truman during the transatlantic crossing on the RMS *Olympic* to New York. I hadn't initially planned to come down this far south, but after all the stories he told of your city and the opportunities here, I had to see for myself.

"It was at this very hotel that I met Laura. She worked here, as a cigarette girl at the Bank Underground." He leaned forward, lowering his voice as he did so. "It was rather fascinating, finding out about the Prohibition laws in your country. Especially all the ways people came up with to work around them."

Pierce chuckled. "I told you we Yanks are an inventive bunch."

"True, you did. Even Paul approved of this one when I told him." A shadow of a smile crossed his lips. "The hotel has a special service, one they made their exclusive clientele aware of before the laws took effect. As a hotel client, you rent space in which to store any alcohol purchased prior to Prohibition. When you wish to drink from your stock, the Bank Underground gives you a venue in which to enjoy it—one with tables, food, entertainment, and dancing. A high-end club with all the amenities, except the alcohol you and your friends are drinking is already your own."

There had been stories in the papers over the years of the bitterness expressed by some at the quick thinking of those who had stocked up on liquor before Prohibition went into effect. Others expressed disbelief that any one man could have stored enough to keep himself supplied for the last ten years. There were many theories on how they held onto it, from having ties to the mafia, to hidden stockpiles the size of warehouses. Rather than solving any of the problems Prohibition had been meant to address, it had created several new ones—giving a foothold and power to the various mob families only one of them.

CHAPTER 11

"Meeting her, truly *seeing* her, was just one of those unexpected things." A ghost of a smile came and went again from William's face. "We'd been going to the Bank pretty regularly. The club area is about the size of a pub back home, so you tend to see a lot of the same people. I was waiting for Truman by the exit at the basement one night, watching the crowd just to pass the time. I don't know exactly what caught my attention, but I started watching Laura. She weaved between the tables with her wares, not calling out like I've seen others do, but observing the people around her. If any glanced her way, she'd flash them a broad smile and already knew what they wanted before they asked for it. She somehow even realized when they wanted nothing, but still gave them that brilliant smile—as if their acknowledging her gave her great pleasure, even if nothing was said."

A muffled snort made clear that not everyone thought it was an endearing trait. I couldn't tell whom it had come from, but I was pretty sure Dai knew. I would ask her later. William ignored it entirely and went on.

"Once I realized that, I started paying more attention. That's when I discovered the other little things she did. Things that she did because she *could*, not because she had to." He placed a lot of weight on the words, as if wanting to make sure we realized this was the important point. "They were small things, sure, but everything stacks and they can make an enormous difference to a person's day. Best of all, she did them not only for the hotel's clients but also its employees.

"If someone left their table and the wait staff was busy, she'd swing by and tidy up. She'd refill water glasses, empty and clean their ashtrays, straighten things—Laura did a thousand little things. By the time they came back, she'd be gone, leaving no one the wiser. Yet she'd improved their day or experience, even if they weren't entirely aware of it."

Dai nodded. "A hidden treasure. I can tell why you fell for her."

His gaze grew brighter. "Yes. Yes, exactly, a hidden treasure. One that needed to be coaxed into the light and shared."

"Our dearest Laura. Such a loss." Shannon perched herself just behind William's chair and laid her hand gently on his shoulder. The look in her eyes belied the honeyed words, however. I was getting the distinct impression that Shannon hadn't liked Laura much, but didn't mind using her death to her own advantage.

"That's when I decided I wanted to get to know her better. To be honest, I may have become a bit of a nuisance. I made sure to come during her shift, and to sit in her designated area. They frown on fraternization between clients and employees, so I took to buying cigarettes or matches from her just to pass a smile and a word or two. Eventually, I asked her out to tea— iced tea, as it turned out. A strange change from hot English tea, but with the constant scalding weather here, I can understand how it would seem more appropriate."

William swallowed hard, his tale bringing up conflicting feelings. "That first meeting outside the club was hesitant on both sides. I didn't want to frighten her off, and she, I suspect, was not quite sure of my intentions. I told her of the things I'd seen her do and she blushed, making her even more endearing. For a half second, I honestly thought she would run for the door, so as Truman would say, I had to do some fast talking to convince her otherwise."

He laughed. "We Brits aren't known for expressing our feelings. Baring my heart to her in that café was one of the hardest things I've ever done. But I needed to convince her she was the best thing I'd encountered in either the New or the Old World. I'm not sure she believed me, yet she stayed. I proved my words in whatever ways I could after that. Two months later, I knew I wouldn't be able to live without her." The life drained from his face and eyes.

Lizzie piped up when the silence lengthened. "Caused quite a furor back home when we received the telegram. Father was beside himself. Paul and I were free, and Mrs. Grey knows William best, so we all came to see what was what. And if necessary, force William to see sense. Not that it was necessary," she quickly added. "Laura really was a dear. It was obvious the two of them were besotted with one another." The last was stated somewhat wistfully, as if her own experience had not been as fulfilling. Looking at Paul and the sneer on his face, it was easy to imagine why she might feel that way.

"She didn't have a penny to her name, but she *was* pretty," Paul said. "If wide-eyed and naïve are your kind of thing."

William jumped to his feet and whirled around, his hands bunched in fists at his side. "I'm about sick of you and how all you care about is money, *Paul*."

Lizzie intercepted her brother. "I'm sure he didn't *really* mean anything by it, Will. Paul, tell him, won't you?"

Her husband shrugged. "We came here to find out if she was a money-grubbing Yank, didn't we? She wasn't. Our job was done. End of story." He pulled his flask back out.

Before he could take a swig, Mrs. Grey plucked it out of his hand and gave it to Lizzie. "I believe, Lord Domberry, that you've had enough for now. Please think of your reputation and the image you're presenting to these Americans."

Domberry's face went through several shades of red and purple, his expression a blank mask. Mrs. Grey met his glare head-on. He was the first to look away. It seemed Mrs. Grey was a dragon in her own right.

Despite losing the encounter, Paul couldn't keep from throwing out another volley. "Lizzie, you really need to teach the servants how to treat their betters." Not meeting the nanny's gaze again, Domberry stormed from the room, swiping a few more hors d'oeuvres on his way out.

"I'm so sorry, everyone. Paul's been under a lot of stress of late. He liked Laura, too; his pride just won't let him admit it. He doesn't mean half the things he says." Lizzie started for the door. "Many apologies, Will."

Once they'd gone, William deflated back onto his chair.

"Perhaps we should take our leave." Dai rose daintily to her feet. "I apologize if we're responsible for making this sad time more unbearable."

"No, please don't say that. If anything, your eagerness to listen has helped me immensely." William stood.

"When will the funeral be, if I might ask?"

For once, I connected the dots on my own: A funeral meant a casket, a funeral home, a body. It was probably one of the most critical pieces of information we might glean here.

"There won't be one. Laura had wasted away and it was beyond the skills of the mortician to make her presentable." He shook his head. "It didn't seem fair to present her to others at anything less than her very best. Instead, we came up with the idea for this... affair. Something to keep me distracted while her body is being cremated."

CHAPTER 12

"I see." The others might not have noticed, not being as well acquainted with Dai as I was, but there was heavy disappointment lacing those two simple words.

Cremations were a recent option in the States, and still uncommon. The facilities for such a choice were few. It seemed a strange option to take.

"Nan—I mean, Mrs. Grey thought it would be the practical thing to do," William said. "Her ashes will be placed in an antique etched-marble urn. I can take it with me, so I can keep her by my side wherever I go."

A somewhat morbid solution, but also a convenient happenstance for the killer.

"She had no living family. No one to care for or visit her grave once I've gone, so…"

"That's perfectly understandable under the circumstances," Dai said.

William seemed relieved at having a stranger affirm his own thoughts. "Yes. Thank you. Yes."

There were never any right words for situations like this. "We're truly sorry for your loss."

"Thank you both."

Taking Dai's elbow, I helped guide her out of the room, Prince Razor at our heels.

"Hold up a minute!" Pierce bolted after us into the hallway.

Just when I'd thought we'd be rid of him.

"China Doll," he said, kneeling down before Dai and pulling out a calling card seemingly from midair. "Take my card, please. I would very much like us to get better acquainted." Prince gave him a warning growl, which Pierce ignored. "Fate brought us together. I would be a fool not to listen."

A fool indeed. I plucked the card from his hand, noting the crisp black paper with gold embossing. Expensive. I'd be dumping it into the nearest trash can as soon as we were out of sight.

"I'm planning to hold a soiree in a day or two," Pierce said. "I'd be over the moon if you'd agree to come."

Dai arched a brow. "Because it would be scandalous and entertaining?"

Pierce's face broke into a devilish grin. "Yes, there would be that. But mostly because I am earnestly interested in you and want us to get to know one another better. You are unlike anyone I've ever met."

For the second time that day, I saw Dai hand out one of her social cards. It made my stomach clench.

"I am assuming Asquith and his family will be attending as well?"

Pierce nodded. "Yes. Figured it might do him good to do something different. Plus you seemed quite interested in their doings. It'll be fun finding out exactly why."

The rich boy stood and bowed like a knight from a fairy story. "As soon as I get the details solidified, I'll let you know. I'll also invite the gold-digger. She was Laura's roommate and possibly the happiest of the bunch that Laura is gone." The devilish smile was back. "Very much looking forward to it." Then he left.

"Dai, this isn't a good idea. He's a spoiled popinjay, and we've no idea as to his true intentions." I took a deep breath, sure that what I was about to say next would not be well received. "You should not associate with his ilk."

She laughed. "Are you jealous, Jacques?"

I made a face. How could she think such a thing? "No. I just don't like him. I doubt he'd hesitate to hurt you as long as it proved entertaining. Plus he could very well be the killer."

Dai shook her head. "He's helping us, which at the moment is all that matters. With the body cremated, we won't be able to get any solid direct evidence of foul play. All we have is the dress and a roomful of likely suspects. We need more information. And the best way to get it is to stay close to them."

While I couldn't disagree, I also didn't want her putting herself in the line of fire. She had a lot more to lose than they did.

"Since we're here," she continued, "why don't we go see this Bank Underground? If we need to, we can use Truman's name and card to get us in."

That made me frown. "I'm not sure it's a place for a lady."

"Please, Jacques. I might be blind, but I am far from naïve. Plus if you don't describe it, how will I know what is there?" Dai 'looked' at me with a dimpled smile, neither one of us believing the last part of her statement.

"They're probably not open. It's early yet."

Dai pouted. "Well then, maybe it's time we took Alphonse's advice and used the service entrance to the hotel. We can speak to some of Laura's coworkers. The ones not trying to profit from her death, that is."

From the mezzanine level it wasn't hard to find one of the service corridors, and from there to find individuals in the hotel's service staff. Between declarations of "¡*Ah, que linda!*" and "¡*Que chiquita!*" from the workers about Dai, I explained in passable Spanish what we were looking for and got directions. Contrary to my supposition, the Bank Underground was open twenty-four hours a day so its clientele could imbibe whenever it suited. The rest of the club activities, however, had set hours.

The freight elevator was noisy, and its operator chatty, as we made our way to the hotel's basement. We walked down a long corridor with stark white walls and giant pipes overhead until we reached the entrance to the club. It was unlike any club entry I'd ever heard tell of. The Bank Underground was literally behind a giant bank vault door. Two men in hotel livery stood to either side to open the massive beast whenever carded clients arrived.

I described it to Dai as we walked on past, and after two more turns we reached a normal-looking door with a sign stating "Service Personnel Only." Turning the knob to the unlocked door, we let ourselves in.

The left wall had a set of metal lockers for the employees, next to a doorway leading to changing rooms. A dumbwaiter was set into the far wall, more than likely connected to the kitchens—a fast way to get food orders filled for the club clientele. A wheeled rack of skimpy but colorful costumes sat ignored in a corner. It stood next to a massive wall-mounted mirror that held sway over a long thin counter littered with makeup, brushes, sequins, and more. Instrument cases sat lined up near the room's only table, which held four men with slicked-back hair, deeply engrossed in a game of cards.

"Excuse me, might we be able to ask you gentlemen some questions?" They didn't even glance my way. "Did you happen to know Laura Cooper?"

At the mention of her name, all four put their cards down and turned in our direction, half curious, half threatening. "Yeah, we knew her. What's it to you?"

Dai stepped forward, Prince back in her arms. "Would you tell us about her? From what we understand she was rather special."

The four men looked at one another, back at us, then seemed to decide we were harmless. "Sure, sure, we can do that. She was a great gal, that one."

The skinniest of the bunch pulled out a pack of Lucky Strikes and, after tapping the box on the table, took one out and lit it. "No doubt."

"She did a lot of stuff she didn't have to," said the third, "like keeping this place tidy and clean. Nobody willingly does any of that shit."

"Too true." The fourth sent a disgusted look at the skinny one as he took a long drag on his cigarette and released the smoke into the room. "Though some around here could learn."

Dai wrinkled her nose at the potent smell of tobacco. "Did anyone dislike her?"

The four looked at one another then shrugged. "What was there not to like? She was easy on the eyes. Always had a smile for everybody. Kept the back room from being a total pigsty. She was a peach."

Nods followed all around. "She kept mostly to herself though. Friendly, sure, but didn't talk much. Kind of an odd duck in a way."

"What about Shannon? Did she get along with Laura?"

The skinny one choked in the middle of a puff.

"They were roommates. Had been for years. Came together from East Texas somewhere. They didn't have any other family, so they put up with each other."

"Shannon sure as heck didn't mind leaving all the work to Laura. Took advantage of her all the time."

The fourth man laughed. "Served her right it was Laura who caught the eye of that British Joe. Not that she took it well."

"Shannon might be more of a looker, but you're asking for a world of hurt getting involved with her." Skinny winced as if speaking from personal experience. "She's the type who'd leave you bleeding in the street rather than take the risk of breaking a nail."

"They both worked as cigarette girls?" Dai asked.

"Yeah, mostly. They were also backup dancers if any of the regular girls were out." The first man grinned. "Shannon was livid when Laura quit after announcing her engagement. She's been having to work extra hours until they get a replacement. Though she's skipped one or two, trying to get the British Joe to take her as a substitute for Laura."

The second one shook his head. "That dame has no shame."

"Oh, nice one, Ricky! I'll have to borrow that." Skinny blew a perfect O of smoke into the air.

"Would it be all right if we took a peek at the club?" Dai asked.

The four men looked at one another and shrugged. "I don't see why not. You two don't look like you could cause a lot of trouble." Skinny grinned.

Oh, he had no idea. "We'll restrain ourselves, I assure you."

As I guided Dai toward the service entry to the club proper, I couldn't help but wonder at her curiosity. Did she want to 'see' it because Laura had worked here and she hoped it would give some clue as to her murderer? Or might it have more to do with the popinjay's mention of the place? It was an unpleasant thought.

The unassuming door opened into a curtained area, minimizing the amount of light that bled out from the dressing/prep room. Though the heavy red drapes kept the light from disturbing the patrons, it was a little disorienting from this side. With the door closed, the curtained-off space got very dark. Once my eyes adjusted to the gloom, I led Dai forward, pushing aside the drapes so we could look at the club beyond.

Black mahogany, red velvet, and bronze fixtures were the headliners in a room done in the increasingly popular Art Deco style. Everything was sleek geometries and visual effects. A small stage took up one end of the open floor, looking like a half-opened package. Light reflected off the angled partitions, entertaining the eyes even when no entertainment was available. More odd-angled partitions hid the area for the band; it looked like they could be easily widened or shortened depending on the needs of the entertainers.

"Prince seems especially interested in the place," Dai said. Still sitting in her arms, his small face turned to and fro, his nose high in the air sniffing for all he was worth. "Do describe it for me, Jacques, won't you? Include all the lovely details."

The bronze-rimmed black mahogany tables were triangular, with plush velvet chairs that looked more suited for an afternoon of comfortable reading in a private library than for a 'members only' speakeasy.

A mahogany bar filled with all manner of glasses and tidbits sprawled next to a bank of recessed wooden safety deposit boxes. They were very similar in style to those you could rent at a real bank, but had more flair. Each box had a small bronze plate with engraved Art Deco numbers.

Instead of being packed close together to maximize the space, the tables were purposely set three or four feet from one another, allowing renters some privacy as they imbibed their libations. Wealth had its advantages.

It being the middle of the afternoon, there weren't many customers, but those who'd made the trek looked fairly comfortable and content. I understood the appeal. Throw in some music, dancers, and cigarette girls, and the younger male set would have a good romp. I had to admit it appeared a lot classier than I'd expected.

CHAPTER 13

Returning to the dressing area after our peek at the Bank Underground, we learned little more than we had previously. Laura had grabbed what few possessions she'd kept in her locker when she turned in her notice, and the performers had told us all they knew, so we took our leave. On the drive home we rehashed all we had discovered. The musicians' information supported much of what we already suspected about Shannon. Getting information about the others wouldn't be anywhere as easy.

The Wu family's second car was nestled under the carport when we arrived, which meant Mr. Wu was home for dinner. The bicycle sitting propped against one of the carport columns announced Mrs. Vega was also here.

The mouth-watering scents that wafted out when I opened the rear door confirmed it. Smelled like we would have Rosa's special *puchero* this evening. A tasty stew of pork, beef, and chicken, it incorporated a wide variety of common and unusual vegetables. Rosa's recipe included a chunk of plantain, chickpeas, sweet potatoes, carrots, onions, potatoes, and rice. Yet it wasn't a heavy meal, and was quite delicious. Mrs. Vega and Mrs. Wu were chatting away at the kitchen table when we arrived.

A few years previously, Rosa had answered the Wus' advertisement for a part-time cook and housekeeper. The ad had stipulated that applicants must be fluent in a second language. This kept most of the whites who would likely take offense at the idea of working *for* a Chinese family from even applying. This also neatly circumvented revealing to the public the nationality of the family living at this address.

Previously, the job had belonged to Mrs. Ping. She'd been a hard worker, but like the employees at the laundry, she disapproved of Dai. She additionally didn't approve of keeping a foreigner in the house, and detested the easing of social barriers between royals and commoners as practiced in the household—despite that being one of the very *reasons* so many migrated to the land of opportunity and freedom. She'd returned home to China to care for family, never once adjusting her expectations the entire time she served here.

Rosa had made a marked change in our lives. Unlike Mrs. Ping, she accepted us as she found us. Her jovial personality was infectious, and she took the job more for something to keep her busy than actual monetary need. Despite the differences in countries, religions, and customs, she and Lien became fast friends, united by the fact that they'd both left their homelands behind and chosen to live here in Texas. Rosa had lost her husband and son during the Cristero War, in which those of the Catholic faith rebelled against the Calle government, which had passed laws against the church in an attempt to loosen the organization's hold on the people as well as its vast influence on politics.

"*Buenas tardes*, Daiyu, Jacques! Your timing is perfect." Rosa rose to her feet, giving us all a welcoming smile. "Dinner is just about ready."

Prince Razor gave a quick bark.

"Oh, and *buenas tardes* to you too, Prince. I saved you a little something to add to your meal." She scratched him behind the ear and he wagged his tail, enjoying every second. Yes, he had *all* the women entirely in his thrall, the pampered runt.

"I made some *jericalla* for dessert, Jacques. So everyone will get a treat today."

Dai laughed out loud. "Prince isn't the only one who gets spoiled around here."

My cheeks grew warm. Was it my fault it was one of my favorites? *Jericalla* was considered a custard, something between a flan and a crème brûlée, creamy and delicious. "Thank you, Mrs. Vega."

"I'm happy to make them. Cooking for just myself is not nearly as satisfying." Her eyes turned sad for a moment, and I was sure she was thinking of her husband and son.

Lien stood. "Go freshen up, then meet us in the dining room. Tye is already there reading the afternoon paper. I'm certain he'll be interested in what you three have been up to today." She studied us as if to give us a chance to come clean before questions got brought up at the supper table.

"Of course, *Mǔqīn.*"

I gave Prince his meal and treat, then cleaned up for dinner. The Wus' spacious dining room was painted in a light mauve, which contrasted well with the walnut trim running along the floor and ceiling. The walnut table comfortably seated six but could be extended to seat ten.

Dai's father sat at the head of the table, with Lien on the opposite end. Wu Tye was middle-aged with a round friendly face, which hid the sharp business mind that allowed him to walk the tightrope of managing a successful business without appearing to be doing *too* well. As a foreigner, he could earn the ire of those who might take it upon themselves to stop the Yellow Blight, just because they resented his success.

Dinner at the Wus' was not what anyone might call typical.

It would never be allowed in other households, but I ate with the family, and so did Rosa. The lines between the employers and the help didn't exist for meals, which made them a lot more comfortable, lively, and warm than mealtimes in other well-to-do households. According to the stories passed down from her parents to Dai and then to me, back in China the Wus were accustomed to dinners of multiple courses lavished upon them by a staff of twenty or more. They'd been lonely meals, however, and the lack of children and other family had been like a weight pressing down on them as their every move was watched and assessed by those around them. Lien and Tye still held firmly to most Chinese traditions and beliefs, but they no longer considered many of the social restrictions valid. That was something Mrs. Ping would likely never have understood, despite the fact that it would have made her time here more pleasant.

"Daiyu, I hear you made a friend today."

"Actually, *Fùqīn*, I may have made two new friends."

I flinched, realizing she probably meant Pierce as the second one.

"I might even be going to a party."

I wasn't sure what type of reactions I had expected to that statement, but stunned silence hadn't been one.

"A party?" Lien sounded half pleased, half horrified. "What kind of party?"

"Just a small get-together, *Mǔqīn*. Nothing to worry about." Dai's hands moved lightly over her plate, cutlery, and glassware, making sure she knew where each item was located.

"I thought you weren't interested in such things, my daughter." Tye's accent was more pronounced than Lien's.

Dai smiled. "I just hadn't met anyone interesting enough to bother going to the trouble."

"Maybe we should meet them before you make any arrangements." Lien's expression turned anxious.

"Jacques will be with me. There's nothing to worry about."

"Good for you, *mija*." Rosa served Dai some *puchero* before placing some in her own bowl. "Having friends is a wonderful thing."

Dai's mother still didn't look convinced. The pointed look she sent me a moment later told me I'd better make sure nothing untoward happened, or there'd be hell to pay. As if I would let anything happen to Dai!

Derailed by Dai's party announcement, her parents asked no more probing questions during dinner. I wondered if she'd done it deliberately, having calculated the effect it would have on her mother, thus curtailing unwanted questions for a time. The dragon sensed something was going on, and she wasn't wrong. But since Dai rarely strayed too far across the line, she couldn't pin down what it might be. With any luck, we would keep it that way.

I was just taking the last smooth spoonful of Rosa's exceptional *jericalla* when there was a knock at the front door. Everyone froze—such a thing was entirely uncommon.

"I'll get it." Answering doors, taking deliveries, and overseeing workmen had always been on my list of duties. I was the 'American' face of the Wu family, the better to keep as many unaware of their nationality as possible. Yet I couldn't help the tingle of apprehension that rose in my stomach as I moved to the front door. Most visitors came to the back for deliveries and other work, and during the daytime. It was now close to seven o'clock, and they'd come to the front door. Most unusual.

Upon opening the door, the first thing I saw was an enormous bouquet of yellow roses. A large envelope with a fancy 'D' on it was stuck prominently amongst the blossoms.

"Good evening! I have a delivery for D?" A grizzled old face came out from behind the flower arrangement with a lopsided grin. "Rarely do deliveries myself, but they paid a pretty penny for it, so I was more than happy to oblige." He craned his neck trying to look past me into the house.

"I'll take that, thank you." Juggling the large vase to keep hold of it, I fished some change out of my pocket for a tip.

"You have yourself a good evening." With a tilt of his hat in thanks, the man hoofed it back to the delivery truck and went on his way.

By the time I closed the door and turned to place the bouquet on the round table by the entrance, I had a full audience.

"Roses? Who would send us roses?"

I pulled the envelope from its perch. "I believe they are for Dai, ma'am." I had a compelling feeling about who had sent them, especially since they'd paid extra money for such a late delivery. At least he'd had the grace to make them yellow roses. Yellow ones stood for joy, friendship, and Texas. Whether he also chose them because of Dai's nationality, I preferred not to think about.

"Daiyu, who would send you flowers? Is there something we need to know about?" Once again Lien sounded both excited and frightened.

Rather than answer her, Dai turned in my direction. "What does the card say, Jacques?"

I opened the envelope and pulled out the message, skimming it quickly to make sure there wasn't anything untoward. It was a good thing I did. "My dear Miss Wu," I began. Pierce had actually written 'My dearest China Doll'— but that wasn't suitable for her parents' ears so I edited it. The tasteless cad. His handwriting was disgustingly neat.

"Please accept these flowers as a token of my appreciation. Your friend, Truman Pierce." What he actually said was 'As promised, I've arranged to have a formal evening party at the Dallas Country Club tomorrow at eight. All interested parties have been invited. Bring Jackie and anyone else you like with you. Let the games begin. Forever yours, Truman Pierce.'

I touched Dai's hand with the card so she'd take it, the better to keep anyone else from seeing what was actually there. Dai tucked it away with a dimpled smile as if she knew that what I'd read out loud was not the actual message. Still, was Truman out of his mind? What if I hadn't been the one to open the envelope?

"They're lovely, Dai." Rosa leaned and took a deep breath, inhaling the roses' scent. "Do you want to leave them here or should I move them to your room?"

"Leave them here or in the dining room, if you don't mind. The perfume is rather strong and might get too heavy in my bedroom." Dai reached out tentatively, and I guided her hand to one blossom while keeping her well away from any thorns. She caressed the large petals, painting a picture of them in her mind. "*Fùqīn*, would it be all right to use the telephone in your office? I want to call my friend and thank him for the thoughtful gift."

"Of course."

I noticed Dai's father give her a worried sideways glance as if realizing for the first time she was no longer his baby girl, and he might one day lose her.

As soon as we were out of sight and earshot of the others, having absconded to the safety of her father's office, Dai brought out Pierce's card and handed it back to me. "Please read me what it actually says, Jacques. No editing is required."

I read it out to her.

"That sounds more like him. And he's unknowingly done us another favor." Her dimpled smile came back. "There's one more person I had hoped we could add to our party. Now we can." Her smile brightened.

"Do you have your notebook with you? I need you to dial Dr. Campbell for me."

CHAPTER 14

The second day of this madness began like most others. The loud ringing bells of my alarm clock attacked my ears and the weight of a fifteen-pound dog settled on my chest, his rough tongue licking my stubbled face.

I rolled to the side, dislodging Prince as I reached over to stop the clock's blasted clanging. I didn't recall winding it up and setting it when I'd gone to bed, but I wasn't surprised. It was such an ingrained habit I must have automatically done it, despite the oddness of the previous day.

Grabbing my robe, I let Prince out to do his business and served him his meal. Milk and other staples had already been delivered and sat in a box under the covered drive, so I grabbed those and brought them inside the house. I then saw to my own toilette and started making breakfast.

Most days we stuck with traditional Chinese items rather than the usual American fare of toast, eggs, and bacon. Congee—a rice porridge that, depending on the toppings, could have a different flavor every day—was a regular item. You couldn't have congee without crullers—twisted pieces of dough deep-fried in oil—so I made a few of those as well. Dipping the crullers in the congee created a morning nirvana.

Wontons and steamed buns with an endless variety of stuffings made for perfect additions to our morning meals. The most important staple of breakfast was the tea—green, oolong, jasmine, and more. They weren't always easy to get, so coffee was an occasional alternative.

"Good morning, Jacques."

I glanced up in surprise in the midst of setting the table. "Dai, you're awake!"

She stepped up to the table and took her usual seat, a slight frown on her face. "You don't have to sound so shocked. It's not that unusual."

I was glad she couldn't see my eyes roll at the statement. Dai was *not* an early riser. Getting her out of bed was a chore all on its own. It had nothing to do with her blindness, either, as her regimented life helped set her body clock. "If you say so."

Her frown became more pronounced. Luckily, Prince chose that time to bark to be let back into the house, and I escaped before the moment became more difficult.

Prince ran in to greet her. He licked her face when she picked him up, and her frown smoothed away as if it never existed. As much as I loved my sister, and as often as she denied it, she was a bear to rouse in the morning. The fact that she was up, dressed, and ready for breakfast before seven screamed of how excited she was about the party tonight. I'd have preferred not to be reminded of the coming ordeal for a while longer. To say I was nervous about the event would be an understatement.

It was somewhat comical to see Dai's parents' expressions of shocked surprise at discovering her up so early when they joined us. Both looked at me for an explanation, and all I could do was shrug. Despite no words having passed our lips, Dai's slight frown returned as they sat.

"It really isn't such a big deal that I'm up this early, is it?" Her lower lip jutted out, making for an adorable image, something I doubted she realized.

"Daughter, I love you, but yes. This is rather surprising,"

her father said. For him to even comment was unusual, and it carried a lot more weight than anything Mrs. Wu or I might have said.

"Dai, is something the matter? If there's something about this party that worries you..."

"No, everything is fine. I'm just looking forward to it." She sighed. "You act as if I've never been excited about anything before."

In unusual unanimity, both her parents and I exchanged looks with one another. Dai being genuinely thrilled by anything was indeed rare, and everyone knew it. In silent consensus, we dropped the subject.

While Mr. Wu headed to the laundry in the coupe with Mrs. Wu, Dai and I went upstairs to go through our morning exercises. These were not the types of exercises most Americans would be acquainted with. The household practiced tai chi, a form of exercise with roots in Taoism, one of the main religious practices in China. Based on the dark and light natures of yin and yang, the aspects of balancing the mind and body were perfect for Dai. Her family practiced the yang style, the one favored by the imperial family, which was less taxing than some of the other forms.

It was a marvel to watch her flow from one form to the next, her balance and movements graceful and precise. It had taken a great deal of work to get to this point, and not just for her. I'd been tasked with learning tai chi with Dai so I might ground myself and additionally help Dai do her exercises every day. Her father had been an excellent teacher, cradling Dai's limbs as he moved them for her, so she would *feel* and know what to do.

Once we finished and changed clothes, we took the sedan to join the others at the laundry. Dai ran through her work preparing the detergent and cleaners for the wash in record time—something the workers made a note of and whispered about when they thought I wasn't paying attention. As if they needed more fodder to justify shunning Dai even more than they already did! While she'd stated more than once that it didn't bother her, it bothered me.

My nervousness over the upcoming evening only increased as the day wore onward. I didn't look forward to being forced into Truman Pierce's company again, yet I was pleased we would see Dr. Campbell. The way she and Dai had hit it off, I felt it had the possibility of becoming a great friendship, something I very much hoped for Dai to have. Much as I relished her relying on me, it would be good for her to have a friend—one with a sharp mind that could keep up with hers and who was, additionally, of the same sex.

All her work done, we left the laundry before noon and drove back to the house for a repast of leftovers. I kept busy preparing lunch and cleaning up, more than happy to keep myself distracted. In all honesty, neither of us had ever been to a party, let alone a country club.

We'd agreed to pick up Dr. Campbell on the way, so I spent a little time looking at maps to plan out the best route to fetch her, then get us north to Highland Park and Mockingbird Lane. Prince got a bath and a brush-down as well as an elegant dog collar in red, white, and blue.

Chauffeurs wouldn't usually be allowed to set foot in the place but I would be attending the soiree as a guest, so I opted for a double-breasted black dinner jacket and bow tie. When Mrs. Wu had insisted, some time back, that I needed the fancy evening wear, I'd thought the expense unnecessary. The dragon enjoyed more wisdom than I.

Rosa couldn't contain her own excitement and came over early to help Dai prepare in Mrs. Wu's place as Lien's schedule was full. Trepidation and admiration clashed as I spotted Dai coming down the stairs once they finished. Rather than a sweeping, low-backed dress in satin or velvet as was the popular choice nowadays, Dai had instead decided on a *cheongsam*, a modern variation of the Manchu dress, in red silk with a black lace overlay with sewn-in shiny black beads. The gown was form-fitting and displayed a Chinese collar, with a closure that folded to the right from the shoulder down the right seam. The frogs of the closure were made in the shape of black dragons with red thread at the edges and red crystal eyes. With her black-tinted teashade glasses and red crystal hair pins, every bit of her screamed foreign, exotic, mysterious. There would be no way anyone would miss the nationality to which she belonged.

My throat closed on itself, and it took several tries to get the words out. "Dai... are you sure this is how you want to dress for this?"

"Truman is doing his part. I need to do mine."

I shook my head, having no clue what she meant by that. "This is a terrible idea."

Rosa tsked at me from the top of the stairs. "It's good for Dai to show her pride in her heritage. And she looks *muy preciosa*." She beamed as if she couldn't have been more pleased with how Dai was turned out.

"Yes, but..." It wouldn't be so great if she got deported. Chinese pride happened to be the worst thing she could show in the current political and social climate.

"Jacques, stop frowning. I can feel you doing it from here. It'll be fine." Dai descended the rest of the stairs and held her hand out toward me.

I had no choice but to take it. "You look beautiful. But this dress is just going to make Pierce even more determined to spend time with you."

She flashed her dimpled smile. "Are you jealous?"

"Of that popinjay? Don't be ridiculous."

Rosa held a hand over her mouth as if not trusting herself not to laugh. Her eyes filled with mirth. She handed over a matching clutch purse, which would include a copy of Dai's papers, money for emergencies, and wrapped dog biscuits for Prince. The purse also contained a red war fan, which held blades for the ribs, and Dai could use it for personal protection. Rosa also gave me a folded wrap for Dai in case the evening turned cool.

"Don't be too late coming home, you two," Rosa said. "I expect Lien will be up waiting to make sure you make it back all right. If not for the fundraiser, she would have been here to see you off—though it's probably better that she couldn't make it."

I groaned internally. It hadn't been a point I'd thought about, though Rosa was absolutely right. I doubted the dragon would have allowed Dai such leeway in what she got to wear. But she would wait up for us, and she'd see what they'd done when we got back. As if the evening weren't stressful enough already! "I'll make sure we're home at a reasonable hour."

"What he means is, he'll *try*." Dai's amusement was palpable.

I rolled my eyes. It was good she was looking forward to the party because the closer we came, the more I *wasn't*. And this type of comment didn't help.

I got Dai and Prince tucked away in the rear seat of the sedan, and made sure the directions to the club still resided in my pocket.

Rosa stopped me as I headed toward the driver's side and straightened my bow tie. "*Mijo*, don't worry so much. Just try to have fun." She smiled. "This will be good for both of you."

Except she didn't have any idea what 'this' was actually about. If any of them had known, they'd have locked us both away.

CHAPTER 15

Dr. Campbell had requested we pick her up at the hospital. The moment I chose a parking spot, she exited the building as if she'd been watching for our arrival. She rushed over, her cheeks red, wearing a long buttoned-up lab coat, sunglasses and a church bowler hat. It was almost as if she wanted to make sure no one saw or recognized her, but all it did was draw attention to her. She wore a pair of open toe shoes with pearls. I could see just the bottom edge of her evening dress, which matched the color of her nail polish.

I jumped out of the car to open the door for her. "Dr. Campbell, are you all right?"

Her face turned even redder at the question. She nodded and dove into the back seat and out of sight, her envelope clutch purse squeezed in a death grip in her hand. Shaking my head, I closed the door and returned to the driver's seat. I unobtrusively used the peep mirror to make sure all was well.

Prince jumped into Aiden's lap, which startled the doctor. He licked her palm.

"Don't worry, he's only saying hello," Dai said. "Dr. Campbell, this is Prince Razor. Prince, this is Aiden, a friend."

Tentatively, she patted his head and then scratched him

behind the ear, which got his curled tail wagging. She was coiled like a spring, but Aiden relaxed one degree at a time as Prince encouraged her attention. It looked like he'd made another conquest. Truman Pierce would never beat this mutt's record for stolen hearts.

"I hope coming with us is not too much of an inconvenience for you."

Dr. Campbell kept her attention centered on Prince. "My, my family was ecstatic to hear I was going. My sisters especially. They insisted I let them help." Her head drooped. "I don't get out often."

Dai nodded. "I have to admit, this is my first time going to something like this too, so I appreciate you coming with us."

Aiden's head rose, her ice-blue eyes shining. "There's a killer on the loose. Of course I'll do what I can to help."

I wondered if she realized how rare that was. Most individuals would prefer to pretend the trouble didn't exist or insist that it had nothing to do with them, rather than put themselves through something they felt uncomfortable with. Though I had to admit there were people out there with more significant problems to deal with, especially in these troubling times, so getting involved wasn't an option for them. Nothing was ever just black or white.

"Well, I wanted to thank you all the same." Dai gave her a smile. "I know it's not how you would have preferred to spend your evening."

"Honestly, it's not a bother."

I doubted Dai believed that any more than I did. From what I'd seen so far, just the thought of going on this outing was making the doctor tense. That made me even more curious as to what she was wearing beneath the lab coat.

Aiden captured all of our attention when she said, "I ran more tests on the dress today."

"Was there more to be found?" Dai sat very still, ready to absorb any new information.

Dealing with something she was comfortable with, Aiden no longer looked as nervous as before. "The high concentration of arsenic was bothering me. There was more there than I would have expected in a dye. So I ran additional tests on samples from different locations on the dress."

"And?"

"I think someone tampered with the gown," Aiden said. "The amounts of arsenic present are not consistent. While I would expect some fluctuation, it wouldn't be to the extent the tests seemed to indicate."

Dai nodded. "So they wanted to make sure Laura wouldn't survive receiving the gift, then they tried to cover it up by sending the dress to the laundry."

"I'm afraid so. The extra arsenic would have been washed away, leaving only the concentration that is actually part of the dye." Dr. Campbell looked deadly serious. "We definitely have a cold-blooded murderer in our midst."

A frosty finger rushed down my spine. What were we getting ourselves into? I concentrated on the drive, trying not to ponder the implications of what Aiden had said.

Using the state's extensive system of highways allowed for faster travel and ate up the miles to Highland Park. Once we turned on Mockingbird Lane, it was easy to tell when we neared our destination, as the landscape changed to green rolling hills and well-cared-for trees. The club owned a vast 117.5 acres, which included the area's best golf course.

Glorious hues of orange and purple splashed across the open Texas sky as the sun set, and reflected beautifully off the calm waters of Turtle Creek. The main clubhouse rose majestically in layers to its three-storied height, and a wide all-around porch encircled the ground floor. Lights glowed from within, beacons to those still playing on the greens so they might find their way home.

The parking area was already half full, speaking to the DCC's popularity. Their logo was a D and a C, with an elongated C superimposed across both. It looked like a branding iron, thus harking back to the cattle driven across the Texas plains.

I chose a spot for the sedan, off to the side, then got out to open the car door for the ladies. Dr. Campbell's lab coat was still buttoned as high as it would go, with the hat set firmly on her head and the sunglasses covering her eyes. Despite how she might feel about her dress or hair, letting her present herself like this would just make matters worse.

"Dr. Campbell, if I may be so bold as to make a suggestion? It would be best if you left your hat, lab coat, and glasses behind in the car. It's doubtful the evening will be chilly."

"Lab coat? Hat?" Dai extended her hand from inside the car so I could help her out.

Aiden's cheeks turned crimson. "Y-you're probably right." With fumbling fingers, she undid the buttons of the coat. Settling Dai's palm on the side of the sedan, I moved to help the doctor take it off and folded the coat before placing in the back seat. She took longer in removing the church bowler, trying to be careful not to displace the hairdo beneath. Last but not least were the sunglasses.

The doctor's short brown hair had been curled around her head, with pearl hairpins used as accents. Her cream colored dress fell in tiers, multiple rounded panels stitched with embroidered pearls. The whole was a mix of Greek and flapper styles. The skirt's innermost layer draped her in flowing cloth from the knees down to her ankles.

Unlike her usual work clothes with the vest, apron, and lab coat, the dress helped shape Dr. Campbell to show she was indeed a woman. The light application of makeup and pale pink lipstick toned down her rugged looks into a more feminine aspect—the blush still lingering on her cheeks and shy, embarrassed expression even more so.

Aiden would never be anyone's vision of a beautiful woman, but to my surprise, I found the look endearing.

"Shall we, ladies?" I placed Dai's hand in the crook of my arm, then presented the other for Dr. Campbell. After a moment of hesitation, she settled her large hand delicately at my elbow, her short freshly-colored nails showing to best advantage.

Prince brought up the rear.

Coming up the stairs to the main entry, we found our host lounging in a white wicker loveseat with rust red cushions. He was smoking a cigarette and his eyes lit up as he caught sight of us. Standing, Pierce half bowed in our direction. "I'm so glad you made it. I've been looking forward to this evening very much."

Blond hair still slicked back, he was the picture of a perfect millionaire. His double-breasted dinner jacket was a rich, deep burgundy and had been tailored for him. A large white carnation served as his boutonniere and was even more noticeable against the jacket's dark color. His crisp white shirt had burgundy colored buttons, and he wore a matching bow tie. The black slacks were straight, the seams pressed into sharp relief.

When Pierce got a good look at Dai, the ensuing bright smile would have blotted out the sun. I was glad she couldn't see it—though she probably felt it, it was so radiant.

I still wasn't falling for it.

"China Doll, you look exquisite!" He came in close, but a low growl from her canine guard was enough to warn him back.

"Prince, be nice." Dai sounded amused.

"Ah, yes, Prince Razor, so good of you to come." A raised brow showed he'd not thought of the possibility. But his invitation had stipulated she might bring whomever she liked. "It's great to see you again, too, Jackie." Flashing a smirk at my frown, the popinjay turned his attention to Aiden. "And who might this be?"

"Allow me to introduce you," Dai said. "Truman Pierce, this is Dr. Aiden Campbell. Aiden, this is Truman. It's thanks to him that we've been able to get close to those possibly involved with the incident."

To give him credit, his smile and manner didn't falter when he inspected his extra guest. "It's a pleasure, Dr. Campbell. Any friend of my beloved China Doll is mine as well." He took her hand and kissed it, lingering over it just a bit too long and making the doctor blush.

I wanted to punch him.

Aiden shyly looked away, her cheeks flushing even deeper at the unexpected gesture. I ground my teeth, my temper trying to get the best of me. I should be happy he had lavished some attention on Campbell, but I didn't trust him. If he was setting her up for ridicule later, I would make sure he came to regret it.

"Shall we go inside?"

Before I could intervene, Pierce took Dai's hand and placed it in the crook of his arm to guide her in.

"Dr. Campbell?" I presented my arm for Aiden, and she accepted it somewhat timidly. Prince trotted after Pierce and Dai as if he owned the place.

Then I spotted Pierce leaning over to whisper in Dai's ear as if the two had known each other for years and were the best of friends.

I might just kill the popinjay before the evening was over.

CHAPTER 16

The interior of the Dallas Country Club was impressive. The founders had spared no expense. Buffed stone flooring filled the entryway, giving way to polished wood set in eye-catching patterns. Pale yellow walls with dark wood trim invited guests to continue forward in several directions. Pierce led us to a wide staircase leading upstairs.

With a jolt of panic, I realized he meant to take Dai up them. Before I could intervene, he surprised me by saying "Steps leading up," and waiting for her acknowledgment before moving forward. He patiently stepped with her, not rushing her and letting her set the pace. I was so astonished at this unexpected courtesy and awareness, all I could do was follow quietly behind them.

Soft orchestral music filtered down, teasing us as to the possible delights upstairs. Though the hour was still early, the party was already in full swing. For a last-minute affair, it didn't feel like one: Buffet tables lined with food filled one wall of the ample open space, while chairs sat against the wall opposite. A live band had assembled in a far corner on the left. The variety of the instruments being played and those in stands nearby proudly proclaimed the band could perform everything from orchestral to jazz and anything in between. Dancers filled the middle of the space, while others stood or sat around the periphery.

From the laughter and glitter of those present, you'd never have guessed we lived in the middle of the worst economic struggle of our age. Yet it wasn't entirely surprising. Rumors abounded over harder-hit states like California and New York, telling of parties of immense excess while people starved on the streets. It was almost as if some believed denying the fact of the catastrophic fall in U.S. stock market prices and the consequent hardships would make it go away.

Heads turned and eyes grew wide as our presence was noticed. Most of the faces looked young, so it appeared Pierce had been selective with his invitations. That implied forethought and organization, two attributes I would not have given him credit for. And I still wouldn't, not until I knew he hadn't just dumped the job on an assistant or secretary to take care of it for him.

"Truman, darling!" A blonde with pencil-thin brows, a low-cut red satin dress, and a glass of champagne swished over to them. I wondered what loophole they were exploiting to be serving something like that so freely.

"You're always so over the top! So utterly shameless. I love it!" Her brown-eyed gaze kept flicking between Dai and Pierce.

"I always aim to please. Linda Carmichael, allow me to introduce you to Miss Daiyu Wu."

Linda shifted her entire attention to Dai. "She's so *Chinese*! Wherever did you find her? Can she speak English?"

"Yes, I can. I am quite fluent in the language, thank you for asking." Dai's tone was pure frost. "Pleased to make your acquaintance."

The woman stared as if a beloved pet had started reciting *Hamlet*. "Oh! *Oh*. How fabulous!" She clapped her hands like a little girl, almost splashing champagne on her expensive dress.

Coming here had been a *terrible* idea. People inched toward us as if sensing something exciting about to begin.

"Linda, please. Daiyu is my guest." For once Pierce's

expression and tone were serious. "There's no reason to be rude."

The woman froze in mid-clap, then woodenly swiveled toward him. Those around us suddenly turned away to hunt for entertainment elsewhere. It didn't bode well for the rest of us.

"This isn't like you." It was an accusation more than a comment. Several emotions crossed Linda's face, too quickly for me to interpret. "Truman, are you *involved* with her?"

Rather than answer her, he gestured for us to proceed, leaving Linda to fume quietly behind us. The conclusion she'd jumped to didn't please me in the least. It was beyond rude. While Pierce might not care about his reputation, there was Dai's to consider, and I would not stand by and allow anyone to tarnish it. Right or wrong, a stain on a woman's character was a grievous thing in our society. It was bad enough they held her race and blindness against her through no fault of her own. Luckily, removing ourselves seemed to do the trick. I was sure the conversation wasn't over between them, but fortunately, it appeared she wouldn't be causing a scene.

"Please accept my deepest apologies, China Doll. Linda isn't always the most astute of people."

"Are the two of you close?" Dai kept her voice low. If it was because of concern or just to keep the question out of nearby ears, I couldn't tell. It was rather worrisome.

"Not especially, though I'm sure she'd like to think otherwise." Pierce shrugged. "We've known each other since we were children. Her father and mine have been involved in several business ventures together over the years."

Wherever we passed, heads turned, conversations died, eyes widened and stared. While she might be blind, I knew Dai was aware of them all. She kept her head held high, her heritage at the forefront for all to see, giving every impression she was royalty and receiving their attention as only her due.

In an alcove at the back of the room, we found the group this soiree had been arranged to gather together. Placed as it was in the corner, and thus out of the central dancing area, it stood as a small island of calm. People came and went, greeting Pierce's special guests and trading pleasantries, without monopolizing their time. Foreign zoo animals on display.

Asquith wore a classic red rose as his boutonniere—appropriate, as one of the flower's meanings was a symbol of deep love for someone lost. Shannon hovered at his elbow, her expression flip-flopping between thrilled and jealous depending on who walked past. Her evening gown looked new, the dark green contrasting nicely with her waved black hair and fair skin. The dress didn't quite hug all her curves, betraying that it had come from a rack and wasn't tailor-made. That and the lack of sparkling jewelry declared she didn't come from money. From the dismissive glances she kept receiving, her merit was being assessed by all the women in the place, and they found her wanting. The men seemed less particular and appeared to approve of what they saw.

Among this crowd, being poor looked to be an even greater offense than being Chinese. At least the latter had the benefit of being entertaining.

Lord and Lady Domberry, on the other hand, looked like a couple of regulars. Paul appeared to be in his element, though the haughty undertones to everything he said and did would not be making him any friends in this crowd. He apparently considered them the *nouveau riche* and therefore not up to his level.

Behind them, sitting in one of the chairs by an open window, was Mrs. Grey. She wore a modest black dress with pearls. Her attention seemed to center around Asquith, her expression markedly neutral.

"Apologies for my lengthy absence, but see whom I've stumbled across." Pierce flashed one of his big smiles at the group.

William's eyes showed some life as he focused on us, as if he'd previously been just an automaton going through the motions. "Miss Wu, lovely to see you again. You look ravishing."

"Thank you, that's very kind." Dai gave him her best smile,

which brought a little more color to his face. It was a little scary how well she knew the effect she might have on others when she chose to. Shannon, her expression sour, didn't appear pleased by this one bit.

"I'd like to introduce you to a friend of mine if that's all right," Dai asked.

"Of course. I'd be honored." Asquith stood a little straighter, meaning every word.

"Aiden, this is William Asquith, fifth son of the second Earl of Oxford and Asquith. Did I get that right?"

William looked astonished. "Exactly right, Miss Wu. You've quite a memory."

Dai flashed him another smile. Shannon turned almost as green as her dress.

"William, this is Dr. Aiden Campbell. She's a pathologist at Baylor Hospital." Dai paused, then lobbed her first volley of the evening. "In deaths involving foul play, she's called upon to perform autopsies and works closely with the *police*."

CHAPTER 17

Dr. Campbell's introduction to the others was something we had discussed the night before. While not technically accurate—it was the justice of the peace who would call the doctor for an autopsy, not the police department—we'd decided the word 'police' would make more of an impact. It was my job to watch the group's reaction, specifically searching for any signs of discomfort or shock. I included the popinjay in the list of suspects to observe. Helpful or not, it was too early to rule him out as the guilty party. He could be doing all this just for a lark.

To my disappointment, Pierce's eyes lit up with curiosity rather than guilt. Asquith appeared intrigued, while Lizzie appeared startled, as if Aiden had somehow changed from a woman to something alien. Paul looked puzzled, apparently not understanding why anyone would care. Shannon's expression turned suspicious, as if she smelled a rat. Mrs. Grey sat as impassively as before, her face growing even more unreadable.

"You... you cut open dead bodies?" Lizzie took a half step back, her face pale.

Aiden gave a soft sigh, seemingly well acquainted with the

reaction. "Not unless it's necessary. Mostly I work with tissue samples and a microscope looking for signs of disease."

Lizzie didn't look reassured in the least.

"Whatever prompted you to go into such an unusual field?" William asked.

Aiden's cheeks reddened a touch. "The first time I looked at a blood sample in science class. All the microscopic components were so beautiful, logical. I decided to learn all about them. You always know what to expect from them. They make sense..." Her voice tapered off at the last.

Dai brought up the next question. "And doing autopsies?"

The doctor's cheeks reddened even more. "That was something of an accident. They needed someone right away for a sensitive case, and I was the only one still in the lab at three in the morning. I, I guess they thought I did a suitable job because they put me in the rotation after that." Her voice brightened. "It's really fascinating, and I don't mind. Plus some of the others don't show the dead the respect they should."

Aiden looked at the ground after that, as if she hadn't meant to say the last part, yet wasn't entirely sorry for having done so.

"Sometimes life is like that, isn't it? Giving us opportunities we never would have sought on our own." Asquith's gaze got a far-off expression. "Wonderful, unexpected opportunities."

"Yes, *fate*." Truman was looking intently at Dai as he spoke. I ground my teeth. *The freebooter.*

William nodded. "Exactly."

"I totally agree." Shannon rested her hand on William's arm, her voice sultry. "My deep friendship with Laura, and meeting you through her, feels that way to me."

Domberry rolled his eyes. "Yes, I'm sure that's how it must have felt."

Shannon sent him a sharpened glare which he returned, invisible daggers flying between them.

Lizzie piped up, her previous discomfort a thing of the past. "It was for me, too. When I met Paul." Her expression turned dreamy. "He looked so handsome and regal at the winter social where we met." She smiled in fond remembrance. "He's a fabulous dancer. Swept me off my feet in more ways than one. Didn't you, dear?"

"Sure." Paul glanced away as if that wasn't how he remembered things.

That was when I recalled one of Shannon's comments during our prior meeting, the one where she'd called Domberry a 'penniless royal.' Had he married the plain-looking Lizzie for something other than love? If the Asquiths were new royalty, as Domberry had insinuated previously, what other reason would he have for marrying someone he obviously considered beneath him? His obsession with money might be the answer. What if he'd targeted her to ingratiate himself into the Asquith family? If so, it put him on the same level as Shannon. Perhaps they disliked each other so much because they were more alike than they cared to admit. Unfortunately, while that might have been a motive for Shannon to rid herself of Laura, it wouldn't hold for Paul. Or would it?

"A winter social? Is that similar to the famous balls they sometimes mention on the radio programs? The ones with the fancy ballgowns?" Dai asked. Only someone who knew her well would know that beneath her innocent tone hid pointed traps.

Lizzie laughed. "Oh goodness no! Nothing like that. You only see those at private parties. Like the kind Paul's uncle loves to throw. Incredibly lavish, exclusive, and *extremely* expensive.

"A winter social is more of a community get-together, open to anyone who wants to come. They're normally held at the local dance hall, at the *palais de dance*. Sounds so elegant, don't you think? With the splendid music and all the new dances, dancing has become terribly popular back home. A way for people to forget their troubles."

"And their morals." Surprisingly, this came from Mrs. Grey. "They are places looking to make trouble by not requiring chaperones to accompany unwed ladies. Shameful."

"Oh, Nanny, these are modern times. Plus, I only ever went

to the ones organized by Father Eustis. Nothing improper would ever happen there." Lizzie brought her attention back to Dai. "I do all right at the waltz, but the foxtrot is a bit much for me."

Dai nodded as if she knew what Lizzie was talking about, even though she'd never seen anyone dance them. "So no fancy ballgowns for you then?"

"It's funny you've asked about those," Asquith said. "Laura was curious about them, too. I'd promised to get her a new gown after our wedding."

"A new one?"

"Yes. I had Lizzie bring her one of my mother's old gowns as a present when they insisted on coming to meet her." Asquith's eyes lit up. "She was so happy when I presented it to her. Over the moon. Said it made her feel like a fairytale princess. Looked like one, too." His eyes misted over. "Please, please excuse me for a minute."

The moment Asquith was out of hearing distance, Shannon snorted and shook her head. "You should have seen her. Laura wore it every chance she got, even slept in it. She pranced around all over the apartment wearing it. It wasn't even her size, and way out of style." Despite her dismissive tone, it was apparent she'd also felt a little jealous.

"I'm sure that didn't matter to her." This surprising statement came from Aiden. "Sometimes it's nice to pretend to be something other than what you are."

Lizzie nodded in immediate understanding, but the lovelier Shannon just gave a flippant smirk.

"If you'll pardon me, I think I'll go look after William." Mrs. Grey wore a slight frown, the first real expression she'd shown all evening. She soon disappeared in the same direction as Asquith.

Paul rolled his eyes. "I would have escaped to another continent too if I was always being babied by that woman."

"Really, what a thing to say." Lizzie smacked her husband lightly on the arm. "She's quite dedicated, you know. You can't find help like that anywhere anymore."

Dai pulled her war fan from the clutch purse and snapped it open to fan herself. Though the sun had fallen, all the people milling around and dancing kept the air in the vast room from cooling. "Has Mrs. Grey been with your family long?"

"Oh, for ages!" Lizzie said. "Her family has served ours for generations. But she'll be the last, I'm afraid. Her husband died in an accident quite young, and they didn't have any children. Mother said they took pity on her not long after and had her move in with us. Taking care of us gave her something to live for. She'd never say so, but Nanny missed William terribly when he left."

"Did she like Laura?" Dai asked.

"Of course she did." Lizzie seemed puzzled at the question.

Paul raised a brow. "You saw her. Always watching, judging. And with that face, probably scary good at Three Card Brag."

"Three Card Brag?" This wasn't a game I'd heard of before.

"It's similar to poker," Pierce said. "Bluffing your opponents to win is one of the most important skills in the game."

"Oh, Paul, Nanny doesn't gamble." Lizzie frowned at him. "It's a sin!"

"Her loss, not mine." He shrugged. "She'd really rake it in if she gave it a go."

Lizzie looked shocked for a moment then turned indignant. "I'm thirsty, Paul. Please fetch me something cool to drink."

"Really, darling."

"Now, *Paul*."

Domberry half turned and rolled his eyes where she couldn't see it, but made sure the rest of us could. "But of course."

Though it seemed to take a lot to get her there, Elizabeth Domberry had a temper.

Removing people from the suspect list would not be as easy as we'd hoped.

CHAPTER 18

"Please don't pay attention to anything he says. He really is sweet, he just thinks it's bad form to show it. Honestly." The desperate look in her eyes stated what we all already knew—what we'd seen was the real Paul.

"It's a stressful time for everyone in your family," Dai said. "Don't worry on our account."

"Thank you. You're very kind."

Skirts rustled behind us as someone approached in a hurry.

"There, you see, Wally? Just like I told you." Linda Carmichael had caught up to us and was pointing at Dai. "An evil temptress spinning her web right in our midst."

An out of breath young man stopped beside her. His ordinary clothes and the large camera clutched in his hand stated what, if not who, he was.

Linda stomped her foot. "You fool, what are you doing? Hurry up and take the picture!"

Red-faced, the young fellow brought the camera up and pointed it in Dai's direction. As if we'd rehearsed it, Pierce and I moved as one to block his view.

There was as a small pop as the bulb went off. The ensuing bright flash made everything go white, and I could see absolutely nothing for several seconds. It was disconcerting—yet this was something Dai lived with every single day.

"I will take that, if you don't mind."

I heard a yelp after Aiden's words, and a warning growl from Prince Razor. After I'd blinked numerous times and the afterimage of the flash abated, I found Aiden glowering down at the newcomer. She gripped his camera in one hand, holding it away from both him and Carmichael.

Whether we wanted it or not, we were now the indisputable center of attention. Even the dancers nearby had stopped, despite the band still playing boogie-woogie.

"Linda, what are you playing at?" Pierce loomed over her, his expression a blank mask but his eyes flashing. "I told you, Miss Wu is my *guest*. Are you trying to embarrass me?"

"No, of course not! I'm doing this *for* you! Saving you from, from this Yellow Menace!"

I turned my back on them, taking Dai's hand and placing it on my arm. "We should leave. This is bound to become unpleasant."

Dai shook her head, not in the least perturbed. "We can't. We don't have everything we came for yet. Take me to where Mrs. Grey was sitting."

I waffled between doing as she asked or trying to lead her away from here regardless. Glancing back at the gathered crowd, I realized I'd never get her past them unscathed, so we gravitated to Mrs. Grey's vacated seat.

"Razor, to me."

Prince jumped to us and set himself as head guard, teeth bared and prepared for battle. I pitied anyone who didn't heed the warning. I stood to Dai's right, the rear wall and alcove corner protecting her other sides. Her war fan with its pointed steel blades, which were concealed by the cloth-covered front, lay on her lap at the ready.

Aiden and Shannon dropped back toward us as Linda's shrill denials of wrongdoing rose in pitch. Amazingly, Pierce appeared calm. He kept his voice low. It seemed this wasn't the first time he'd had to confront a tantruming Linda. From the rolling eyes of several of those watching, it looked like it wasn't theirs either.

"Why are you so blind? You're being taken for a ride. She's just out to get your money, Truman. But you never have to worry about such things with me. I love you for who you are, not what you have. But that's all she's after. Can't you see? I'm *protecting* you." Linda's tone drew out into a whine. She reached out to grab Pierce's hand, but he deftly avoided her attempt.

For the first time, Pierce let his annoyance shine through. "Enough is enough, Linda. Go home. We can talk about this later, when you're calmer—maybe even sober. Take your man with you on the way out."

Linda stared at him as if he'd slapped her. "Wha-what?" She flipped from shocked to flaming in an instant, her entire face turning red and splotchy. "You *dare*? You dare say that to *me*? Daddy will hear about this, Truman. Your father will get an earful and so will you. You wait and see!"

She stomped off into the crowd, shoving at anyone who didn't move out of her way quickly enough. Wally didn't even ask for his camera back, just slunk off after Linda with his head down, like a doomed man walking to the gallows.

Shannon was smirking, looking every bit like the cat who ate the canary. "So much for *polite* society."

She wasn't wrong.

CHAPTER 19

Linda's banishment and her huffy departure seemed to take most of the life out of the party—almost as if it had been the culmination of the evening, and those present no longer had anything to look forward to. Over the next hour, in ones and twos, they dropped by to excuse themselves, many adding whispered condolences on how things had turned out.

Pierce ignored the comments, acting as if nothing untoward had occurred. A few of those leaving looked disappointed by this. Despite appearances, maybe our host wasn't universally liked. There was plenty about him I didn't approve of, so perchance others weren't fooled by him either. But it hadn't stopped them from eating his food or enjoying his alcohol.

I doubted I'd like them any better.

"Prince, here you go." Dai slipped him a treat from her clutch, having him stand down from guard mode. The saying of his second name alone was the signal for more abrasive behavior, his first name an indicator his duty was done. He lay down at her feet to contentedly chew away, alert but no longer showing teeth.

With Pierce occupied, Dai turned her attention to Shannon, who was now in a pleasant mood. Without Asquith as a distraction or Domberry as an adversary, it would most likely be our best opportunity for information gathering.

"Miss Daugherty, how long had you and Laura been roommates?"

Shannon stepped back a little to draw closer to Dai, but her gaze remained on the rest of the room. The music continued to play, now switching to a lively waltz, despite the thinning numbers of the dancers. "About three years, I guess."

"Met her at work?"

Shannon chuckled. "She would never have thought of working there if it weren't for me. No, we'd known each other for years. Raised in the same backwater in East Texas."

"So the two of you came to Dallas together?"

She chuckled again. "Laura *begged* me to let her come with me. Winona was too small for her. There's a big wide world waiting for us, she said, and we should go take it."

I raised a brow, not quite believing her. It didn't mesh with the image I'd been building of the deceased, but it fit Shannon to a T.

"So you have no ambitions yourself?" Dai cocked her head. "Now that Laura's gone, will you be returning to Winona?"

Shannon's eyes narrowed and she stared at Dai as if trying to make sure she wasn't being made fun of. I bit the inside of my cheek to keep from laughing.

"No. I have a job, a place to live. And I have my eye on a few possibilities. It would be a pity to waste the opportunities Laura helped find, don't you think?"

Dai cocked her head in the other direction. "Will you be looking for another roommate then? A friend of mine is searching for an apartment to share."

Shannon hesitated. "I haven't decided. Laura felt bad about leaving me in the lurch, so she used money she'd stashed away to cover her share of the rent for six months. She was stupid that way."

For the first time, I saw a glint of grief in her eyes.

"Would it be all right for us to see it, anyway? If you do eventually decide you'd like a roommate, we'd be ahead of the game."

"I suppose."

"Splendid." Dai smiled. "If you'd give Jacques the details, we can come visit whenever it's convenient for you. Sometime tomorrow, perhaps?"

Shannon eyed us as if unsure of what we were up to. "Sure, I guess that works. But it needs to be before three."

She pulled a social card from her small fabric purse, which matched her green dress. Someone came prepared, though I doubted she'd had much opportunity to use them.

Our lost party members returned one by one. Domberry brought with him a glass of chilled white wine for his wife in one hand, the other holding a tumbler filled with something stronger. From the slight waver in his gait, he'd drunk at least a couple before returning. He presented Lizzie her glass with a flourish. "Your drink as requested, madam." The 'as' came out 'ash.' He'd definitely had several drinks while he'd been gone.

"Thank you." Lizzie's cheeks colored in a combination of pleasure and embarrassment.

Asquith returned a minute later with Mrs. Grey in tow. By this point most of the floor was empty. Pierce rejoined them, looking tired.

"Well, the evening didn't go exactly as I'd hoped. Apologies."

Asquith looked confused. "Did something happen?"

Domberry snickered. "I was downstairs, and even *I* heard about it. You must have been hiding in a deep hole, Willy old boy." He snorted at his own comment.

Lizzie elbowed him in the ribs, hard. "It was nothing to worry about, Will. Just someone who drank too much." She aimed the last bit at her inebriated husband.

"Normally Linda's more restrained." Pierce gave a slight smile, one bereft of humor. "This was over the top, even for her."

"I truly didn't mean to cause you any trouble." Dai bowed her head. "I should have thought more about the possible consequences of coming in traditional dress, even if it's a modern variation. My vanity got the best of me, and for that, I apologize. As you may imagine, the opportunities for me to wear evening dress are rather limited."

"No, don't you dare take any of the blame for this." He flashed her a grin. "It's been a privilege seeing you dressed this way. It's worth any inconvenience."

Did he never stop? I fought the urge to roll my eyes.

"Perhaps we should call it a night ourselves? Just in case someone decides to send more trouble our way." Aiden still held the bulky camera, her gaze scanning the room looking for other possible undesirables.

I thought her suggestion an excellent one. I doubted there was more we would glean from the suspects tonight.

Pierce looked deflated. "We've not even had the pleasure of a dance yet. You'd not deprive Miss Wu of such a treat before leaving, surely? Without the crowds, it should be safe enough. And the band is paid up for at least another hour. "

Dai sat up straighter, apparently intrigued by the prospect. "I wouldn't mind. I'd be loath to waste the chance. But I have no experience with dancing. I don't know what to do."

"That is simplicity itself. We'll do something slow and without a lot of steps. It is the man's place to take the lead, and I won't steer you wrong." Pierce looked over at me and grinned. "We've just the right amount of people, too—four boys and four girls. Excluding Mrs. Grey. Though I can find her a suitable dance partner if she would like to join us."

"I most certainly would not." Mrs. Grey huffed her lack of interest.

"So, China Doll? What do you say?"

I didn't like this one bit. But I also didn't want to take the opportunity away from Dai, if she wanted it. The cad probably had this planned all along.

Dai held out her hand in acquiescence. Pierce took it in his and gently pulled her to her feet and led her to the dance floor. He signaled the band, and they wrapped up their current number before smoothly shifting to the Arabian Dance from *The Nutcracker*. Slow yet erotic. I was right—the bastard had planned this from the start.

There was only one way to be close enough to stop anything untoward before it got too far. "Might I have this dance, Dr. Campbell?"

Her wide mouth opened in a silent O, the bulky camera dropping to the floor as if it no longer existed. When I presented her with my hand and a half bow, she tentatively placed hers in mine. Perhaps Dai would not be the only one having a wish fulfilled this evening.

"Paul, it's been ages. Shall we?" Lizzie's excitement at the prospect made her face glow.

With a small sigh, he offered his hand to her in turn, and she took it.

"Will, I know you would prefer for this to be with Laura, but since that's not possible," Shannon suggested, "maybe we could dance to honor her? We'd been practicing together. She wanted to make sure she wouldn't embarrass you."

Shannon's ploy was as rehearsed as Pierce's. I glanced back to see what William would do. He nodded, extending his hand to hers. Mrs. Grey glowered at her before her expression returned to its careful, disapproving neutrality.

Interesting.

"I've had some lessons, but haven't actually danced much." Aiden stared at her feet as if fearing to make eye contact.

"Same here."

She looked up, surprised.

"I filled in for Mr. Wu whenever he couldn't get away for their private classes. Dai said it would be good for me, and she seemed to enjoy the music and the sounds the dancers made as they moved." I raised my left hand, gently grasping her right hand, then placed my right at her hip, keeping a modest distance between us. Aiden's free hand rested on my shoulder.

Out of the corner of my eye, I spotted Pierce and Dai doing much the same. If he'd brought her too close to his body, I would have intervened. I noticed his lips moving, but he spoke softly enough that I couldn't overhear.

Their heights were off-kilter, but neither seemed to mind.

They started swaying to the beat of the music, Pierce seemingly content to keep it simple, with the occasional small step to point them in a different direction.

Aiden and I began the same way, but soon added more steps to make it an actual waltz. To my surprise, Dr. Campbell was light on her feet and followed my lead smoothly. It was nothing like my struggles when dancing with the dragon.

Lord and Lady Domberry swooshed across the floor even with the slow tempo. Lizzie had been correct in her assertion that her husband was a talented dancer—good enough to compensate for what she lacked. She couldn't have seemed happier.

Shannon and Asquith proved to be evenly matched, their dancing smooth and unforced. Though she looked thrilled and was enjoying herself, William appeared pensive, struggling to hold it together. Shannon was the farthest thing from his thoughts.

Aside from the occasional glance to make sure Pierce was behaving himself, I tried to keep my attention centered on Aiden. She was here at Dai's behest, after all. It wouldn't be proper to be rude by making her dance yet focusing my interest elsewhere.

"You love her very much, don't you?"

There was no need for the doctor to say about whom she was speaking. "Yes, I do. We may not be related by blood, but she is my sister and must be protected."

"I agree." Aiden threw her own glance in Dai's direction. "She is quite formidable."

It made me smile to know someone else saw Dai in the same light I did. "The mystery has her pushing beyond her usual boundaries. She can be a handful even at the best of times. I'm grateful for your aid in all this."

"Of course," she said. "But it's nothing at all, really. Just trying to solve a murder."

"Come now, don't sell yourself short. You've gone through a bit of trouble and hardship to help us out. You're a good egg."

Aiden's eyes widened with astonishment, and her cheeks took on a red hue. It was a pleasant look on her. But then she shook her head and frowned, looking away. "You really shouldn't say things like that. They might be misunderstood."

Before I could make heads or tails of what she meant, the music faded, signaling the end of the piece. We both let go, and I thanked her for the dance. Glancing toward Dai, I saw Pierce doing the same. Her cheeks were flushed, and a serene smile showed on her face.

All the men led their partners back to the alcove. Aiden was still frowning, but the other three looked to have enjoyed themselves thoroughly. Of the men, Pierce looked the happiest. Asquith seemed pale and forlorn. I was still struggling to figure out what had gone wrong with Dr. Campbell.

"You've had your dance." Mrs. Grey stood looking ready to go. "We have a long drive back to the hotel, so I think we should leave. We wouldn't want to overstay our welcome, especially since the party is over. It's been a full day for everyone." Her gaze strayed to Asquith, not that we weren't already aware of whom she truly meant.

William nodded. "Yes, I think it would be best as well. Thanks again for your generous hospitality, Truman."

"It was my pleasure. On many fronts." He flashed one of his smiles in Dai's direction, despite the fact she couldn't see it. I wished I could say the same.

"What are your future plans, if I might ask?" Dai sent the question in Asquith's direction. "Will you be staying in Dallas, or will you be returning home to England?"

William looked away. "I haven't decided anything as yet. The family wants me to return right away, but I never completed what I came out here to do in the first place. Yet everything seems so unimportant now."

"You may feel that way at the moment, but it won't stay that way forever." Mrs. Grey hovered over him but made no move to touch him. "Family will get you through it. Being back in a familiar setting and surrounded by those who care for you will help you put all this behind you. It helped me in my time of need." For the first time, her face filled with emotion.

"I know, Nanny. But I'm not sure it would be the same for me as it was for you." William hung his head. "No matter how hard everyone tries to convince me of it."

"I apologize, I didn't realize," Dai said. "It wasn't my intention to make this harder on you."

Asquith shook his head.

"They've been pressuring him to leave almost from the moment Laura died." Shannon glared at the others. "As if she'd perished from a plague and we were all contagious."

Lizzie looked put out. "Well, she *was* sick off and on for a week or two, wasn't she? Despite modern medicine, there's still a lot we don't know about diseases. Natives build immunities, we all know that. But we aren't natives. Surely you don't begrudge us for wanting to stay healthy?"

"She'd been sick for two weeks?" Aiden was suddenly at the forefront, her eyes flashing. "Did she see a doctor?"

Shannon snorted. "As if we could afford one. And the free clinic was no help. Besides, Laura's always had a weak constitution. We just figured the cramping and stuff was because she wasn't used to eating all those fancy foods. By the time we realized something was really wrong, it was too late."

"I should have insisted she see a private doctor. I was more than willing to pay the fee," William added. "But she was so sure it was nothing. Even Nanny agreed it was something that would pass." He shook his head, tears welling in his eyes. "I should have *insisted*."

CHAPTER 20

There was no more that could be said or asked that wouldn't have seemed rude or ghoulish at that point, so we set off to go our separate ways. Full evening had descended upon us. Fortunately, the staff was prepared with lanterns to light the way to the vehicles.

The popinjay insisted on escorting Dai to the car. There were matters we needed to discuss, but not in front of him.

"China Doll, it's been a pleasure." Pierce bowed and kissed Dai's hand. Prince growled a warning, to make sure Pierce knew he was too close. I half hoped he would ignore it so Prince would have a reason to leave teeth marks on the man's ankle, but no such luck.

I opened the rear passenger door for Dr. Campbell.

"Will you honestly be all right after all this?" Dai asked Pierce. "Miss Carmichael seemed set on causing you trouble." With Pierce's help, she settled into the car's back seat. Prince jumped on her lap to stay between them. I wanted nothing more than to yank the popinjay out of there and away from Dai.

"It's nothing I haven't been through before," he said. "This will pass. It always does."

Why did she insist on wasting her breath on this man? "Will it? Because she seemed determined to cast dirt on Dai on your behalf. It would create no end of trouble for Dai *and* her family if your girlfriend did anything untoward. The law is *not* on Dai's side." Belittling the damage that might be brought on the Wus didn't help his cause one bit.

Pierce raised a brow. "I'll make sure she behaves herself, Jackie. Also, she is not my girlfriend."

"You may want to tell her that. And my name is *Jacques*."

With a wave, Pierce left to say his goodbyes to the others.

I got in the car and slammed the door shut. I had no faith he'd take care of anything—or in my ability to handle things if they got out of hand.

"Isn't Jacques just adorable when he gets all protective like that?" Dai's tone was laced with amusement.

I gritted my teeth, fighting the urge to glance at the peep mirror. Not one bit of this was humorous. I started the car and got us underway.

"He has a point though, doesn't he?" Aiden's voice whispered to the front, a balm on my shattered nerves. Finally, a voice of reason. "If that man had taken a picture of you and slathered it all over the newspapers…"

"But he didn't, and it's not," Dai said. "Besides, we have other more pressing things to worry about."

"We do?" This time I couldn't help but glance in the angled mirror. Even with the lack of lighting inside the car, I could tell Dai's expression was grave.

"Most of our suspects are foreign. While William might stay behind, there is no such impetus for the rest of them. If the guilty party is one of them, we need to solve this before they can leave the country. This leaves us with little to no time to get it done, and we still have a lengthy list of things to check."

"Leave the free clinic to me," Aiden said. "I might be able to obtain more information there about Miss Cooper's visit. I also want to verify if the doctor who was on duty knows what to watch for regarding arsenic poisoning. Ever since the Marsh test was published and the method proven reliable, the use of arsenic as the poison of choice has dropped dramatically."

Aiden shook her head. "It might not even be something they'd think to look for. Symptoms vary with how the poison is applied, the duration of exposure, the amount breathed or ingested, and the victim's own physiology. The tragic part is that it's possible they could have saved her with dimercaprol, if they'd been able to diagnose her properly and the damage hadn't yet become too extensive."

"That would be a great help," Dai said. "Jacques and I will visit Laura's apartment tomorrow. With any luck, we'll find more clues there, and possibly remove Shannon as a suspect."

"So you don't believe it was her?" I half thought she wasn't the one either, but Dai might have realized more factors than I.

"No, I don't. Shannon had motive and opportunity, but despite her airs and the things we've heard about her, I believe she cared for Laura, even if she was jealous of her friend's good fortune. An opportunist, yes, but a murderer? I'm not so sure."

Something about her tone prompted me to ask a question. "You have someone in mind now, though, don't you?"

Dai gave me a wry grin. "Perhaps. I have an inkling of an idea, but it's too soon to mention it. I need more facts." The grin changed to an impish smile. "Speaking of facts. Aiden, dear, what is your opinion of Jacques as a dancer? Did he make you swoon?"

It was too dark to be sure, but it looked like Dr. Campbell's face turned beet red. "He, he did well. It wasn't unenjoyable."

I felt strangely satisfied at her words. I too considered the dancing not unenjoyable, and I wouldn't be averse to dancing with her again. As long as Pierce was nowhere in the vicinity.

"I'm so glad." Dai sounded like she was. "This was an evening of many firsts for all three of us."

While I was happy for her in that regard, there existed too many bad firsts that might still come out of this. Similar to the unlit road before us, where the car's headlights revealed only a minor piece of the path ahead, there were too many objects hidden in the surrounding darkness that could pose all manner of unexpected trouble. Trouble we might not see until much too late.

CHAPTER 21

Dr. Campbell had us drop her off at the hospital. She quickly bundled up again, hiding any hint of her made-up hair or lovely dress. As she walked away, I realized it was a shame there hadn't been a party photographer. Seeing Aiden dressed up was probably a rarity. A photo of Dai in her Chinese finery would also not have gone amiss, aside from the risk that unscrupulous characters might use the negatives to damage the family. Perhaps having no evidence of either was for the best.

Speaking of what was best... "Did Pierce behave himself during your dance? The cad obviously meant to do it from the start."

Dai laughed, startling Prince from a sound sleep. "Jacques, he was a total gentleman. You worry too much. I thought he was rather attentive and sweet."

"He has an angle of some kind, Dai. Steering well clear of him would be best."

She said nothing to that for several seconds. When she did reply, I almost choked.

"So you believe that since I'm Chinese and blind, nobody could have a genuine interest in me as a woman?"

I stared hard at the road before me. "No. That's not what I

meant, and you know it."

"Do I?" From the teasing tone that crept into the quick question, I knew she did. Thank goodness. The last thing I wanted was for her to think no one might love her for who she was.

I might as well take the plunge. "You could get anyone you wished if you put your mind to it. I've no doubt of that. But I don't believe Pierce is sincere. I don't trust his intentions."

"His intentions, you say. Hmm. I will admit we know little to nothing about him. But so far he's done nothing but help us. Arranging this party so quickly would have involved both his money and time. We owe him a great debt."

That was not what I wanted to hear. "What he'll want in payment for that debt is exactly what I'm worried about."

She made no reply to that.

The rest of the drive home was quiet. Distantly spaced streetlights showed the way, though most homes in our area had already gone dark. I breathed a sigh of relief as I shut down the Ford once we were safely tucked away under the carport.

"I doubt I'll sleep much tonight," Dai said as I helped her out of the car. She couldn't have looked happier. "There's a lot of pondering I need to do."

"When did you want to call on Shannon tomorrow?" I asked.

"Sometime between mid-morning and lunch would seem appropriate. That should give us ample time before her three o'clock deadline."

The kitchen light shone from inside the house, but I didn't think much of it. That is, until I opened the door and found the dragon and Tye in their robes, waiting for us.

"Mr. Wu, Mrs. Wu, good evening."

The dragon sent me a scathing glare. Prince had just trotted in and immediately scampered back outside when he sensed the danger before us, leaving me alone in the direct line of fire.

"*Mǔqīn, Fùqīn*, were you waiting up for us?" Dai squeezed past me, a vision of angelic innocence and naïveté.

109

The dragon inspected what Dai was wearing and gasped, both in awe and horror. "Oh, Daiyu, you shouldn't have! To wear that to a party!"

"I'm not ashamed of my heritage," Dai told her. "And where else would I wear this, if not to my first party?"

"Oh, Daiyu." Lien's brow furrowed with worry.

"But she looks beautiful, doesn't she, *qīnai de*?" Tye smiled at his daughter with pride. "My little Black Jade." After a moment he took off his glasses and wiped his eyes with the end of his sleeve, then jumped to his feet. "I'll get the camera!"

Before the dragon could protest, her husband had hurried from the room.

Lien sighed. "He is not wrong. You look lovely. But still… You should know better than this. So many things could happen. You don't want to risk your future." Lien's accent thickened, a definite sign she was upset.

"I won't be kept in a glass jar, *Mŭqīn*. To live is to take chances. My path must be my own." Dai's tone softened. "But it makes me happy you worry for me. Though I never intended to make you do so."

Lien sighed again. "I know. I know. Come, let's go to the living room so your father can have his pictures. He'll never forgive us if we let the moment pass."

As Dai moved past, the dragon came out in force and aimed a baleful glance directly at me. It looked like I would get an earful sometime soon. But not while Dai was in hearing distance.

By the time we made it to the living room, Lien had quickly combed Dai's hair and straightened her stole and dress to her satisfaction. Tye hurried back with his latest toy, a Zeiss Ikon Kolibri with 127 film. Photography was Mr. Wu's one passion, and his favorite subject was Dai—much to her chagrin, though she never let him know it.

The next half hour was spent sitting, standing, posing. Dai insisted her father also take pictures of us together or with me alone. I was happy with the former, if not the latter. Why would I ever need a dressed-up picture of myself? But Dai would not be denied, despite the fact that she couldn't see the photograph. I sensed some kind of ulterior motive, but couldn't fathom what it might be.

At eight pictures a roll, we went through several before Mr. Wu was satisfied.

"I'll process the film for you, *Fùqīn.* Just give it to Jacques to bring with us in the morning."

Thankfully, we all retired after that.

CHAPTER 22

Just like the day before, Dai was up unusually early. I had expected it this time, so was able to hold back from showing any surprise. The dragon showed up earlier than usual as well. I was sure she'd hoped to regale me with everything she did not get a chance to tell me last night. She obviously thought yesterday's early rising by Dai was a fluke and planned to 'talk' to me this morning while Dai was still asleep. I'd dodged a bullet, but for how long?

"*Mǔqīn*, good morning."

"Good morning, *Nǚér*. What are your plans for today? Should I meet you at home for lunch?"

Making no eye contact with anyone, I served breakfast.

"I'm not positive I'll be back for lunch, so no reason for you to go out of your way on my account. I need to develop Father's photographs, and I was hoping to go on a drive before the day gets too hot." Dai's fingers reached out as she acquainted herself with the location of the plate, cup, and other utensils, making a mental map as she went.

"Daiyu, if something were wrong, you would tell me, wouldn't you?" Though she addressed the question to Dai, Lien was looking at me.

"Of course I would, *Mǔqīn*."

I added a nod in turn, acknowledging the same. Nothing genuinely untoward had occurred, so why worry the family with those details? With any luck, I would never have occasion to do so. It was my duty to keep Dai out of trouble, after all.

"Lavender suits you." Lien looked her daughter up and down, a slight smile tugging at her lips.

"So this *is* a new exercise suit, is it?" Dai fingered the lacy collar of her loose blouse. Each night, Lien set out everything Dai would need for the following day. "You realize no one will ever take me seriously if I continue wearing things like this."

More than once Dai had tried convincing her mother to let me take charge of buying her clothes and setting them out for her each day, knowing she'd then have a lot of say in what she wore. But the dragon would not be swayed, and appeals to her father had fared no better. Though I would never tell Dai this, I too enjoyed seeing her in frills and lace. Anything else, aside from the mandarin dress she'd worn last night, would seem awkward and unsuitable on her compact frame.

"Why would you need anyone to take you seriously?" Lien's gaze sharpened, like a shark coming across the scent of blood in the water.

"Why wouldn't I? I've heard you say more than once how important first impressions can be, and how most are based on how one looks. What are they to make of me looking like this?"

Tye walked in with the latest copy of the *Dallas Morning News* tucked beneath one arm. "That you are the most adorable creature in the city, that's what."

"*Fùqīn!*"

I bent and hid my face behind the open refrigerator door so no one would see the grin on my lips. If Dai even suspected my amusement at her expense, I would get a bruise or two.

"It's the truth, *Nǚér*," Tye said. "We'd be remiss as parents if we didn't present you to your best advantage."

Dai pouted, unwittingly proving his point. "This might have been fine when I was younger, but I am no longer a child. I should dress more appropriately for my age."

While Dai had broached this subject with her parents many times before, my amusement dried up at this new tactic. Might this have something to do with the popinjay? About the impression she made on *him*?

Glancing at her parents, I saw from their expressions they'd come to a similar conclusion.

"Daiyu, is there someone you are interested in? Is this why you wish to change what you wear?"

Dai stirred her congee but had yet to take a bite. "No, not particularly. But if there was, I wouldn't want them to think of me as just some foreign doll."

My heart sank. The rest of my breakfast held no flavor at all.

CHAPTER 23

The rest of the meal was subdued. The dragon kept trying to make eye contact, so I made certain to keep my gaze riveted only on what was before me. Prince sat in a corner and watched events like a silent witness, doing nothing to attract attention to himself.

We ran through our tai chi forms after breakfast. I was sure Lien and Tye had started dissecting the entire conversation the moment we were out of sight. I doubted Dai had an accurate idea of how much her parents worried about her. Or how much I worried for her myself, for that matter.

She remained silent until after we'd completed our morning routine and got underway. The loose-fitting lavender suit was exchanged for an even frillier violet dress.

"It has nothing to do with him, you know."

My gaze darted to the peep mirror before shifting back to the road. Dai had her face turned toward the window as if staring at the passing view. Prince was curled up on her lap, and she softly fingered his new purple collar.

"Doesn't it?"

She shook her head. "No. Although the events of the last few days *have* given me things to think about, topics I'd not bothered with before."

That sounded ominous. "Such as?"

She shrugged. "My future. My place in the world. What I want to do with my life. How I wish to be *perceived*." A small sigh escaped her. "I'm not particularly interested in love one way or the other. If it comes, it comes. If not, not. But things can't stay as they are forever. I refuse to be kept in a glass case for the rest of my existence."

She turned her face in my direction. "Have you no thoughts regarding your own future, Jacques? Shouldn't you be looking for your own path, rather than just remaining chained to mine? Whatever you may think you owe me or my family has long been repaid."

My eyes suddenly itched, her words dredging up odd cutting feelings within me. "You're tired of me? Am I holding you back?"

She slapped the door beside her with a resounding smack. "Don't be a fool. Of course not! But surely you want more out of life than just taking care of me."

I gripped the steering wheel harder than necessary, searching for words until my hands went numb. If not for her, I wouldn't have had a life to live. "I am quite happy with my lot, thank you. I found my purpose a long time ago, and until you tire of me, I don't see a reason to look for anything else."

Dai laughed. "I don't deserve you, you know that, right?"

"I've no idea what you're talking about."

Yet the thought of one day not being useful to her, of being set adrift, sat like a pile of heavy rocks inside my gut.

Slipping the car into its usual parking space behind the laundry brought with it an unexpected sense of relief. This was normal and had naught to do with weird thoughts about the future. Whatever Dai decided on, I would support her all the way, but that didn't mean I had to look forward to it. Especially if it meant having to let her go. I wouldn't know what to do with myself.

"If you'll set out what I'll need for preparing the cleaning mixture, I'll go down to the lab and get *Fùqīn's* film processed so he can make prints later." Dai held out her hand so I could help her from the car.

"Should I check the supplies in the lab before you start?"

She shook her head. "I restocked after the last time, so it should be fine. The sooner we can get these chores done, the sooner we can turn to today's true business."

Once inside, she headed for the lab with Prince at her heels, and I proceeded into the laundry proper. "*Nǐmén hǎo,*" I said in greeting, half-bowing to the workers as I walked past.

Two of them acknowledged the greeting since I was alone, but the rest moved to finger their gourd talismans and avoided eye contact. Despite this being my country, I was a foreigner in their eyes—and the demon's minion to boot. I kept hoping they would someday come to their senses and see Dai for who she was rather than what they assumed her to be. Yet all her triumphs were viewed as only more evidence they were right, instead of belonging to someone who strove to overcome her limitations. Not for the first time, I wondered what it would take to change their perceptions of her. Not that it mattered to her in the least. She was doing her part to keep the business profitable and the workers employed; if they didn't deign to acknowledge it, that was their problem.

It didn't make it any easier for me to swallow, however.

Mrs. Zhang and her daughter Mei Ling were busy at the front counter as people on their way to work dropped off clothes to be laundered. A couple of hours from now, the second rush would begin as secretaries around town brought in or picked up items for their employers.

Mei Ling was a native Texan, so her English was impeccable and her clothes modern. This did much to disarm customers coming in for the first time. Mr. Wu had long ago hired Robert Cline to be the face of the laundry's commercial business so as not to give rise to any paranoia about the Yellow Peril. Both these things though seemingly small were of great importance in the incessant juggling act to keep White Laundry and the Wu family alive and well.

No new items had been left overnight without information

on their tickets, which was a relief.

I pitched in where I could and kept busy. I was taking a brief break upstairs with the morning newspaper and a glass of iced tea when Prince rushed in with Dai not far behind. "All done?"

"For now. Let me freshen up, and then we can be on our way."

I folded the newspaper, leaving it on the table for anyone else who might be interested. I'd not found any articles in the paper talking about the party at the DCC or Dai's presence there, which was a relief. But then, the *Dallas Morning News* might not have had time to add the information before they had to go to print. I'd have to check the *Dallas Times Herald* when their evening edition was released later in the day. By the time I washed out my glass and placed it on the rack to dry, Dai was ready to go.

It was time to see where the late Laura Cooper had lived.

CHAPTER 24

The Jefferson Hotel at Ferris Park Plaza sat close to Union Station on Houston Street. Only a half-mile from the Adolphus, it was a very convenient location for Laura to have lived. The original hotel had been expanded with a second slightly taller building. Like most hotels in the city, they catered to both transient travelers and long-term residents.

It was an unremarkable, red-bricked structure, one built for functionality rather than aesthetics. The only attempt at elegance was the white first floor with balconies extending out from part of the second floor over the entryway to protect customers from the weather. A park across the street helped soften the view with its manicured lawns, walkways, and an artistic fountain which was illuminated at night with colored lights. The Waiting Station stood at one end so those coming into the city by train would have access to the streetcars and interurban trains between Dallas and Fort Worth.

The interior of the hotel was utilitarian, with only a few potted plants to give the lobby any kind of identity. I escorted Dai to the elevators, and after giving the information to the operator, we rose to the sixth floor. The employees at the reception desk paid us no attention at all.

The door to Room 603 was as non-descript as the rest of the doors on both sides of the plain hallway. I was at a loss for words when trying to describe this to Dai, not having expected such a drab place.

My knock was answered after a minute, the door opening only a crack—enough for the owner to take a peek at us. An apparition wearing a faded house robe, curlers, and face cream stared us up and down. After a shocked second, I realized it was Shannon.

She looked in no way as appealing as the other times we'd seen her. Perhaps being attractive enough to snag a husband required more work than I imagined. I wasn't sure if I should be offended by the fact that she didn't seem to care about me seeing her like this. I was confident she'd rather drop dead than let Asquith find her in such a state.

"So, it's you two, is it?"

A soft bark from Prince admonished her that there were actually three of us.

Shannon hissed, "For pity's sake, keep him quiet." She poked her head out into the hallway as if verifying that our presence hadn't been noticed. She opened the door wider and stepped back. "Hurry up and come inside."

As drab and ordered as the rest of the hotel had been, the tiny apartment exploded with color and chaos. It consisted of a central common area and kitchenette, and two bedrooms that were but alcoves placed at ninety degrees from each other. The bays provided room only for a miniscule bed and a set of shelves placed overhead, with a bar at the bottom for hanging up clothes. A curtain rod with thick drapes was the sole means of obtaining any privacy. A diminutive bathroom opened on one side, nylon hose and ladies' undergarments dangling willy-nilly from the shower curtain rod.

Noticing my gaze, Shannon rushed to close the lavatory door to hide the items within from prying eyes.

The color I'd noticed when we first came in emanated from the back wall above a battered couch. Posters of bands and singers had been plastered in a giant mosaic of talent—from jazz to ballroom and everything in between. It was the most attractive feature of the entire place.

"Did Laura do that?" I asked Shannon, quickly explaining to Dai what I was talking about in an aside.

Shannon turned to look then sighed. "Yeah. I thought it was a goofy idea when she first suggested it, but the wall came out well. Plus the posters were free. They always print more than what they'll need, so we could typically swipe a copy or two."

"That's a vast array of talent." I found it difficult not to be impressed.

"It's the Adolphus. Nothing less than the best for our guests." She laughed, making the face cream on her cheeks jiggle.

"Which alcove belonged to Laura?" Dai set Prince on the ground. He immediately started sniffing around.

"He's trained, right? I can't afford to lose the deposit."

Dai smiled. "Prince Razor is better trained and more refined than a lot of people."

Shannon laughed again. Perhaps the comment had brought someone to mind. "Good to know."

"But perhaps having him stay still would be for the best." Dai turned her attention to our mutual canine friend. "Prince, sit by the door, please."

With a soft bark, he scampered to the entrance and sat down, trying to keep his awareness on everything.

Shannon pointed to the nearer of the two alcoves. "That one was hers."

I guided Dai closer and described the contents, not that there was much to see. The mattress lay bare, and though it had been cleaned, you could still see discolored outlines of where it had stained. A battered box sat atop it with an open suitcase beside it. A Raggedy Ann doll and a newer-looking teddy bear were nestled at the top of the container, with books and small knickknacks supporting them beneath.

"She died here." There was no doubt in Dai's whispered comment. "The scent of her death still lingers. I can also smell a faint trace of burned garlic."

If she could still smell the arsenic, it begged the question of how much might even now be scattered about the place. The thought gave me goosebumps. Shannon sat on the arm of the ratty couch, watching. How much arsenic was falling around her right now? She'd mentioned that Laura wore the dress often and danced in it about the apartment. She may well have flailed the deadly powder into everything. How much had already worked itself into Shannon's lungs, her skin? How much was settling on us as we stood here? We should have never come.

"Calm yourself." Dai's gloved hand touched my cheek. I almost flinched from it. "This happened over weeks if not months. The concentration in the rest of the rooms would be less than her alcove. She wore the dress, hung it in the same space. The circulation of the air is poor. It would confine most of the poison to the alcove."

"What are you two whispering about?" Shannon was frowning in our direction.

I chained down my panicked imagination and tried to pretend all was well. "Apologies. We were just trying to envision if there would be room for everything if our friend became your roommate. She has an unpleasant habit of collecting all sorts of odds and ends, and she's loath to part with any of them."

"Yeah, well, as you can see, there's not a lot of room for keeping extra stuff here." She looked at us as if we'd just revealed ourselves to be a couple of idiots.

"Laura's fancy dress—did it come with a box, by any chance?"

Shannon's brow rose. The movement jiggled the goo on her face in a rather disturbing way. "It did. Might still be under the bed. Why do you ask?"

I kneeled down, glad for my uniform, glad for my gloves, wishing I had even more on. To my surprise, the area beneath the small bed was a little dusty but generally clean. There were two shoe boxes and a fairly large and sturdy white box. A giant bow and matching ribbon were folded on top, as if they had been wrapped around the container at one time.

Assuming Shannon was the person who'd put Laura's things together, she'd not bothered to gather everything.

"We're just curious, more than anything," Dai said.

I touched the box with only two gloved fingers and pulled it out, then placed it on the bed. I took a slow, steady breath to fortify myself before taking off the lid. The container was empty except for some colored tissue paper most likely used to nestle the dress. My pulse pounded at my temple. I didn't want to touch it, to look at it, to breathe anywhere near it.

"Do you have a use for this? Or might I take it off your hands?" Dai's voice was at its most angelic. "Boxes like these are getting harder to find these days. I'm more than willing to buy it from you."

Shannon's eyes narrowed—a rather dangerous move with all that face cream. "What are the two of you really doing here? And you can stop pretending about this 'friend' who's looking for an apartment while you're at it." She got off the armrest of the couch, looking defiant.

Dai tipped her head in Shannon's direction as if conceding her a victory. "We're just wallowing in some morbid curiosity, to be honest. I'm sorry if we've caused you an inconvenience." From her small clutch, she pulled a ten-dollar bill and set it on top of the suitcase.

I took the hint and put the lid back on the box, then tucked it under my arm with a shudder. Shannon's gaze was riveted on the money as if looking away from it might make the cash disappear. She might cover all sorts of expenses with that kind of money.

"It doesn't bother you that she died here?" Dai asked her.

Shannon shrugged, still staring at the money. "Not like I have a lot of choice about it. Like it or not, it's where I live."

"If I might ask, who took care of her?"

Shannon threw her a glare, suspicious that Dai was implying something. "I did, when I could. But Laura knew I had to work, and she was never a baby about being sick."

Though she continued to stare at the money, her eyes suddenly shimmered with unshed tears. Whether or not she'd ever admit this, she had loved her friend in her own way. "William barely left her side close to the end. His family was here, too, on occasion. Although that bastard, Domberry, never stayed more than the absolute minimum and kept a nasty expression on his face the whole time. As if not being rich was a disease he could catch or something."

I had no trouble picturing that, from the sneer of disgust to the leap to the door the moment he could manage it. I was sure he had come in and stood in the center of the room the entire time, making certain to look at little and touch nothing.

"I was on shift when she passed." Her expression was hard to read under the cold cream. "I didn't find out until I got home."

"I'm sorry for your loss."

Shannon said nothing.

"Thank you for your time." Dai turned to Prince and me. "We should go."

I opened the door of the apartment, ready to get out, eager to be rid of the bomb under my armpit, but Dai pivoted in Shannon's direction one last time.

"By the way, what will happen to Laura's things?" Dai asked.

Shannon had crossed the room and snatched up the money. She half spun, looking like a startled Gorgon who'd thought her prey had already turned to stone. "William wants them. Laura has no family, so I didn't see the harm. Nothing of actual value in the bunch."

Dai tilted her head. "What about the ballgown? It wasn't in her belongings."

Shannon's eyes grew wide, seeming to realize for the first time that the dress was missing. "It should be here." Her gaze raked the room as if the clothing might somehow have hidden itself when she wasn't looking.

"What about her key? Is that missing, too?"

"No. It wasn't in Laura's purse, but I found it on the coffee table. She must have forgotten it there?" Shannon no longer looked sure of anything.

Satisfied, Dai nodded and let me escort her from the apartment.

CHAPTER 25

When the door closed behind us, I breathed a lengthy sigh of relief. While most of the panic was my doing, I was still only too happy not to be in the possibly contaminated space.

We made our way toward the elevators, and I knew what Dai would say before she said it.

"She's definitely not the one."

"I have to agree." Unless Shannon was absurdly stupid, she couldn't be the poisoner. I'd had trouble being in the same apartment where the arsenic might have come in contact with other items or suffused the air. So committing the crime and then continue to live unfazed in the same small quarters seemed farfetched. Add in the possibility of the poison having spread around the place and leaving yourself exposed to it day after day? It would drive anyone insane. While she might be a gold-digger, we'd noticed she'd been fond of Laura in her own way. Only someone truly heartless or overflowing with hate could have watched as Laura withered away and not felt anything. Nothing we'd seen so far showed either, as far as Shannon was concerned. She didn't seem to be the type who'd be able to keep any ill feelings hidden for long.

"We need to get this box to Aiden."

I'd momentarily forgotten about the thing, and I wasn't all that happy to be reminded of it. "You think it's evidence?"

"Possibly. I want her to take samples and test the interior of the box. There might be some residue. The lethal potency of the dye on the ballgown has been bothering me. If there's a residue, then we can link the dress to Laura. Shannon has verified that Laura wore it. The dress itself is proof of the poison. With those three things, we can relate the facts to each other. Then we can see if that's enough for the justice to open an investigation."

"And if it's not?" I was sure I already knew the answer but had to ask.

"We keep pursuing this ourselves." Dai frowned. "Even if the police become involved, they might not act fast enough. The more information we can gather before those on our list try to leave the country, the better the chances the murderer won't get away."

Returning to our car, I put the possibly-poison-filled box into the trunk attached to the outside of the Ford in the back. It would keep the container safe from curious canine prodding while I drove us to Baylor Hospital. After giving Prince some water and kibble, and rolling the rear windows partially down, Dai and I headed for the cafeteria. Prince would guard the Ford and its cargo until our return.

Through the use of a courtesy phone, I was patched through to Dr. Campbell's work area and let her know where we might be found. Settling Dai at a corner table, I then bought us lunch. It was bland and unimaginative fare, but healthy. By setting the plates and silverware in the usual configuration and spacing, Dai would know where everything was to eat her meal without having to hunt for them.

Ten minutes later, the doctor appeared with her own tray of food and joined us. I noticed several nurses and other people in lab coats raise their eyebrows or show other expressions of surprise at seeing her there, and their number increased as she settled at our table. It would appear Aiden getting a meal and then using the common eating area was an unusual occurrence, and that she would sit with others even more so. It was a little sad to realize, but not entirely surprising. In many ways, Dai was the same.

"Thanks for calling me. How did it go at Laura's apartment?"

"We brought back a gift—the dress box. Jacques will bring it to you after we're done here." Dai took a bite of her salad.

Aiden nodded. "I'll get it tested right away. If our suspicions are correct, there'll be evidence there of the additional poison added to the dress, which would indicate a definite intent to murder the deceased." Dr. Campbell dug into her Salisbury steak as if in a hurry to get started.

"Did you get a chance to visit the clinic?"

Dai's query slowed Aiden to a halt. She stared at her plate for a long moment.

"I did." Her voice was low. "It was disturbing."

Neither of us pressed her. I could see she was struggling with what she'd found there. Dai must have sensed that as well.

"I arrived before they opened and there was already a line of people waiting to come inside." She took a swallow of her iced tea, still grappling with the words. "Everyone tried their best, but they were overwhelmed. They had files on all the patients, though most were incomplete. No time to truly study the people, to consider the cause of their troubles for any amount of time. They just tried to get through as many as possible. It was easy to see why poisoning never occurred to the doctor who saw her." Her large hands curled into fists. "It frightens me to think of how many others they might have saved if only they'd been able to take the time to examine them more thoroughly."

As money became more scarce, the problem would only get worse; more people would have no choice but to go to the clinics rather than personal doctors. There was nothing I could think of to say.

"Well, well, well, if it isn't Aiden Campbell."

Her fists tightened further at the sound of the gravelly voice. "Dr. Stewart."

The newcomer wore a three-piece suit and a pristine doctor's coat. Washed-out gray eyes twinkled as he looked down, looming over her.

"Decided to scurry out of your lab and mingle with actual people, did you?"

I shot to my feet before I realized what I was doing. This Neanderthal was being more than rude. "What did you just say?"

The man glanced up. From the quickly hidden shock on his face, I was pretty certain he wasn't used to anyone reacting negatively from anything he said or did. "Pardon me."

He rushed past me as if that had been his intention all along. I stared hard at his back, making sure he wasn't tempted to return. He spoke brusquely to a gaggle of nurses, who hurriedly dispersed out of his way.

"Who was that?" Dai asked in a quiet voice. "And is he always that bad-mannered?"

Aiden sighed. "That's Dr. Henry Stewart, the hospital's chief of staff." She shoved the food around her plate. "He's that way with everyone. Well, almost everyone."

It made me angry. More than it should have, truth be told. "Let me guess: If they're wealthy or on the board, he's goodness personified; otherwise, he's a well-dressed bully?"

Aiden nodded slowly, as if amazed that I'd been able to put that together from just a few words. Sadly, I'd met the type before. Gary, my tormentor at Buckners Orphan Home, and this Henry Stewart would have gotten along famously.

"Does he trouble you often?" The question came out more briskly than I intended.

"No. Only if we accidentally cross paths or he needs something at the lab, which is rare." Her ice-blue eyes looked up into mine. "But I appreciate your concern."

My stomach churned at that look, though I didn't understand why. So I just nodded and sat back down to finish my lunch.

I noticed from the corner of my eye that Dai wore the smallest of smiles, as if she knew something I didn't. I wasn't sure that was a good thing.

"You said they cremated the body, correct?"

Dai nodded. "Yes, that's right."

"I thought of something last night." Aiden took a sip of iced tea, a momentary delay as if checking her idea for any holes one last time before presenting it to us. "Arsenic is considered a heavy metal. Even though it's a volatile poison, some of it would have turned to arsenates in the bones. As arsenates are non-volatile, cremation wouldn't necessarily destroy them. It's possible that running tests on the ashes could prove it was present in her system."

Dai's face lit up with the possibility. "If we could do that, it would show an undeniable link to everything else we've gathered so far. It would give weight to the assertion that Laura was murdered."

"That's all well and good, but it presents us with a different problem." I suddenly found myself pinned by their full attention. "How in the world are we going to get a sample of the ashes to test them?"

This new conundrum put a damper on the rest of the meal.

CHAPTER 26

"There must be a way to get a sample of those ashes." Dai scratched Prince behind the ear as I got us underway in the Ford. "We just need to be creative."

Creative wouldn't begin to cover it.

At least the toxic box was no longer in our possession, so no one would come in contact with it and accidentally poison themselves. That Aiden would make sure to lock it away and mark it as hazardous, I did not doubt.

"Asquith has the ashes, so maybe we just need to come clean with him," Dai suggested. "I believe he had nothing to do with Laura's death, so getting his consent to take them shouldn't be an issue." Her expression grew thoughtful. "The trick will be to get him alone so we can talk. Someone seems to always be hovering around him."

She was right about the last part. I had other misgivings about this course of action, however. "Dai, this would be a major shock for him. At the moment, Asquith thinks it was just fate that tore him and Laura apart. If he finds out she was murdered, how will he react? We don't know him well enough to guess at what he'll do. He might fall into despair from the news or go into a murderous rage. *If* he even believes us." It would be a hard pill to swallow for anyone. It would only make it worse when he realized she could have been saved.

"Perhaps we'd best leave that as a last resort then," Dai said. "We can't have him giving the game away."

I wished it were only a game. In a game, a mistake might cost you a playing piece or numerous fake dollars. But here, if the murderer grasped what we were up to, the consequences might well have a cost we couldn't afford and didn't want to pay.

"I wonder how difficult it would be to bribe a maid at the hotel to get the sample?"

From where did she pull out that idea? "That sounds like a recipe for getting us into trouble. The Adolphus caters to clients who demand top service and discretion. I doubt the employees there can be swayed easily—or that we have enough capital to *afford* to sway them."

Her lips pursed into a slight pout. "I suppose you're right. Though it could have been fun to explore it as an option." Dai sighed. "I guess I'll have to come up with something else."

By the time we returned home, we were no closer to a plan of action.

I left Dai with her feet curled up in the living room with the radio on to continue pondering the problem while I dived into a few of the household chores. I was in the midst of making lemonade as part of a mid-afternoon snack for us when the doorbell rang.

Traveling salesmen usually pursued their house to house calls on foot, hitting an entire neighborhood at one time. But even they weren't daft enough to do so in the middle of a scorching Texas afternoon. Not unless they were hoping for a case of heatstroke. So the fact that someone was at the door at this time of day didn't bode good tidings.

Grabbing a handy kitchen towel, I dried my hands as I moved to the front of the house. Prince beat me there, sitting at attention as he waited for me to see who'd come to our door.

My heart skipped as I got a peek at our visitor. The peaked

hat in dark blue with the Dallas County emblem instantly proclaimed him to be a police officer. The Ford Model A parked at the curb, with its white and black paneling and the word "police" written on the side, also left little doubt as to the visitor's identity.

"Good afternoon, officer. How may I help you?"

A blank expression met my query. Despite the porch cutting off the direct glare from the sun, perspiration clung to the man's neck. The short walk from the car to the house was taking its toll. "Afternoon. My name is Officer Davis, and I'm with the Dallas Police Department. Is this the Wu residence?"

His question left little doubt—his visit was not an accident. "Yes, it is. What can I do for you, sir?"

The policeman shifted where he stood as if my answer annoyed him. I doubted it was a good sign.

"We got a call stating that the members of the family are illegal immigrants. I'd like to speak with Mr. Wu, if I may. I'll also need to check the family's papers." Officer Davis had a bit of a southern twang, though nowhere near as pronounced as Constable Higgins' had been.

I guess we now knew what shape Linda's retaliation would take. "Mr. Wu is currently at work, I'm afraid, and not available. I can, however, show you a copy of the family's residence papers." I would also give him the contact information for the Wus' lawyers. "Won't you come inside while I get them? Might I offer you some fresh-squeezed lemonade to refresh yourself while you wait? Or perhaps you'd prefer some iced tea. It's a scorcher today."

The officer's eyes lit up for a moment. "I wouldn't want to put you to any trouble on my account." Though his stance was still guarded, he seemed to relax just a degree or two.

"It would be my pleasure. Please, come on in."

Inviting him inside was more for his benefit than mine. I wanted to make sure he got a good look. That he saw for himself how normal and American the household was.

"And who might you be, exactly?" As expected, the officer was glancing around to see what could be seen from his current vantage point. He politely removed his hat and used a handkerchief to soak up the sweat gathered at his hairline and the back of his neck.

"Jacques Haskin, I work for the Wus."

That got me a strange look. "Like a butler or something?"

"More of a handyman and driver than anything else. I do odd jobs for them here and there."

Officer Davis seemed to take the information at face value. With the steep economic downturn, I was sure he'd seen his fair share of unemployed masses coming through the city looking for any kind of job they could find. That many of them would rather starve than work for a Chinese family didn't need to be mentioned.

I left the officer in the foyer, hoping he wouldn't venture too far while I was absent. Dai wasn't visible from his current spot, and I preferred it to stay that way. She realized he was there—with her acute hearing, little of what happened in the house was kept from her.

I fetched the offered lemonade and a coaster for the table in the foyer.

"That's a nice bouquet of yellow roses you got there."

Of course he'd notice the popinjay's extravagant gift. An aspirin dropped in the vase's water made sure the flowers remained beautiful and fragrant for several days—no point in wasting them unnecessarily. "A gift from a friend of the family."

"Some friend. Roses aren't cheap. And that's a heap of them." He looked rather impressed.

The less mentioned about the darn things, the better. "I'll go get a copy of the papers for you now."

By the time I returned, Officer Davis had gulped down half the glass of lemonade and appeared all the happier for it.

"Here you go. Everything should be in order. I've also got a spare card for Thompson & Knight, the family's legal representatives. In case you have any further questions about the papers."

The last gained me a raised brow. The Thompson & Knight

law firm had been established in Dallas in 1887, and were a well-known and respected firm. They'd been hungry to get into international law. So when they'd been approached by intermediaries from London, hired through firms in Peking, they'd been more than willing to take on the needs of the Wu family and forge relationships overseas.

Officer Davis drank more of his lemonade, paging through the documents. They confirmed the Wus' ownership of the house, the land it sat on, and their business downtown, and included forms proving their legal status in the country. "So the only Chinese residents are Mr. and Mrs. Wu and their daughter Daiyu. Is that correct?"

"Yes. Though I also live here. I have a small room by the back door."

"I see." He straightened the stack of papers and handed them back. "Everything seems in order." He took one last swallow of the lemonade then set the glass on the coaster before putting his hat back on. "Sorry to have disturbed you. And many thanks for the fine lemonade."

"Glad you enjoyed it." I moved to open the door for him. "It's just sad how some people try to get others in trouble for no actual reason. I know it's your job to investigate when a complaint is made, as you can never be too careful, but it's a pity all the same."

I got another raised brow at the comment. "Not the first time you've had a visit about this, I take it?"

I shrugged. "It happens on occasion. Despite the fact that the family's been here for twenty years and made Dallas their permanent home."

Officer Davis tipped his hat. "I'll make a note in the file. Might help cut off another visit at the pass."

"We'd really appreciate that, sir. Thank you very much."

It wasn't until I saw the police car drive off down the street that I allowed myself a sigh of relief. That had gone rather pleasantly, though there'd been no guarantee it would. There were plenty of prejudiced people in the world, and you never knew when you'd encounter one.

"That was an interesting visit." Dai's voice pulled me away from the window.

"Hopefully that will be the end of it."

Dai shook her head. "She's been foiled twice, Jacques. I'm not sure that's happened to Linda Carmichael before. She didn't seem the type to handle failure well."

That hadn't occurred to me. It left a somewhat bitter taste in my mouth.

CHAPTER 27

As if things hadn't already taken a somewhat sinister turn, the call we received later that afternoon didn't make me any happier.

"Wu residence, may I help you?"

"Jackie boy, is that you?"

I couldn't stop a grimace. "My name is *Jacques*, as you're well aware. What do you want?"

"Why, to speak to my dear China Doll, of course."

I seriously considered hanging up on him. "What is this regarding?"

"There's no need to sound so formal, surely. And can't a friend just call another to say hello?"

There wasn't much I might say to that, but it made me no happier on the matter. "Please wait a moment."

Fighting the temptation to 'accidentally' hang up on him, I set the receiver on the desk before going to get Dai. I needn't have bothered—when I turned, she was already walking into the room. "You have a phone call."

"Is it Truman?" Was that a slight tone of eagerness in her voice?

I picked up the receiver again and put my palm over the

mouthpiece. "I can tell him you're busy."

"Whatever for?" She held her hand out as she reached my side. "His timing is perfect."

I grudgingly handed over the receiver.

"Good afternoon, Mr. Pierce." Dai sat on a nearby chair, keeping the earpiece of the receiver partially turned away from her so I might listen to both ends of the conversation.

"Come now, call me Truman. I insist," he said. "We've plotted together. It seems only right."

What would be right was for my left fist to show him a thing or two.

"All right, Truman. To what do I owe the pleasure?"

"Believe me, China Doll, the pleasure is entirely mine." He was almost purring as he spewed his suave playboy fare.

He deserved both of my fists, multiple times. If he didn't hurry and get to the point, I *would* hang up on him, regardless.

"I wanted to find out if you got what you needed from the party last night. It turned out to be a tad more eventful than I'd anticipated, but hopefully everything went as planned?"

Dai took longer to reply than I expected. A soft smile lit her lips. "Perhaps. It was somewhat enlightening and quite memorable. Have you heard from Asquith today?"

"I have." At least his tone was normal again. "His family's driving him a little batty, so we've arranged to meet for drinks later this afternoon. I'll be introducing him to several business friends of my father's. People and topics of no interest to the others, so it should buy William a bit of peace for a while."

"You're a good friend."

Truman laughed. "Maybe, maybe not. It'll help get *my* father off my back as well. He'll believe I'm showing some interest in the dealings around town. So we both benefit."

"I see." Dai hesitated for a moment. "Might I ask a rather bizarre, and perhaps morbid question?"

Truman's voice perked up. "Those are the best kind. Fire away!"

"William mentioned that Laura was being cremated and that he was having her ashes sealed into an urn. Do you know if he's picked them up yet, or are they still with the funeral home?"

"You are a creature of genuine wonder, China Doll. I could not have anticipated that question in a thousand years!" He truly sounded like he was enjoying himself. The cad. "It's my understanding he collected the ashes and added them to the marble urn this morning. Now that he's got them, his family's become even more insistent about returning home and making sure he comes with them. It also appears they were none too happy that he set the thing next to his bed instead of into a shipping crate." He laughed. "Quite gruesome, but who am I to judge? I had no choice but to take pity on the man and give him a way out of all that. For a short while, anyway."

"I'm confident he's very grateful to you for your help. By any chance, do you know how or if the urn was sealed?" Dai asked him.

"No idea whatsoever, but I'll be sure to work it into our conversation when we're on the way to the meeting this afternoon." The line seemed to crackle with his anticipation. "I've got a feeling you know something worrying."

Was the popinjay about to confess? If only.

"I can't really say much regarding that at this time." Her tone was serious.

All the levity left his voice. "Of course. I'm willing to wait until you can tell me. Just remember, you may rely on me for anything you need."

Dai gave another little smile, her cheeks picking up a hint of pink coloring. "I'll keep it in mind. Thank you, Truman. Goodbye."

I took the phone and placed it back on the receiver a bit more forcefully than I should have. "Nothing good can come out of using this man. If he truly suspects what we're up to, we should trust him even less."

"Jacques, honestly." She shook her head. "There's nothing to be worried about."

What in heaven did she mean by that?

Before I got a chance ask her, a familiar voice rang from

the back of the house.

"Daiyu, I have news!" It was the dragon. Rosa must have dropped her off after their charity work before going for groceries for tonight's dinner. I wasn't sure I'd ever heard Dai's mother sound so elated before.

We met Lien in the foyer, where she was removing the pins from her hat and veil, this being the means by which she disguised her nationality from those who didn't know her.

"What is it, *Mŭqīn*? Did something good happen?"

"Yes! At least I hope so." Her face was flushed. "Rosa and I have worked so hard to be accepted by the other ladies. Volunteering, taking on more on than our share—anything we could think of. It looks like someone finally noticed." She pulled a gilded envelope from her purse and waved it in the air. "We got an invitation to a small gathering tomorrow! All our patience and hard work are about to pay off."

Dai smiled brightly. "That's wonderful! I know how much you've wanted to be accepted by the ladies from your group."

Despite Lien's years of trying, getting the community to accept her despite her nationality had been an ongoing struggle. I was happy for her, though I'd never understood her deep need to be accepted by others. Like Dai, it wasn't something I cared about one way or another.

"Yes—and they didn't invite just me and Rosa, but the daughters of the attendees are to come as well! This will be a grand opportunity for all of us, don't you think?"

Somehow Dai was able to maintain her smile, though I glimpsed a crack or two at the edges. "*Mŭqīn*, have the ladies ever invited their daughters to one of their social get-togethers before?"

Lien gave Dai a puzzled look. "I assume so, although I can't be sure, not having received an invitation before. Why?"

"I was just curious."

Lien took a hesitant step toward her, her expression suddenly clouded. "I know it's not something you're used to, but you will come, won't you? It would mean a lot to me. You might even make a few more friends."

"Yes, of course I'll come." Whatever had crossed Dai's mind was no longer anywhere in sight. "Jacques can even drive us there so we can arrive in style." The fact that she was making sure I would be there indicated that she definitely thought something else was going on. I just couldn't for the life of me figure out what.

CHAPTER 20

"It's such a beautiful area. So many trees and parks." Rosa sounded impressed. "I hear they're even planning to build a shopping village. So progressive."

The morning had dawned bright and clear, Rosa and Lien rushing us around until we could depart for the get-together. Dai had said little since she'd been told of the invitation, and I assumed she was thinking of other matters.

We were once again north of Dallas, near the DCC, as we drove into Highland Park. Just like the club, this residential area was meant for the more affluent residents of Dallas. Anyone doubting it needed only look at the extensive manicured lawns and lavish homes to realize they were no longer where normal humans trod.

"I can smell the trees," Dai said. If Prince had been with us, he would have been plastered against the partially open window, sniffing for all he was worth. "Isn't there a famous pecan tree in Highland Park? I remember one of the radio programs talking about it. How they light it up during Christmas."

"I believe that's right," Lien said. "It's somewhere south on Armstrong Avenue."

The tree was also known as the 'Million Dollar Monarch,' owing to the price paid for the land it sat on—but moreover for the unusual stipulation in the contract that the tree stay untouched, just as Joseph Cole did when he'd found it as a sapling in his fields after the Civil War.

The address we drove to was in the first developed area of Highland Park, down Versailles Avenue. Our destination sat on a double plot with a circular driveway and covered entrance. The two-plus story edifice showed all the hallmarks of Hal Thompson's architectural designs. He'd become famous for his French Eclectic style, which also featured Renaissance detailing.

The white outer walls and domed first-floor windows, the dark gray shutters and roof, and the three-foot-stone balustrades on the drive and main entrance oozed elegance and proper breeding. It was both gorgeous and intimidating.

As I parked by the front door, I realized there were no other cars here. It was only two minutes before the assigned time; I would have expected that at least one or two of the other attendees would have arrived before us.

Lien lowered the veil on her hat and Dai opened her lace umbrella after I opened the car doors for them, to obscure their faces from any passerby. Rosa wore a floppy sun hat, which would hide her face from anyone not directly in front of her. Dai had insisted that ruffles be kept to a minimum, so she wore a dark green silk day dress with puffed sleeves. Lien and Rosa were dressed in blue and red for subliminal support—the colors were part of both the Texas and US flags.

I set Dai's hand at the crook of my elbow and led the party to the large front entrance. Mere moments after ringing the doorbell, an older man in a somber butler's uniform and sporting an old-fashioned cravat opened the door. The man's expression remained blank and unwelcoming—somewhat off-putting, especially for a social event.

"Good afternoon, sir." I passed the ladies' cards and the invitation to him for inspection.

The butler barely glanced at us before stepping back to

allow us entry. Grecian style columns surrounded the foyer, and the polished marble floor gleamed in the sunlight. Without a word, he took our hats and gloves and motioned for us to follow him.

I made a note of the artfully curved staircase, more grand columns, and a posh formal dining room with lustrous wood-paneled walls. Only a blind man could miss the lavish chandeliers that hung from the ceilings as we moved from the foyer to the sitting room.

From the moment we stepped into the space, however, it was apparent something wasn't right. The expected side tables and comfortable seating were gone, leaving only an occupied settee and three stiff chairs set five or more feet away facing toward it. Nothing welcoming about this arrangement at all.

"Please take a seat." This came from the occupant of the gold-cloth and wood-trimmed settee. The woman was reedy, ideally suited to the tube-like fashions currently in vogue. Her sandy blond hair was coiffured in perfect waves, her brows pencil thin. Pearls hung from her ears, wrist and neck, each one separated by diamonds set in platinum. Her gold- and silver-colored dress was tailor-made and fit her like a glove. Every inch of her screamed wealth, refinement, entitlement— and something about her seemed strangely familiar.

"Mrs. Pierce, thank you so much for inviting us to your lovely home." Lien chose the center of the three stiff chairs, in no way revealing that she understood things weren't as they should be.

I settled Dai in the chair to her mother's left and took a position behind her, trying to keep the shock at Lien's words from showing on my face. This was the popinjay's *mother?* Had he somehow maneuvered this meeting? But for what reason? It was only then that I realized there was a sixth person in the room. She came in from an arched opening beyond the settee and stood behind it, on Mrs. Pierce's right. The smug look on Linda Carmichael's face spoke volumes. Mrs. Pierce did not introduce her to the group.

Now I understood Dai's troubled expression from the day

before. She'd somehow pieced together that this social event was actually an ambush.

"I'm so glad you could make it." The sentiment of the words wasn't reflected in Mrs. Pierce's cold blue-eyed stare. "I realize this is unorthodox, but I wanted to have a private conversation with you. One of a rather sensitive nature."

"How can we help?" Lien still appeared completely unperturbed, despite the obvious effort that had gone into placing them in uncomfortable chairs and lining them up before the queen of the house like errant servants in need of discipline.

From Rosa's tight-lipped profile, I knew she understood precisely what was happening and was none too pleased about it.

"Please understand, I am not in any way invalidating the contributions you've both made to the Dallas community and our charity organizations. Despite troubled times, you do your part and should be commended in that respect. It would behoove others to follow your example."

The half eye-roll from Linda Carmichael made her thoughts on the matter clear. The fact the two women had not been welcomed for anything but doing the work spoke of Mrs. Pierce's own.

"However, it is my understanding that your crippled daughter has been seen in public in the company of my son. As I am sure you're aware, my husband is a very important man in this state—a position others envy and would like any excuse to deprive him of. That being the case, it's essential that we maintain the highest of standards in all things."

She gestured vaguely around them, as if using her very home as an example.

"We wouldn't want any... *blight*, intentional or otherwise, to blemish our excellent family name. It would be even more damaging if certain associations were allowed to proceed and taint the purity and influence of our bloodline. While I am sure she is everything a mother might wish for, despite her obvious impediments, it would be in everyone's best interest if you kept your daughter at home and away from the members of my family. We don't want there to be any ugly misunderstandings."

Lien had gone still as a statue, yet her pleasant expression remained unchanged. I felt the storm building around her. " 'Ugly misunderstandings'? Is that right?"

"Yes. We want to avoid those at all costs. Your people suffer from an atrocious reputation—one you wouldn't have if not for entrapping good, faithful Christians into using opium. We understand quite well why you do so much charity work. Guilt is a heavy burden."

The words were preposterous, yet something in the way she said the last of them had the ring of understanding. What might that be about?

Lien rose to her feet with deliberate slowness. Once standing, her presence solidified and continued to rise, the dragon coming to the fore. Whatever advantage Mrs. Pierce thought she'd ensured with the setting and her demeanor was a mere pittance compared to what the dragon could bring forward without any props or trappings.

"I see you are under many misunderstandings. Allow me to *enlighten* you." Lien's tone was soft, but edged.

Mrs. Pearce sat stoically as if already prepared for unpleasantness from the rabble she had allowed into her home.

She had no idea what was coming.

"First, despite your assumptions, we do not do charity work from 'guilt.' Far from it. We understand how blessed we have been and wish to share those blessings with those who have not been as fortunate.

"Second, it would behoove you to be a better student of history and to learn your facts, rather than accuse others of misdeeds without substance. My people did not bring the blight of opium to *you*. It happened the other way around. China enjoyed everything the Western world wanted, but you possessed nothing we needed. So Westerners decided to create a need, and by combining opium with your North American invention of smoking, you did just that, subjugating thousands to the chains of addiction. Profits came rolling in. Then you could buy what you did not possess, while simultaneously bringing destruction to everything we'd built in five thousand years of civilization."

The dragon's presence intensified, her authority almost more than the house could bear. "Third, you speak of the importance of your bloodline. How far back can you trace yours, if I might ask? Two, three, maybe four generations?"

Lien appeared to grow even taller. Such was the power of the dragon when fully unleashed—something I had learned early on to avoid provoking.

"*I* can trace *my* lineage twenty-four generations. That's a span of over a thousand years—and ours is an *imperial* bloodline, unlike yours. If there were to be concerns regarding the tainting of a heritage, it would be yours polluting *ours*."

Despite her lack of jewels and other accouterments of significant wealth, Lien's bearing and confidence alone proclaimed her royal lineage, leaving no doubt whatsoever she spoke the truth.

"Yet *we* do not concern ourselves with such matters any longer. *We* came to America to be free of such tethers, free of pointing blame, free to be whoever we want. To give our children the right to choose, to be free, to be happy. You? You yearn for the very ideas this country was created to reject. You're just too blind and ignorant to see it."

Lien nodded to Rosa and then myself. Without prompting, Dai rose to her feet.

"Thank you so much for your lovely hospitality. I've learned a lot today, and for that, I am grateful." Lien gave their host her brightest smile, hiding the dragon from sight, as if nothing untoward had occurred. "Don't get up. We'll see ourselves out."

Out of the corner of my eye, I caught Mrs. Pierce's blooming shock and befuddlement. It made me wonder what Linda had told the woman about Dai, and whether either of them had bothered to do any research before plotting this little scene. Linda stood ramrod straight, face beet red, and she looked about ready to explode. I was sure Mrs. Pierce's presence and Linda's desire to join that family were the only things keeping her in check.

The butler was nowhere in sight, so I scooped up our hats and gloves as we made our exit from the premises. No one said anything until we sat safely ensconced in the car.

"*Mǔqīn*, that was exquisite." Dai smiled brightly.

"I agree with Dai. Your handling of those *brujas* was amazing!" Rosa threw a dirty look back the way we came. "I can't believe they did this. If you hadn't put them in their place, I might have been tempted to ram the fear of God into them. What nerve!"

Lien only sighed. From what I could see of her in the peep mirror, she looked wrung out. "I've not had to do that in a long time," she said. "I forgot how tiring this is. Not once have I missed playing these idiotic games." She sighed again. "But it's so disappointing. I thought we were finally making progress."

"I'm so sorry, *Mǔqīn*. This is my fault." Dai bowed her head, the smile gone. "I met the younger woman at the party on Thursday. She's quite taken with Mrs. Pierce's son, though apparently the feeling is not mutual. The fact he was interested in talking to me and did not hold my race or my disability against me made her fairly vexed. It never occurred to me she would do something like this."

Except it had, hadn't it? Last night when her mother had mentioned the social get-together and the fact their daughters were invited. Though to be fair, it would have been impossible to convince the dragon of what she suspected. Lien had been so excited about what appeared to be a genuine breakthrough, and I imagined Dai hadn't wanted to rob her of that, even though the truth would be revealed in the end.

"Don't fret, Daiyu," Lien said. "This isn't your fault. I should have known better."

Dai half turned in the seat. "Why is that?"

It was Rosa who answered. "Rumors we've heard from some of the people we've helped." She shook her head. "It's been said Mrs. Pierce was once a member of the Ladies of the

Invisible Empire. Everyone who belonged to the organization has distanced themselves from it; the corruption of several of the leaders was exposed in the twenties, leaving most of the members disillusioned. But that doesn't mean their core beliefs changed."

So the popinjay's mother had once been a member of the women's branch of the Ku Klux Klan. That was a rather frightening thought. Definitely something to tuck away for later.

There was, however, one outstanding thing that had come out of this most unusual and unpleasant meeting, I thought: We might have just found a motive for the death of Laura Cooper.

CHAPTER 29

"Dai, just how seriously do you suppose someone might take this whole concept of diluted or tainted bloodlines?"

We'd returned home not long before. Lien and Rosa were busy in the kitchen trying out an oatmeal scone recipe from Ida Bailey Allen, a famous cookbook author who had a regular show on the radio. Scones not being typical Chinese or Mexican fare, the two hoped to lift their spirits after the morning's debacle by attempting to make something new.

Dai scratched Prince behind the ear. His curled tail thumped against the couch's cushions, more than content at the attention. "It had occurred to me, but until today, I hadn't considered just how much it might mean to someone. Asquith is the son of an earl, making his father, and therefore his line, one of nobility. Laura was not only an orphan, but a commoner and an American. It could be regarded as scandalous or beneath him to marry her, even if he's not the heir."

"But to murder somebody over it?" I shook my head, not able to get my brain wrapped around the concept. What actual difference did it make who your ancestors were? Yet even to the Americanized Wus, filial piety still played a part in their lives—as shown by the altar to their forefathers upstairs. Perhaps it didn't matter to me solely because I had none.

"Sadly, it would appear so." Dai shook her head. "It's just another type of discrimination. And we've witnessed firsthand how violent or petty that can become.

"I've thought before that prejudice appears to be more about feeling superior over someone than anything else. Of having a person or group to blame for the things they can't control. For example, blaming the Jews for money problems or accusing blacks and Mexicans of stealing people's jobs. Or even Texans denying that the current economic troubles will fully ever reach here."

"Still, as you said, William is not the heir. Would it truly be that scandalous for him to marry Laura? What am I not seeing?"

Dai grinned. "So you need the blind girl, to show you the way?"

"You know that's not particularly helpful, right?"

Her grin turned impish. "I do indeed."

I was both gratified and mortified at her humor. This 'murder' business had been weighing heavily on her small shoulders. It was good to see her feeling better, even if it was at my expense.

"Emotions aren't always cut and dried, and definitely not regularly logical. Regardless of the fact that he's not the heir, I believe the issue is blood or status related, if not both. Though such things are fairly unimportant here, they most certainly are not for the British. Theirs is an empire that has control of a quarter to a third of the world. Even a British pauper probably imagines himself superior to any of the native people under the empire's thumb."

Domberry sure believed it with his entire heart. The way he looked down on even Dallas' most wealthy was proof of that. The way he behaved, and the hints we'd heard indicating that he might have 'married down' into the Asquith family to offset his own lack of funds, gave credence to what Dai postulated. But did that make him a murderer? Laura marrying into the family wouldn't have a direct bearing on Domberry's lineage—though it might affect how much capital would be left to his wife once her father passed. Could money also be a motive for Lizzie herself?

"I can sense the wheels turning in your mind from here." Dai laughed. Prince gave a soft bark as if agreeing with her.

"There's a lot to contemplate. Though I don't think we're any closer to solving this. Or at least, I'm not."

Whatever she would have said to that was cut off by the sound of the doorbell. Had Linda sent the police after us again? Or had she come up with a more malicious idea? I headed to the foyer with a heavy dose of unease.

I opened the door, only to find something even worse waiting for me there.

CHAPTER 30

"Jackie!"

My worst nightmare, in the flesh. The last thing we needed.

"Mr. Pierce." It proved hard to fight the knee-jerk reaction of slamming the door in his face. "This is highly irregular." I frowned my displeasure, but he appeared to take no notice of it.

"Is Dai in? Her mother as well? May I speak to them?"

The rapid-fire questions brought me up short. It was only then that I noticed Pierce wasn't his usual popinjay self. His sandy blond hair was windblown rather than slicked back. Though he was wearing a stylish double-breasted day suit and vest of golden brown with blue diagonal stripes, they looked as if they'd been thrown on in a hurry. Even his bright blue tie was askew.

"Truman?" Dai came into the foyer, Prince nestled in her arms.

"China Doll!"

"Has something happened?"

Her sharp tone brought to mind our other worries. Had something transpired regarding the murder? Surely no one else had been killed! A wave of trepidation overrode all my earlier irritation at our unwanted visitor.

I had only a moment to register the flash of confusion that crossed Pierce's face before Lien walked into the room, wiping her floured hands on a kitchen towel.

"Jacques, who's at the door?"

I turned around, blocking her view of the entryway with my body. "No one—"

"Mrs. Wu?" Like an eel, the popinjay wriggled past me into the house. Before I could grab him and hurl him back outside, he'd reached the foyer table, and its still-lovely bouquet of yellow roses. He gave the startled dragon a full, formal bow.

"Please accept my deep and most sincere apologies for the events of this morning. I can offer no excuse for them." He dropped the bow even further. "Though undeserving, it's my fervent hope you will all find it in your hearts to forgive us."

Pierce stayed as he was, looking as if he was willing to hold the uncomfortable position for days if need be.

The dragon sent me a surprised inquiring look, but it was Dai who answered the unvoiced question.

"*Mǔqīn*, please allow me to introduce to you my friend, Truman Pierce." Dai set Prince down and moved to stand beside her. "Truman, this is my mother, Lien Wu."

I spotted Rosa peering out from the kitchen, curiosity plastered all over her face. Truman still maintained his bowed pose, waiting.

"Jacques, close the door, won't you?" Lien's voice was smooth and even, her shock of a moment ago tucked away out of sight. "Please, Mr. Pierce, we're in America. There's no need for such formality." She smiled ingratiatingly. "Won't you come into the sitting room? Would you like something to drink?"

I closed the door without turning around, so as not to miss anything. Truman held his pose a moment longer before standing up straight. Even from the back, I could tell that he'd somehow smoothed out his hair and straightened his clothes in the moments before he'd slithered past me and bowed. Like Lien, he had become totally composed, as if the rattled, unkempt figure I'd found at our doorstep had never been.

"I wouldn't want to put anyone to any trouble." Pierce stepped aside so Dai and Lien might proceed him into the sitting room.

"It would be no trouble at all, I assure you."

He nodded his capitulation. "Anything at hand would be fine."

"Jacques, would you mind asking Rosa for some drinks, and snacks if we have them. Then if the two of you would join us as well?"

"Right away, madam." While loath to leave the popinjay unwatched, I knew I had nothing to worry about. With Prince and the dragon in attendance, he wouldn't be getting away with anything untoward—not without losing some skin, at least, if not a finger or three.

"Who is that? What's going on?" Rosa could barely contain herself, her curiosity eating at her. Expecting Lien's needs, she already had a tray on the table loaded with glasses, and was taking ice from the icebox.

"It's no one to get excited about, believe me." I checked the cookie jar; we still had a few oatmeal raisin ones left, so I put them on a plate. "Just a new friend of Dai's. He's also the reason for the scene this morning."

"He's the one who sent the roses, isn't he?"

I couldn't quite read her expression. It looked like a mix of excitement and worry, with a dash of pity thrown in. For *whom*? I wondered. Surely not me.

"Lien wants all of us, so two more glasses please." I reached into the refrigerator for the pitcher of *agua fresca* Rosa had made that morning. Fresh melon juice and sugar in a jug of water. No caffeine punch like iced tea, but as refreshing—if not more so—in the heat. I was curious to find out what the popinjay would make of it.

We took the lot into the sitting room. Everything appeared the same as when I had left, so Pierce must be behaving himself.

The Wu sitting room didn't see many outsiders, but was always ready to receive them just in case. During certain times of the day it was cooler than the other rooms, so Dai and I tended to loiter there. In the late afternoon and evenings, it was where the family would gather to listen to radio programs, music, or newscasts. Currently, however, the radio—the prominent piece of the room, a tall Zenith model in the Art Deco style, dark walnut with silver and gold chrome accents— sat silent.

An elegant gold and glass abstract sculpture hung on the wall across the windows, reflecting the dulled light passing through the sheer curtains. Curved couches in deep green and wood faced each other with an oval walnut table nestled between them. It was here that Rosa and I set down our burdens and served everyone. It was a much more relaxed environment than what we had been presented with at the Pierce home.

Truman Pierce stood when Rosa entered the room, displaying proper manners. Rosa sat with Lien and Dai after the cookies and drinks were passed around, and I was left with little choice but to share the second couch with the popinjay.

"I once again wholeheartedly apologize to you three wonderful ladies for what you endured this morning. If I'd had the faintest inkling of what was planned, I wouldn't have allowed it to happen." He flashed an impish grin. "Though from what I gather, you took care of matters quite well on your own."

Dai let slip a dimpled smirk, while Rosa decided now was the best time to take a sip of her *agua fresca* and hide her own expression. Lien, in true dragon fashion, let nothing slide past her pleasant-faced façade.

"My mother was extremely vexed with Linda by the end, so I doubt she will join her in any other ill-conceived shenanigans."

"So you think Linda will try something yet again?"

Both Pierce and Lien turned their full attention to Dai and simultaneously asked the same shocked question. "*Again*?"

Dai sat prim and proper, glowing with angelic innocence. "Oops—a slip of the tongue. Apologies."

In another bizarrely synchronized movement, they both pointed questioning, stabbing stares in my direction. It was all I could do to give a shrug of the shoulders with open hands and try to appear as befuddled as them.

'A slip of the tongue,' my ass. I just hoped Dai hadn't doomed me to being cornered later by one or both of them and pounced upon for further explanations. Watching the popinjay and the dragon act in concert was disturbing enough.

"I'll make sure she doesn't." I'd never seen Pierce look so grave. "Sometimes I'm not so sure she understands all the possible repercussions of her actions."

My brow rose of its own accord. I was sure Linda wasn't the only one, the popinjay could stand to do some reflecting himself. Yet despite how I felt about him, I had no choice but to give Pierce credit for being man enough to apologize in person. It would do much to counter the rebuff Lien and Rosa had suffered that morning.

"Don't worry yourself," Lien said. "It will be as if nothing happened. I doubt they'll share this with the other ladies, so no harm done."

If the dragon ever found out the details of Linda's other attempts to cause trouble, naught would be forgiven and more than likely blood would flow. I could only pray she never discovered any of it.

"Dai doesn't have many friends, so I am always curious. Might I ask how you two met?"

I froze in place. My brain reeled in a panic trying to remember if we'd ever mentioned anything about how they knew each other. Nothing came to mind, but I wasn't sure. The fact that I could not control how Pierce would respond sent goosebumps of trepidation rolling down my spine.

"We met downtown. They needed directions, and I was happy to help. We got to chatting a bit, and I found your daughter to be truly fascinating and quite intelligent. Such a combination is hard to find in my usual circles, so I was more than pleased to have her as a friend." His bright expression darkened just a touch. "It was never my intention to cause her, or yourselves, any trouble."

I glanced at Dai, and she had a little secret smile on her face. As if she had thrown a hurdle to test him, and Pierce had overcome it and admirably so. She was enjoying herself immensely.

"Not everyone is willing to give my daughter a chance to show them her real self, and for that, I thank you." Lien stood, bringing Pierce and me to our feet. "Unfortunately, Rosa and I were in the middle of a project when you arrived, and we should get back to it before the work we did is ruined. However, please feel free to stay and chat with Dai a while. Perhaps you'd care to join us for dinner later this month? I'm sure Mr. Wu would love to meet you."

"Nothing would make me happier, ma'am." Truman's smile blotted out the sun.

This gave me no peace of mind whatsoever. The last thing I wanted was his insinuating himself further into Dai's life.

CHAPTER 31

A muffled giggle echoed back toward us once Lien and Rosa were out of view. I was sure the two would dissect everything that had gone on until now, the dragon plotting courses of action to subtly ferret out more information during the aforementioned dinner.

Disaster after disaster. I couldn't keep from giving the popinjay a look of disgust as I switched to the sofa where Dai still sat. With the dragon gone, Prince moved around the table and sat peering into Pierce's face, waiting for him to make a move. It gratified me to note he was on the same page as me regarding the intruder.

"China Doll, I want to give you my personal and deeply heartfelt apology for what happened this morning. Linda is a bit daffy, but to go this far, and to drag our mothers into it—this is a new low."

I snorted. "You're no better. I told you, you've no idea what you're playing at. This is not some embarrassing but inconsequential matter. It's not something to be glossed over with a measly apology. If your girlfriend had taken that picture, if we not been prepared with paperwork and lawyers for the police she sicced on us, if Dai's lineage were not so far above anything that might be found in this country, the family might well be in jail now, tarred and feathered, run out of town, or worse."

"Jacques, please. Calm yourself." Dai's hand rested on my knee, pushing encouragement to do so to my frayed nerves. To my surprise, my hands were shaking.

For once, the popinjay said nothing, merely glancing from her to me and back. I'm not sure what he found in what he saw, but he blanched a little before looking away.

"So the 'yet again' was not a slip after all."

Dai nodded. "Our situation here is not typical of other countries' immigrants. They have more options than those given to the Chinese in current times. So we need to tread lightly in most situations lest someone take offense and cause trouble for us. Very few of us remain, even in a progressive city like Dallas."

I could tell from the puzzled expression on his face that Pierce had never thought one lick about immigrants—in general or otherwise. The biggest thing he'd possibly ever had to worry over was what color his latest tailored hundred-dollar suit should be.

"I've a lot to learn, don't I?" He gave a self-deprecating chuckle. "But it makes me no less earnest and my apology no less heartfelt. If there's some way for me to make amends, you need only ask."

To my surprise, he included me in that statement. The one thing he might have done was let me stay mad at him. *The cad.*

"If the truth be told, this is all on me," Dai said. "You've done nothing but to try to help since we met, which is more than I would ever have expected from anyone, aside from a person or two." She patted my knee then removed her hand. It always felt good to be appreciated.

"Now, before they can't take it anymore and look in on us, do you have any news for me?"

When Pierce didn't answer, I glanced over at him, wondering why. He was staring at Dai's face. At her eyes. It was only then I realized she wasn't wearing her teashade glasses. They were most likely in their case, as she did not usually wear them in the house. He'd seen her blind eyes at the hotel, at least momentarily, but now could do so without impediment. "You know, staring is *rude*."

Pierce jerked back as if I'd hit him. "Sorry." He turned to Dai. "China Doll, your eyes—they're truly mesmerizing. Why do you keep them hidden?"

Though I felt the same way, the sight of her eyes typically disturbed anyone other than the family. Contrasting with the dark hair that framed her heart-shaped face, the pearly smoky-white gray of her eyes seemed almost luminescent. Angelic. When I first looked upon her all those years ago, I would have sworn her blind eyes let her see more than nature ever intended.

It brought me no joy at all that Pierce appeared to feel the same way about them as I did. But for Dai's sake, I was glad of it.

"Not everyone is as discerning as yourself." She sounded pleased. "Most people simply find them disturbing. Unnatural. So it's best to shade them from view."

"Everything about you is fascinating. Exotic and yet familiar. As if I, myself, had been blind before now."

This was getting out of hand. I gave a short cough. "Might we stay on topic, please?"

At least the fool had the grace to appear embarrassed. The last thing we needed was for the dragon to hear this soppy foolishness.

"Forgive me," Pierce said as he sat back. "What was it again?"

Dai laughed. "News. Do you have any news or information for me? About Asquith?"

He appeared befuddled for a moment then seemed to make the connection in his mind. "Oh, right! Between this morning's debacle and everything else... Sorry. Yes, I have news. Regarding the... sealing of certain items," Pierce said, his voice dropping low as he leaned forward, "it is my understanding that the stopper is affixed with a simple sealant. The kind found at any hardware store. He took care of the deed himself."

I could sense Dai's mental wheels turning as she examined the possibilities opened by this information. If what had been sealed could be unsealed and then sealed again...

"How do you think they'd feel about us inviting them to tea? Or perhaps dinner? I believe the Adolphus has a grand reputation for both. It would only be Jacques and me, yourself if you like, and the Asquiths."

Pierce grinned. "The Brits do love their afternoon tea. It would be a little piece of home for them, so they'll probably be willing. I hear the hotel rearranges the French Room for it. Bringing in special tables and potted plants to create a private atmosphere. I've never been—I don't really care for the hot version. But for you, I'll brave this new, possibly doily-filled frontier."

He looked at his Cartier Tank wristwatch. "It's half-past eleven now. If I could use your telephone, I can call in a reservation and get the ball rolling. If for some reason they turn us down, it would still make for a pleasant afternoon diversion."

I didn't like the sound of that. The cad might spoil Dai's plans just to grab a few hours alone, or semi-alone, with her. I would need to keep a close eye on him. "I'll show you where it's at."

Dai stood. "I'll let *Mǔqīn* know we'll be going out. I don't believe they've started on lunch yet."

Not a conversation I envied. Out of the way of prying eyes and ears, I was sure a giggle-filled inquest was about to start in the kitchen. I guided the popinjay to Tye's office so he could use the telephone. "Do you need a directory?"

He waved the question away as he picked up the receiver. "I know the number."

I hung around, listening to his side of the conversation as he first spoke to the front desk, then was rerouted to the French Room. Once the reservation was in place, he got routed once more to the front and then to Asquith's room.

"William! Glad I caught you. Do you remember Miss Wu? Yes, that's her. She wanted to invite you and your family to tea this afternoon in the French Room. It would be a novel experience for her, and a chance for you lot to show us Americans what is it about hot tea that's so enticing. They informed me it's 'low table,' whatever that means."

Pierce nodded to whatever was being said on the other end of the line. "I'm sure she'd be happy to get a full explanation of the custom when you see her. The reservation is for two thirty. See you then." He replaced the receiver and turned to me with a grin. "Voilà—all done."

That smug face, with wealth and confidence dripping off him… I didn't like him, and I didn't trust him. Then I realized I'd been given the perfect opportunity to make such things quite clear. "You're not fooling anyone, you know."

That earned me an arched brow. "Fooling anyone about what?"

"Who you are. *What* you are. That Dai is merely entertainment for you. That as soon as you've had your fill, you'll shunt her to the side like you do everyone else."

Pierce's jaw twitched, but otherwise his expression didn't change. "Jackie, that just isn't so. You know nothing about me."

"The name, you impertinent cad, is *Jacques*. And I know *all* I need to know." I stepped up close. "I'm warning you, you better watch your step, because I'll be keeping an eye on you. I won't allow you to hurt this family."

Rather than look offended, he beamed at me. The popinjay had the cheek to smile at me! "Lighten up, Jackie. That makes two of us. Should be fun."

CHAPTER 32

The man was insufferable. 'That makes two of us.' What did that even *mean*? If my confrontation had any effect on him, he wasn't showing it.

"I'll leave you to doll up before the meeting." Pierce headed for the foyer and the front door. "Do give my goodbyes to the ladies. I want to go change and get downtown so I can corral as many of them as possible to join us. See you, Jackie."

I slammed the door closed in his wake, grinding my teeth. He *must* be doing it on purpose. And like a fool, I was letting it get to me.

"Is something wrong?"

I tried to school my expression into neutral before turning around to answer Dai's query. Blind or not, she'd be able to tell a lot from my tone and resonating 'chi,' if you will. Tension, anger, and intense emotions fill the air somehow, and Dai could pick up such things. Different senses, yet ones capable at times of conveying as much information as would be gleaned by eyesight, if not more.

"No. Everything's fine. He just needed to go get things ready." I took a deep breath, still trying to center myself. "We have a reservation for half past two. Asquith has agreed to join us. Pierce will get there early to encourage the others to come, too."

"Hmm." Dai tilted her head slightly. At her feet, Prince did much the same while staring at me.

It looked like I might not be fooling anyone. "Do you want me to pick an outfit, or should I get Rosa to help you? I'll need to change as well before we go."

"They've both already demanded I let them dress me." Dai gave a deep sigh. "They've both heard about British afternoon tea parties, and we've been tasked to record every detail of the event to regale them with later." She shook her head. "The experimental scones are safely tucked in the oven, so they're heating some leftovers for a quick lunch to tide us over until teatime."

Laughter and whispers drifted toward us from the kitchen.

"Did the grilling over you-know-who already happen?"

"Not exactly." Dai grinned. "I was able to push them off until you could join us."

I stifled an internal groan. "Lovely."

"Oh, cheer up." Her grin widened. "We have commitments to meet, so there's only so much time to spare. We should come through pretty unscathed this round."

I hoped she was right.

When we made it to the kitchen, I took over setting the table. Rosa stood at the stove, already reheating some leftover tortillas and other odds and ends. The back door stood open, helping the heat from the oven seep outside, though soon it would be too hot for the trick to work even with a fan blowing.

Dai answered most of the questions regarding the popinjay and the Asquiths, leaving much thankfully unsaid. The dragon's expressions swayed from one extreme to the other, both elated by and worried about her daughter's unexpected social strides.

As soon as we finished eating, Rosa prodded Dai upstairs and I started on the dishes. Lien moved to go with them but then hesitated, and waited until the two were out of sight.

"The hotel won't refuse to serve you?" she asked. "Are you certain of this? I don't want Daiyu exposed to... such an awkward situation. I'm sure I can come up with some excuse to make her stay. She's already seen more than she should have of the ugliness in the world for one day."

The dragon had no idea how much Dai was actually aware of. It was amazing how close people could be yet not know each other at all. Like her namesake, she was strong, stable, and fearless, not at all the innocent naïve flower they liked to pretend she was.

"The reservation is under Pierce's name. He's well known there, or at least his father seems to be. Dai is his guest. They won't want to get on his bad side. Or inadvertently offend the Brits, since they're staying at the hotel."

Lien considered my words for a moment, then nodded. "It will have to do, won't it?"

"I'll be there, and so will Prince. Dai is *always* our primary concern."

She relaxed even more. "Yes, you're right. Despite your unexpected arrivals into our lives, you've done nothing but support her. For that alone, I am forever grateful."

I looked away, heat rising up my neck. For the dragon to compliment me was a sure sign of the depth of her distress. "Prince and I feel the same about her, I assure you."

She gave me a slight bow with her head and then trailed off after her daughter.

Knowing my time was minimal, I finished cleaning the dishes, washed off a bit, and put on my finest afternoon chauffer/companion ensemble. I suspected Lien and Rosa would take this opportunity to present Dai in the best light possible, so I had no choice but to do the same. Prince would go through his own transformation, getting wiped down and brushed, and a collar found for him to match whatever color they decided on for Dai.

As I discovered a few minutes later, this afternoon's hue was forest green. She looked like a pixie plucked from an enchanted forest. The ruffles at the elbow-length sleeves, below-the-knee-length skirt, gloves, and beret were stitched with leaf patterns, enhancing the effect.

She couldn't have appeared more adorable. From her mortified expression, I was reasonably sure Rosa and Lien had both assured her of this multiple times. For my own safety, I would keep my opinion to myself.

Within moments, I had tucked her and Prince into the car, and we were on our way.

"How bad is it? Be honest now." Dai grimaced as if steeling herself for the worst news imaginable.

I glanced at her in the peep mirror. Time to walk the razor's edge. "Not bad. Minimal ruffles. No ribbons in sight. The full skirt is straight rather than flared. They restrained their natural impulses quite well."

She fingered the half sleeves then sighed. "I have no choice but to take your word for it."

Though still utterly charming, it was true Rosa and Lien had held back from the usual doll-like appearance they frequently forced on her. I had a bad feeling this tapering off had more to do with Pierce than anything else. They wouldn't want a potential suitor to look at Dai as a child. The thought was rather sobering.

After the morning's debacle, it amazed me that they might even be thinking in that direction. Yes, Pierce was Dai's first-ever gentleman caller, but his mother's opinion of her origins would not be softening, despite having been led astray by Linda. Prospects for a blind woman and a foreigner might seem bleak, but you didn't settle for the first smooth talker who came along.

I was so caught up in my own thoughts I almost forgot to stop by the hardware store on the way downtown.

After leaving the Ford in the capable hands of the smartly dressed valet at the hotel, I steered Dai inside. Prince followed at our heels, sporting a matching green collar and leash, tail and chin held high, proclaiming with every step that the patrons should be honored at the privilege of seeing him in top form.

Pierce must have advised the concierge of our impending

visit, because no one approached us or tried to stop us as we crossed the lobby and headed toward the French Room. The restaurant was spectacular, with molded high-vaulted ceilings in white, and arches embellished with embossed scrollwork. All the fancy tables and chairs had been removed, and dozens if not hundreds of potted ferns and palm trees now created private nooks in which gold-colored wrought iron padded chairs nestled around small glass-topped tables. The setup had the ambiance of being outdoors in a garden, without exposing the clientele to the wilting Texas afternoon heat.

We were shown to our secluded nook in prompt order. Pierce and William stood to greet us. Lizzie was there, but her husband and Mrs. Grey were absent. Judging by the lack of additional chairs, it appeared they'd not be joining us. More confounding were the strained expressions on Lizzie's and William's faces.

"Good to see you again." I shook hands with Pierce then got close to Asquith. While my right hand shook his, my left checked his jacket pockets. After running away from the orphanage, I'd collected a set of particular talents before Dai discovered me. She'd insisted I keep them sharp, so I'd continued to practice to humor her. Aside from occasionally filching an extra cookie or other tidbit, I'd never thought I would use them in public again.

I slipped Asquith's pilfered room key into my pocket, which already housed a brush, glue, and a folding knife. The test tube, rubber stopper, and a small wooden spoon were in the other. We had achieved the first step in our plan.

"China Doll, that dress suits you." Truman took her gloved hand and kissed it. The cad didn't call her adorable or cute, or any of the other diminutive endearments Dai so loathed. I'd been looking forward to hearing him use one and thus lower himself in her estimation. No such luck.

Lizzie's face lit up as she got a good peek at Dai's outfit. "You look like a fairy, or perhaps a pixie. It's utterly delightful!" She glanced at the rest of us. "Do they have those in America? Fairies and pixies, I mean."

Truman's expression showed he didn't know what she was talking about, but thanks to Dai's appetite for information, I knew what they were. "I'm afraid not, Mrs. Domberry. It's much too hot for them in these parts."

Lizzie laughed, and Asquith half-grinned for a moment.

Pierce still looked confused. "The only fairy I know about is the Tooth Fairy. It's always been quite generous. Is there more than one kind?"

The tea cart for the first round appeared as Lizzie began explaining for Truman's benefit. Once Dai was settled in a chair, I moved on to the next step of her plan.

"Please excuse me for a minute." With everyone busy, I left the group and headed for the elevators in the lobby. A quick glance at the room key I'd absconded with gave me the room number and thus the floor. Less than two minutes later, I was opening the door to William's room.

As one would expect from a hotel with the Adolphus' reputation, the space was well appointed and immaculate. Tasteful art on the walls, comfortable-looking chairs, and a wide bed in a color palette revolving around reds, golds, and browns. But Laura's urn was nowhere to be seen.

A quick search of the room confirmed it wasn't there. Had the killer beaten us to the prize? Leaving everything as I'd found it, I made my way back downstairs before I was missed.

Lizzie was telling the group about leprechauns when I arrived. I nodded to her in apology and took my seat. The first round was mint tea, served with a myriad of finger sandwiches cut into rounds, squares, and rectangles. Dai was nibbling on a cucumber-butter sandwich, and I lightly touched her arm to let her know I'd returned.

Further taps in our code informed her I had been unsuccessful in my quest. Her brow furrowed for a moment, then straightened. I noticed Prince had placed himself next to Lizzie's chair. Mrs. Domberry would take a small bite of one of the sandwiches then sneak the rest of it down to his waiting mouth. Occasionally she'd reach and scratch behind his ear. The mutt had made another conquest while I was gone.

The second round featured Assam tea, a rather strong black tea, offset by sweet berry scones and chilled lemon curd. By then Lizzie had run through her topic, leaving it open for other conversation. Despite her exhaustive explanations, Truman still appeared befuddled by the notion of the fae. Asquith, though going through the motions, seemed elsewhere, the tightness around the eyes that I'd noticed when we first arrived still in evidence.

"I am sorry that Mr. Domberry and Mrs. Grey weren't able to join us. I'd hoped to thank all of you properly for allowing my intrusion into your lives the last few days." Dai took a sip of her tea while waiting to see if her lobbed bomb would have any effect.

Lizzie's expression soured, and William frowned. They both avoided looking each other's way. Something had definitely gone down between the siblings.

"Paul didn't feel very well after lunch. He didn't want to be a damper on the activities, so he stayed in our room to rest." She petted Prince as she gave her explanation, plainly wanting to avoid seeing if we believed her or not.

"And Nanny—I mean, Mrs. Grey needed to make some last-minute travel arrangements, so she also had to excuse herself." Asquith glared in Lizzie's direction as he spoke, as if blaming her for both Mrs. Grey's absence and the need for the change in their travel plans.

Truman jumped in. "Hold on, does this mean you're leaving us?"

"I wasn't left much choice." Asquith sounded both bitter and angry.

Lizzie's shoulders slumped. "Will, I already apologized. I only did what I thought best. I can't take it back now, no matter how much I regret it."

A prickle of foreboding teased my neck. Dai asked what I could not. "What do you mean?"

Petting Prince rather than look at us, Lizzie's response was almost a whisper. "While Will was out this morning, I snuck into his room and took the urn. Paul helped me pack it up, and we asked the hotel to ship it home.

"By the time he realized Laura's ashes were missing, the package had already gone."

We'd been outmaneuvered yet again.

CHAPTER 33

"Yes, I am being blackmailed by my family." Asquith's hand shook so much from his pent-up anger that he had to set the teacup and saucer down. "How did you so delicately put it again, dear sister? Oh, yes: 'If you want her back, you must come home with us.'"

Tears rose in Lizzie's mortified face. "It wasn't meant to be that way at all!" She glanced at the rest of us, looking for allies. "You have to admit sleeping with her ashes right next to you is not normal. You need help! Being home with your family is the best place to get that."

Asquith shot to his feet. "I'm sorry, everyone. But it's gotten too hard to continue pretending to be civil." He half bowed in Dai's direction. "Miss Wu, I appreciate the gesture, but no matter how you look at it, I'm not fit company at the moment. Perhaps we'll have a chance to say goodbye before I leave for England."

He bowed one more time in apology and left. We all remained silent while the second course was cleared and they brought the third. By chance, or perhaps by divine design, the final tea was chamomile, known for its soothing properties.

Once the waiter left, I surreptitiously offered Lizzie a

handkerchief. She took it, offering me a trace of a smile, and dabbed at her eyes. "I knew he would be unhappy, but I never expected this. He's been so miffed with me. All I ever wanted was to help. If I'd known the consequences when she suggested it..." All three of us had to lean in to hear her next words. "He punched Paul in the face. That's so *unlike* him." She hid her face in her hands.

Dai held up a finger so we would give her a moment. "You didn't come up with the idea on your own, I take it?"

Lizzie hiccupped and lowered her hands after dabbing at her eyes again. I passed her a cup of the chamomile, hoping it would help calm her.

"I... I don't know. This morning we were discussing what we should do." She sighed. "Paul was making fun of things, asking if we'd be buying a ticket for the urn if Will decided to come home. The whole idea was so macabre, it gave me the creeps. I said I'd have nothing to do with that. So, of course, Paul pursued the ugly topic, painting all sorts of scenarios in which Will might take the urn with him. Dinner parties, Sunday socials, church—even the cinema."

I could see the goosebumps rising on her arms just from talking about the subject.

"Nanny came to my rescue and replied that, of course, we wouldn't be getting the vase a ticket or anything else. That we would ship it home. That led to a completely different discussion. But we got no closer to figuring out what to do. Then Paul said—or was it Nanny?—that if we shipped the urn home and Will really did have an unhealthy attachment to it, he'd follow it and come back to England. At the time that sounded like a grand idea. No creepy vase on the ship, and something to encourage Will to return home. It seemed perfect!"

Lizzie dabbed at her eyes again and sipped more of her tea. "It never occurred to me he would be so angry about it. So very, *very* miffed."

Prince gave a soft whine. Lizzie reached down and petted him, which appeared to calm her more than the chamomile.

"We were all at luncheon, grabbing something light to tide us over until tea, when Nanny told Will what we'd done. He stared as if he'd never seen us before, then he got this half-crazed look on his face." She shook her head as if not wanting to revisit the particular memory. "If it weren't for Nanny being there and the fact that we were in public, I don't know what he'd have done. It's not like it could matter to Laura; she's gone. But he acted as if we'd insulted her, insulted him." She sighed again.

"When we got in the elevator, I could feel him seething. But Nanny, ever the voice of reason, said there was nothing to be done about it. That we would ship the urn back to him once it arrived if he wanted. But Paul wouldn't leave it alone. He joked with the operator and made some comment about loads of packages getting lost in the post, and before anyone saw what was coming, Will *punched* him! I thought I would faint." She started talking faster. "Nanny stepped between them—not that Paul was in any condition to do anything about it. He'd fallen to the floor when Will hit him. She pulled Paul up and helped keep him steady until we reached our floor. It seemed Will was going to come with us, but Nanny stopped him and told him he needed to go cool off—that I would meet him in the lobby before our appointment, and that she'd see to the arrangements for his return home. He didn't argue with her. He only scowled, fists bunched at his sides, and stepped back into the elevator. The operator was staring at us the *whole time*."

Lizzie sipped at her tea and sighed again. "No offense, Miss Wu, but I desperately wanted to cancel. I was just so nervous about seeing Will again. But Nanny would hear nothing of it. Paul was ranting, blaming *me* for what happened, and the last thing I needed was for Nanny to be unhappy with me, too. So I came. When Will showed up, he wouldn't talk to me, wouldn't even glance at me. I don't understand any of this at all!"

I wasn't sure if the woman was an outstanding actress or merely clueless.

"Your brother just lost the love of his life," Dai said.

"Whether Laura's essence is still a part of the ashes or not, it's all he has left of her. You took that from him, making him feel as if he lost her all over again. I'm sure it was a horrid shock."

She stared at Dai, her mouth opening into a shocked O. "Truly? I did *that*? Truly? I never thought... Oh, no, he'll hate me *forever* then!" The waterworks came on then, and tears rolled unimpeded down her cheeks.

Though she already had my handkerchief, the popinjay extended his as well. Lizzie grabbed it and buried her face in it, trying not to sob as she struggled to get herself back under control.

"I'm sure he'll realize you didn't mean to hurt him. Just give him some time." Dai took a sip of her own tea, her brow furrowed as if working to fit all the fresh pieces together. "When are you leaving for home?"

We all waited for the answer to this most pertinent question.

Lizzie sniffed and quietly blew her nose. "We leave the day after tomorrow."

CHAPTER 34

"We've been soundly outmaneuvered. Our window is closing rapidly." Dai sounded energized rather than despondent. "We must act."

Lizzie had left us moments after her debilitating answer. With the afternoon tea concluded, we'd settled our account and made our way to the hotel's parking garage. I dropped Asquith's room key on the floor of the French Room, where a waiter might discover it and return it. Truman accompanied us, despite my having told him there was no need. I wished Dai had waited to broach this topic until after we got rid of him.

"So Jackie didn't find whatever it is you sent him to search for?"

She flashed him a smile, as if pleased the popinjay had figured that much out on his own. I found it bothersome.

"No. As you heard, they shipped off the urn, so we couldn't retrieve a sample of the ashes for testing."

Truman frowned. "For testing? Testing for what, China Doll?"

"Dai, don't." My dislike of the cad notwithstanding, it would be safest for her to let as few people in the know as possible.

"Sorry, Jacques. We'll need his help if we've any chance of succeeding. He should understand the stakes. It's only right."

That didn't make me like it any better. "Not here, though. And we should include Dr. Campbell. Nowhere flashy or too public." The last I added specifically for the popinjay.

Pierce looked more intrigued than bothered by my objections and demands. "Where should we go then?"

"The offices above the laundry should do," Dai said. "It's private, and a Chinese showing up there won't seem out of place."

I nodded. "That should work." Maybe seeing the family business would also deter the popinjay a bit. I was sure being around people who were actually doing *work* would make him break out in a rash.

"Offices over a laundry?" Truman looked intrigued.

"White Laundry is my family's company," Dai told him. "We own the building, and there are offices on the second floor."

"I'll give you the address," I said. "You can meet us there."

"Don't be silly, Jacques. We can offer him a ride. Why take two cars when one will do? It will also be less conspicuous."

She had me there, but I still didn't like it. I loved it even less when I caught Pierce smiling my way and threw in a wink. Opportunistic bastard. The harder I tried to get rid of him, the more he seemed to insinuate himself into our lives.

"Let me open the door for you, China Doll." He helped Dai into the car, then walked around to the other side and got in. Luckily, Prince beat him inside and set himself up in the back seat between the two of them.

Trying not to grind my teeth, I slipped behind the wheel and got us underway. En route, I stopped to call Aiden from a local payphone.

I kept one eye on the road and the other on the peep mirror, and we made it to the laundry in record time. I didn't want the popinjay in such close proximity to Dai any longer than necessary.

Rather than try to pump her for information on what we'd

been doing and why, Pierce spent the ride making conversation—or more like mining for information. Knowledge about Dai. Her likes and dislikes. What she'd done or hadn't. She seemed as curious about him as he was about her, something I didn't like in the least. No, I wasn't jealous. He just wasn't right for her. He wasn't *worthy*.

This brought up a sobering thought. Perhaps someone hadn't believed Laura worthy either, and had killed her for it. While I might want to choke the shenanigans out of Pierce, killing him was a whole other thing altogether. Or was it? Where exactly did one draw the line? I hoped to never find out.

"This is a good location. Near to downtown but not in it, leaving you accessible for other types of clientele."

Rolling my eyes, I parked the car. Pierce was out the door and around to open Dai's before I'd even had a chance to remove the key from the ignition. He was really starting to irritate me.

Pierce stopped for a moment to observe the entirety of our building before going inside. I took a fresh look at the familiar structure, to be sure nothing seemed wanting. Two stories of white brick and gray cement. A sizeable forest green awning with the company logo of a stylized white sandwort flower mirrored the one in the edifice's front. The one at the back provided a bit of shade and relative coolness for our employees, and the one in front offered the same for the customers. A stout door in green and a small loading dock resided beneath it. There were no immediate neighboring buildings, and tall fences on the sides offered the workers some privacy, keeping them from direct view when they came and went. Every month or so, the brickwork, awnings, and outside windows were cleaned to keep White Laundry looking as pristine as possible. No point in advertising you made things clean if you couldn't keep your own place in such a state.

Pierce guided Dai inside, forcing me to bring up the rear. Once inside, I was happy to see her disengage herself from him and take the lead on the set of stairs leading to the second floor. The popinjay stared in astonishment as she bounded upstairs, then laughed and followed her. This was her domain; she'd require little help here, being more than familiar with the layout and where everything was placed.

Dai led the way to the laundry's compact conference room. I left Prince guarding her while I walked downstairs to tell Mei Ling to bring Dr. Campbell upstairs when she arrived. I made a quick stop at the break room to pick up some glasses and a jug of iced tea for Dai and our guests.

Laughter rang into the hallway, but that wasn't what made me halt in my tracks. It was the sight of Mr. Wu, pressed against the wall, trying to peek inside without being seen. "Sir?"

Dai's father jumped back, startled, not having noticed me before I spoke. He put a finger to his lips and motioned for me to follow him toward his office. As soon as we were out of earshot, he pulled on my sleeve. The lenses of his thick reading glasses made his worried brown eyes appear bigger than they were. "Daiyu! She's laughing. Who's in there with her? She never laughs out loud! *Never.*"

Her father wasn't wrong. Dai smiled, grinned, occasionally chortled, but she didn't outright *laugh* often, and it was even rarer for her to do so in her parents' presence. Or at least, it had been until this mystery took hold of her. I understood how it might unnerve him. He wouldn't like my answer either.

"His name is Truman Pierce."

"*His?*" Wu paled before my eyes, his mouth drooping. "Is this the one Lien called about?"

"Yes." I could think of nothing else to say. I wasn't the only one who'd thought they'd never have to worry about Dai having an interest in other men.

He took off his glasses and cleaned them with a kerchief, his gaze focused far away. When he put them back on, he straightened his face and composed himself. "I am not here. You understand? Under no circumstances am I to be introduced to this, this…" He waved a hand in the direction of the conference room to fill in for what he could not say.

"Yes, sir. It would probably be for the best." I'd hate for the popinjay to get any weird ideas that he'd want to discuss with Dai's father. Like asking permission to pursue her affections— or worse. It wasn't worth even thinking about.

We nodded to one another in perfect understanding, then Mr. Wu scurried quietly back to his office and locked the door behind him. It was only then that I resumed my path to the conference room.

CHAPTER 35

Aiden arrived and Mei Ling brought her upstairs, her face full of questions regarding the odd assemblage. Dr. Campbell was attired much as before, wearing slacks, a blouse, and a vest. Without her work apron, it was obvious she was a woman if one bothered to look.

"Thank you, Mei Ling, I'll take it from here." I nodded my thanks and ignored the pout she sent my way. Her curiosity would have to go unsatisfied. I shut the door to keep her from trying to ask anyway.

"Things have taken an unexpected turn. I felt it would be worthwhile to get everyone together to fill you in, and then brainstorm about what to do next," Dai said. "Truman, the big secret is that Laura didn't die of natural causes, but was in fact, murdered."

I didn't know what I had expected him to do at the news, but the soft sigh and the sad look in his eyes definitely hadn't been it.

"I was afraid it might be something like that." He stared at the polished tabletop. "Murder seemed to be the only thing that fit. But it made little sense, so I was hoping it was something else entirely."

Aiden was the one who appeared shocked. "You've been helping Dai all along without knowing why?"

Pierce shrugged. "At first, it was on a lark, but then I realized it also gave me a chance to get to know her. Plus, I figured she'd tell me why when she was ready."

I had to fight the urge to roll my eyes. I'd guessed the initial part already, the cad. The second I wasn't sure what to make of.

"So, why do you all believe she was murdered?" Pierce sent a questioning glance at the rest of us. "And why aren't the police involved?"

Dai quickly filled him in on how she'd grasped what had happened and the fact that we didn't possess sufficient evidence to take it to the police.

"I take it the plan to get a sample of the ashes failed?" Aiden asked.

"Completely." Dai shook her head. "We were outmaneuvered, and not for the first time. I don't know if the culprit has realized what we're up to, or is just being thorough and unwilling to leave anything to chance."

"You think it was someone who knew her, don't you?" Pierce said. "And I was on that list." The popinjay had the temerity to appear wounded, as if by merely meeting him we should have known he had nothing to do with the murder. How pompous could he get?

"You weren't on it for long, if that's any consolation." Dai sounded amused. "We've also removed Shannon from the list, as well as Lizzie. But we're out of time to narrow it circumspectly or to find more evidence. With all of them going back to England the day after tomorrow, we need an alternative approach or Laura's murderer will go free."

The silence lay heavy around the room. Since the popinjay was with us, however, it didn't last long.

"But why would anyone want to kill her?" He asked. "She was a sweet, inoffensive creature, and madly in love with William. The two of them glowed whenever they were together. Might jealousy be the motive? I felt a twinge of it here and there myself, seeing how happy they were."

Dai shook her head, a quirky grin adorning her lips. "We considered that with Shannon, but it doesn't appear to be the right motivation for someone else. I believe the reason is something much less direct. The problem wasn't who Laura was, but *what* she was."

"And that would be?" Pierce asked.

"Something I will keep to myself a little while longer." Dai smiled.

Rather than look irritated, he laughed. I would have preferred the former.

Pierce moved on to a different track. "You mentioned there was arsenic in the dress's dye, but that more had been added?"

She nodded. "That's correct."

"Is that something one can get a hold of easily?"

Aiden answered Pierce's question. "It depends. Arsenic occurs naturally as an element and tends to combine with sulfur. So the majority of it is mined. It's also a by-product of some metal refining processes. Several brands of rat poison use it as an ingredient, and it's even in some medications. From what I understand, you used to be able to buy it in drugstores without being questioned, mostly to use as a pest deterrent."

"Are they all the same?" A nibble of an idea was forming in my brain. "Dai mentioned oxidation once, and you also referred to something similar. Would that change the chemical composition, making the various sources produce not exactly the same arsenic?"

Aiden's eyes grew wide. "Yes, yes, of course! There might be differences. Something we could use to narrow down where the arsenic did *not* come from—and perhaps even where it did!" She glowed with excitement. "One of my old professors is a chemist. His lab is more extensive than the one at the hospital, and better suited for this kind of research."

"Excellent," Dai said. I thought I heard a note of wistfulness in her voice. Owning a full laboratory would be a dream come true for her, even if she couldn't use all the equipment because of her lack of sight. But then, she had me for that.

Pierce was frowning. "I'm assuming the last people on your list are Mrs. Grey and Domberry?"

"Yes."

"Would either take the risk of having to find the arsenic here? It's a foreign country, after all. They wouldn't be familiar with the laws or restrictions here. It would be much easier to just bring it with them," he said.

The comment gave me chills. That would mean the murderer had planned Laura's death even before they met her.

"Using it in the States would also make it harder to trace," Dai added. "If it's a regulated substance or if the purchases are tracked back in England, the authorities wouldn't be looking for it getting misused overseas."

That showed an unexpectedly ugly side to the concept of planning ahead. More disturbing was the fact that if not for Dai, no one would have ever been the wiser.

"I'll call Constable Higgins when we're done," Aiden said. "If the justice has any contacts in England, he'd be the one to know. Maybe he can start an unofficial inquiry on that end about the arsenic."

Dai gave her a dimpled smile. "That's a marvelous idea. Thank you. If we can find a connection there, it would definitely add weight to the evidence we found here."

"But there's no guarantee they'll be able to get any information before the suspects leave the country. So we still need some kind of plan." I hated to deflate the growing enthusiasm regarding the grand ideas being brought forth, but they didn't address our most immediate problem.

"We ought to tell William." Pierce frowned as he spoke. "He should know before he leaves, especially if we're not able to get the proof we need."

I sighed. "We've no idea how he'll react at the news. He might tip our hand and let the guilty party escape. Worse, he might decide to resolve the matter with violence."

Prince barked once as if agreeing with me.

"Yet he's the only one who might hold the information we

need to determine who is responsible—or, at least, he's the one who'd be able to delay their departure," Dai said. "If we can come up with some other way, good. But in the end, we may have no alternative."

An hour later, we were no closer to a better solution. I had to admit we really didn't have a choice. Approaching Domberry or Mrs. Grey directly would seem unusual, and would put the murderer's guard up. Only through William and his well-established friendship with Truman would we stand a chance to get close and keep them from suspecting anything.

Pierce would be in charge of getting Asquith away from the others for a private conversation. Aiden would call on the constable to see if they'd contact Scotland Yard to start an inquiry. She would also reach out to her old professor and have the arsenic analyzed. Dai and I would wait to hear from Pierce, then show up to tell Asquith what we knew. I was most definitely not looking forward to that last part.

CHAPTER 36

I dropped Dr. Campbell off at the hospital, and took the popinjay back to the hotel so he could get his car and also try to contact William. Then I steered Dai, Prince, and myself home to wait and rest. We'd forgotten all about Lien and Rosa, who wanted every detail of what had gone on at our afternoon tea.

It was a verbal dance, telling them what they desired to know while avoiding all mention of the associated drama.

"You were gone much longer than we expected. Did you go somewhere else after tea?" Lien's expression was guarded as she asked the question. Rosa rolled her eyes but was no less eager to hear the answer.

Dai took a sip of her *agua fresca*, letting the tension build just because she could. "He came with us to the laundry. Dr. Campbell met us there, and the four of us had a long chat."

"Dr. Campbell?"

Another sip of her drink. "Yes, the new friend I made the other day. She's interested in all sorts of things, but is rather shy. With her there, it was like we were a foursome—two boys and two girls."

The women exchanged a glance, and as one turned their

entire attention in my direction. "Really? Two couples?"

I inwardly groaned. The last thing I wanted was to have these two asking me all kinds of embarrassing questions about Aiden and my feelings. I would have thought Dai and Pierce would be more than enough to keep them busy. From the dimples showing on Dai's cheeks as she drank her *agua fresca*, I knew she had phrased her answer to get just this kind of reaction.

"Not couples, ladies. Friends, *only* friends." Though one of them was far less than that, in my opinion.

The dragon seemed to take me at my word. Rosa, however, smiled at me, her eyes crinkling with hidden delight.

"Your father was at the office, did he not see you?" Lien asked Dai the question, but looked to me to answer it.

"Mr. Wu was there, and I spoke to him briefly. But he didn't want to interrupt the group."

"Tye didn't call me." Her eyes flashed.

She would have some choice words for him when he got home. I felt terrible for him. He'd already gotten enough shocks for one day.

"We found out during tea that the Asquiths will go back to England on Monday. Truman is trying to arrange a small get-together tonight for his friend and inquired if we'd come. Would it be all right if we go?"

It was almost comical to watch the dragon's battling expressions as she mentally tabulated the implications of what Dai had just asked.

Rosa looked ecstatic. "Two dates in one day? *Chica*, we will doll you up so pretty, he won't remember his own name after taking a look at you!"

"Daiyu, are you sure you're not overdoing it?" Lien asked. "You've been doing so much lately. I'd hate for you to push too hard. It's already been a very full day, you must be exhausted."

"I'm all right, *Mŭqīn*." Dai raised a hand before her mother might protest further. "But I'm willing to take a quick nap if it will make you feel better."

"It would." Lien's face relaxed. "Plus, it'll give Rosa and me time to plan your outfit. We might even go shopping."

Dai grimaced, and I tried to hide a grin. She wasn't the only one with a devilish streak.

The moment Dai retired upstairs, both women turned to me once more. "Tell us about the two of them. Were they getting along? Could this turn serious? Details, give us details!"

I now wished *I* were the one taking a nap. Even Prince had left, following Dai upstairs. I'd have to tackle this on my own. The more they squeezed out of me, the higher their excitement rose. "I doubt it will come to anything. They have nothing in common."

"Unlike you and Dr. Campbell?" Rosa grinned.

"What? No! That's not what I meant at all." Where had that come from?

Luckily for me, the telephone rang, the sound echoing to the kitchen from Mr. Wu's office. "Excuse me." I was more than grateful for the reprieve.

I closed the door before picking up the receiver, the less to tempt the ladies to eavesdrop. "Wu residence. How may I help you?"

"Jackie!"

I wasn't glad anymore.

"Yes?" I tried to put as much frost in my tone as possible—not that it made any difference.

"I have an update. Is Dai around?"

"Sorry, she's indisposed at the moment." I rather savored telling him that. "You'll just have to deal with me for now. So *spill* it."

"Loosen up, Jackie." Pierce barked a laugh. "You're way too serious. It'll send you to an early grave if you're not careful."

"Did you call to inform us of something, or just to hear yourself talk?" Dai would be cross with me at my attitude, but the guy rubbed me wrong every time he opened his mouth. We needed his help, but I didn't have to like it—or him.

"Will has agreed to meet me after dinner. I can bring him wherever Dai deems is appropriate to break the news."

That was when I realized we hadn't discussed that aspect of the plan at all. We'd all agreed it would be best to tell Asquith somewhere away from his family, but we had made no decision as to where. Most places were too public, too noisy, or too restrictive. Then I remembered the small office area in the morgue. Aiden had access, there were multiple entrances and exits to the hospital, and if he got violent, there were medications there to make him calm. "Baylor Hospital, room B301. Will nine o'clock be doable?"

"I should think so," Pierce said. "What's in room B301?"

"You'll find out when you get there." I ended the call before he might ask anything else. Picking up the receiver again, I dialed Aiden's number to inform her of the arrangements.

Once that was done, I realized I had a new, unexpected battle ahead of me. If we were all meeting at the morgue, I needed to curtail whatever Rosa and Lien were concocting for Dai to wear. The setting and the topic were somber. Having her show up all dolled up and wearing an evening dress would be highly inappropriate.

I had to come up with a more casual yet believable setting—something that would keep them from getting too carried away. When I opened the office door, it was to find both of them waiting for me, hats on, purses and gloves in hand.

"Was that about the date?" Lien shot Rosa a veiled look. "I mean the small get-together?"

"Yes." I latched onto the first thing that came to mind. "He wanted to make sure where we'd meet and to let us know the setting would be outdoors and casual. I suspect an ice cream parlor or social, though he was loath to give specific details. I guess he wants to surprise Dai."

"Casual? Outdoors?" The two women exchanged frowning looks. "We will have to think this through again."

Rosa's expression lightened. "We could do a variation of the dress she wore to tea. I have a muted flower print at home that would be perfect!"

"When would you need to leave?" Lien asked me.

"No later than eight, if possible."

She turned to Rosa. "That doesn't give you much time."

"With you helping me, I think we can be done by supper, if not sooner."

The dragon shifted her gaze to me. "There's a roast in the oven. I'll need you to turn and baste it in an hour, and place the potatoes in there as well. You'll want to start the water for the corn a half-hour after that. And don't let Dai nap too long, I want her rested, but I'd hate for it to disrupt her regular sleep cycle."

Since she'd been blind from birth, it had been a struggle for Dai's parents to get her on a regular sleep routine. Dai herself had come up with the best ways to train her body when to sleep. Yawning was an oddly contagious action, so her parents or I starting one off had proved an effective means of getting her sleepy and stabilizing her sleep cycle. Almost as if the yawn set a starting point for her internal clock.

"Leave it to me."

I accomplished all the tasks left in my care and set the dinner table. Prince was licking Dai's face to wake her by the time I made it upstairs to do so. She flipped him on his back and rubbed madly at his exposed belly in retribution. As if that would ever discourage the scoundrel.

"Is no one else here? The house sounds quiet." Dai grabbed her housecoat and rose to her feet.

"Lien and Rosa left to prepare your casual summer dress for the evening. Your father hasn't come home from the laundry yet, but should be here soon."

"Casual? So Truman called, I take it?" She sat down before the vanity so I might brush her disheveled hair back into place.

"Yes, we'll be meeting him at Baylor Hospital around nine."

"Room B301, I assume?"

I shrugged. "It seemed the most prudent location."

"Well done, Jacques."

I tried not to react. Dai's praise meant more to me than I cared for her to know.

Her delicate nose sniffed at the air. Prince was already at the door, busily doing the same. "We're having a roast for supper? It's been a while."

"With baked potatoes and corn on the cob."

"Really?" Dai laughed. "I wonder if they're trying it out to be sure the meal will appeal to a certain Texan when we invite him home to dinner."

That was a sobering thought. "Surely not. They've only just met him."

"But she asked and he agreed. Within the month, I believe. I guess we'll have to wait and see, won't we?"

Her dimpled expression brought nervous pangs to my stomach. The sooner we were done with this murder business, the quicker we might shove Pierce out of our lives. Or so I hoped.

"We should get downstairs; Father's home."

At least Tye would be on my side regarding the popinjay. Even if not for the same reasons.

CHAPTER 37

Mr. Wu was unusually silent when he came in, just nodding in our direction before grabbing the paper and heading for the dining room. Lien and Rosa returned not long after, looking pleased with themselves.

They served supper, and upon seeing what we were having, I could swear Tye shrank into himself a little. He'd jumped to the same conclusion as Dai did. While we often had what would be considered 'American fare,' there were always side dishes that weren't. The fact that all the items for this meal derived from the same culture must have sent up warning flares.

Throughout dinner, he kept sneaking glances in Dai's direction—almost as if to make sure she'd not already been taken away.

"I hear we had visitors at the laundry today," the dragon said.

Tye looked up from his barely-touched meal. "Yes, that's right. I believe Dai invited some friends over." He pushed his meat around the plate. "I didn't get a chance to meet them, though."

"What a pity, dear. Perhaps, next time, you will."

Although the words sounded innocuous in and of themselves, there were tense currents shifting beneath them. It was highly unusual—almost like the continuation of a previous argument, but one disguised as polite conversation.

"You'll be interested to know that your daughter is going out again this evening."

"*What?*" Tye dropped his fork.

The dragon smiled. "She's becoming quite the social butterfly."

"D-Daiyu, is this true?" Tye's eyes were nearly round with panic.

"Don't worry, *Fùqīn*," Dai said. "It's just an opportunity to spend more time with an acquaintance who is heading back to England on Monday. It's just this one time."

"Oh, I see." His relief at her words was palpable.

"But, *dear*, don't forget, there's always a chance a friendship might become more. You need to be prepared."

Tye stared blankly at his plate, moving the meat around some more, and wisely made no comment.

The dragon disappeared, and Lien took its place, steering the conversation to other topics. I had another item to add to the popinjay's list of offenses. There'd never been much of this type of friction between Dai's parents until he came sauntering along.

Even Rosa seemed worried at the odd exchange. "We should probably get Dai upstairs and changed. We don't want her and Jacques to be late."

I started picking up the dishes in silent agreement. Dai looked thoughtful as she rose from her seat. Tye picked up his partially read copy of the evening edition of the *Dallas Times Herald* and retreated to his office. Only then did Lien rise and follow Dai and Rosa.

Pierce had much to answer for. The sooner he moved out of our lives, the better.

I took out my aggression on the dishes and pans, making them spotless. I left a wrapped plate of reheated steam buns on the kitchen table for Tye in case he got hungry while we were away.

When they finished with Dai and brought her downstairs, it said much about Tye's distress that he didn't leave his office to take a picture or two, or even just to get a look at her. It made me a little sad, though I was sure Dai was happy to avoid the chore.

Rosa had once more worked her magic, her sewing machine skills a treat to behold. The fabric was a light gray, bordering on white. Pink blossoms in a bunch trailed loose petals, picked up by a soft breeze. The skirt was pleated, adding to the illusion of wind, with wavy sleeves at the shoulders. Gray Mary Janes adorned her feet. She looked utterly lovable—a fact I would, as usual, keep to myself.

"Have a wonderful time, you two!"

Prince gave a bark, not wanting to be forgotten.

"Sorry, all three of you."

Lien raised a brow. "Not *too* good a time. And make sure to bring her back at a reasonable hour." The promise of what would happen to me otherwise was implied by the fire in her eyes.

"I'll do my best."

Handing Dai a wrap, her gloves, hat, and cloche purse, I escorted her outside to the car.

We were already well on our way toward downtown when Dai asked, "Did Father seem down to you?"

I glanced at Dai in the peep mirror. "A little. I think he's having a hard time with the concept that you might be courting and what might come from that."

"Really?" Her confusion was obvious.

I shrugged. "It's not something he's had to contemplate before. I am assuming you noted that he and your mother seem to be on opposing sides about the entire thing?"

"Huh."

Could she truly not have noticed? That would be a first. I wasn't sure how to feel about it.

We arrived at the hospital with ten minutes to spare, the sun only now lowering on the horizon. Prince stayed in the car, the back windows cracked open and a water bowl on the floorboard. Typically, we would have left him at home, but tonight that would have aroused the dragon's suspicions.

Aiden was already waiting for us in room B301. She wore a long lab coat, dark trousers, a white shirt, and a black vest. I hoped the solemn location and her professional air would give weight to what we were about to reveal to Asquith.

"Evening, Dai, Jacques."

"Evening. Thanks again for helping with this."

Aiden shook her head. "I'm glad to. Anything that will get us closer to catching the person who did this."

She had set up five folding chairs in anticipation of the meeting. I steered Dai to the nearest one.

"Speaking of which, were you able to contact the constable and your professor?" Dai asked.

"Yes, to both. George said he'd send a cable to the British police. I told him a little about what's going on, and he agreed we should at least go through the motions. The judge is out of town for the weekend, so he took it upon himself to take care of it. I think you made a big impression on him, Dai. He remembered you immediately."

Dai flashed me a dimpled grin.

"I also got hold of Professor Brogan. He was quite interested in the possibility of trying to distinguish specific types of arsenic. I sent him a sample of what remained in the box by courier two hours ago. Hopefully I will hear from him tomorrow."

"Splendid. Your help's been invaluable. Thank you."

A splash of red colored the sizeable woman's cheeks, her quickly-hidden pleased smile making her appear almost like a child. It seemed Dai wasn't the only one who could look adorable. I was pleasantly surprised.

Further conversation was pushed aside as we heard voices and footsteps coming from down the hall. Our guests had arrived.

CHAPTER 38

"Truman, I still don't understand what we're doing here. Why did you bring me to a hospital?" Asquith sounded both irritated and confused.

"All will be revealed, I promise you. We're almost there."

The popinjay opened the door and signaled William to go inside.

He took two steps in and stopped, having spotted us. "What is this? What's going on?"

"Mr. Asquith, won't you take a seat?" Dai asked. "I realize this is highly irregular, but we needed to talk to you in private."

"Truman?" Asquith glanced back at Pierce, his bewilderment clear.

"Do sit, Will. What they have to say is rather important." Unlike some of Pierce's other suits, this one was tame, light gray with even lighter diagonal stripes. The cad's clothes actually complimented Dai's. I was sure that, if he got the chance later, he'd make some weird romantic statement about destiny and the universe contriving to show how they were meant to be.

Looking more confused than ever, Asquith complied. The rest of us took our seats as well.

"What is this about?"

"It's about Laura, Mr. Asquith, and the true nature of her death."

His expression became guarded, his full attention on Dai. "I don't understand."

"I'm sorry to have to tell you this, but Laura didn't die of natural causes. She was poisoned."

The room grew unnaturally still. He glared at all of us and slowly rose to his feet. "That's *tosh*! I don't know why you're doing this, but this farce is in poor taste. Maybe all the rumors about you *Americans* are true."

He made as if to leave, but Pierce got in the way.

"William, I'm very sorry, but this isn't a joke. Listen to what Miss Wu has to say. Then you'll understand. Please."

Aiden stood. "It's important. Please hear us out."

As if against his better judgment, Asquith sat down again. "Say what you have to say and get it over with."

Step by step, in a soft voice, Dai recounted everything from the beginning. He didn't interrupt, but his expression grew more and more troubled. By the time she finished, he was shaking. But whether from grief or anger, it was hard to tell.

"We're hoping you can give us more information. Information we can use to figure out the guilty party."

"*Guilty party*?" Fury flashed from his eyes. "Call them what they are. A filthy, depraved *murderer*!" He jumped to his feet, fists at his side, his face growing redder by the moment. "Laura never did any harm to anyone! She was a pure soul. *Destroying her took light from the world!*"

Dai gave a slight nod in acknowledgment. "That is why we mustn't let him or her get away with it. It's why we've done what we've done. The reason we need your help."

"It doesn't make sense. This just doesn't make any bloody sense at all!" William started pacing like a caged animal. "Laura was an orphan. Kept to herself. She helped others when she could, even if they never realized it. I'm not rich. I own no property. I'm not even all that important! There was no reason to *kill* her."

"Yet she was still murdered all the same."

Asquith turned to scowl at Dai. She faced him squarely, hands on her lap, her expression serene. She was a point of calm in the seething maelstrom of his clashing emotions.

"Did anyone try to dissuade you from marrying Laura?"

He brought his fists up as if fighting with himself to find the information. "No. Yes? I didn't pay all that much attention. She and I were meant to be. I didn't care what others thought about it. Why would I?"

He suddenly stood stock still, eyes growing wide. "Domberry, the spineless, ugly snake. Looking down his nose at everyone and everything." His eyes flared, his expression turning murderous.

"Will, we don't know for sure it's him," Pierce said. "That's why we need your help."

But Asquith was no longer listening. "The bloody bastard. He did this. He must have done. I'll get the truth from him, even if I have to beat it out of him." The look in his eyes stated that he would prefer it that way. He started for the door.

Pierce cut him off for the second time. "Will, listen to me. We have to do this right."

"Truman, get out of my way. I know what needs to be done."

Not trusting the popinjay to hold Asquith back on his own, I moved to stand beside him. "You need to listen to us. If you tip our hand, you might let the murderer go free."

Unthinkingly, I reached out for him. He jerked away, then let his fist fly at my face. I couldn't get out of the way in time, so pain flared along my jawline as he made contact, making me stagger backward.

Pierce rushed him, grabbing hold. I ignored the throbbing ache in my face and jumped in to help.

"*Let go of me!* The bastard needs to pay!" Asquith thrashed like a man possessed. I feared the two of us wouldn't be able to hold him.

Aiden suddenly loomed behind him. She plunged a needle into his shoulder, squeezed the plunger, then moved back. He continued to fight, cursing at us, but slowly his movements became less violent, and his words slurred. Not long after that, he stopped struggling altogether and slumped in our arms, out cold.

"What's happened? Is everyone all right?" Dai's tone was sharper than usual. She'd never been witness to a struggle, so even with her superior hearing, the sounds wouldn't have made much sense to her.

"Mostly. Aiden came to our aide and sedated Asquith." I took a moment to catch my breath. "He was proving a bit of a handful." Pierce and I dragged him over to the two chairs Aiden had pushed together, then sat down ourselves. I rather liked this winded version of Truman, since it rendered him speechless.

"Who was hit?"

Or perhaps I was wrong and she did understand the sounds more than I thought. "That would be me. But I'm fine." I'd have to think up some kind of story. Dai might be blind, but her parents weren't and I was sure I would show a bruise before long.

"My thanks, Dr. Campbell," Pierce gasped. "He was becoming a rather big problem."

Aiden nodded, not looking directly at him. "I figured it'd be best to come prepared."

Surely she wasn't *also* falling under the popinjay's spell? It might be too much to bear. Though I wasn't entirely sure why I thought that. My rationality always seemed to take a left turn around him.

"And my thanks to all of you for stopping him from leaving," Dai said, sounding more like her usual self. "I'd hoped he would prove more level-headed, but I suppose we can't blame him. This, however, has given me an idea of how we might move forward." She flashed us a devilish grin. "Now, we just need to set the stage for the next act of our melodrama."

Her words brought me no comfort whatsoever.

CHAPTER 39

"What are you up to, Dai?"

She shrugged. "Something along the lines of the original plan. But this will work better. With William incapacitated, we now have a most excellent excuse to gather everyone. One they won't be able to ignore." The devilish smile was back. "Assuming we can overcome a few obstacles first."

"China Doll, what exactly are you planning?" Pierce swept his hair into place and straightened his suit and tie. He at least had the decency to sound concerned. I knew I was.

Rather than answer his question, she threw another at him. "Truman, how would you feel about using your charms on a bully?"

"What do you mean?"

"I need you to woo Dr. Henry Stewart, the hospital's chief of staff. We require the use of a private patient room for a few hours. Do you think you could manage that?"

Pierce's brow rose, and then he grinned. "So, you only want me for my money, charm, and good looks?"

"At this moment, yes."

He shrugged. "I can live with that."

Dai shook her head and laughed. I was nowhere near as

amused. But since I didn't have those things, I had no choice but to leave this to him.

"So, where do I find Dr. Bully?"

"He may have left for the day, but if not, I know who can give you his contact information. You shouldn't underestimate him." Aiden gave him directions even as she checked Asquith's vitals. She didn't appear amused by the popinjay's little joke. I didn't blame her.

I wasn't sure what Pierce did, but within ten minutes, he returned with an orderly and wheelchair in tow. Thankfully, he had left Stewart elsewhere. I doubt the doctor would have been convivial if he realized Aiden and I were involved.

Soon after, we had Asquith in a bed in "his" private room on the second floor of the hospital. Against the stark white sheets, he looked pale and somewhat diminished. Laura's death had had a significant impact on him. Learning it was murder, and going into a rage, hadn't helped matters. I wondered when he'd last eaten a full meal.

"How long will he remain unconscious?" Dai and I stood near the room's wide window, staying out of the way.

"An hour or two, most likely," Aiden said. "He might slip into a regular sleep rather than waking. He's had a strenuous evening." She frowned. "If he needs to stay unconscious, we'll require one of the doctors to get involved. I've had little experience with these substances and prolonged dosages. I'm not sure it would be a wise course to drug him further in any case."

"Hm, moral and logistical issues are in play." Dai bit her lower lip. "Waiting until morning would increase the tension in those we suspect, but it would not be fair to drug Asquith any more than necessary. If I go home and try to get away tomorrow morning, I may encounter stumbling blocks. Better to get in trouble for staying out too late tonight than to risk finding our way blocked tomorrow.

"If we're able to convince Shannon to come, fine, but it's not essential. She's most likely working. The rest of them are crucial, however. Truman, how would you feel about doing a bit of playacting? If it were overnight, a phone call in the morning would do, as they could easily discover he had been missing all evening. But since we must do it tonight, they'll require a catalyst. Something to ratchet up the tension to a level where they won't question what's happening and might even make a mistake. For that, you must rouse them from their rooms in person. Tell them Asquith's collapsed and had to be taken to the hospital, then you can bring them here."

The room's harsh lighting glinted off her teashade glasses. "Aiden, would you call the constable and see if he wants to join us? We'll need him as a witness. Jacques will try to contact Shannon, then smuggle Prince inside as added muscle."

Aiden and Pierce looked confused at that last bit. They both sent me questioning looks, but I said nothing. If things turned bad, they would learn soon enough.

"Friends, one way or another, this will be over with tonight."

CHAPTER 40

Our general stayed in the room watching over Asquith as the rest of us left to carry out our assigned tasks.

"Jackie, hold up a moment!"

"The name is *Jacques*." I tried to push down my irritation, but it was a struggle.

"Sure, sure, whatever. Just stop for a minute."

It was hard, very hard. I wasn't sure why I even bothered. He *had* to be doing it on purpose.

"What do you want? The longer all this takes, the more trouble we're likely to be in at home."

"Yeah, I understand that," Pierce waved my concerns away as if they weren't relevant. "Someday soon I'll have a whole slew of questions for you, but for now, I'll be patient."

As if I'd ever give him any information about Dai. "Get to the point."

"This ratchet up the tension bit. I want to make sure I do what she needs me to do. How do I sell it?"

That surprised me. As a popinjay, I'd assumed he was an expert. "Just show up like you did this morning—disheveled, unkempt. Pretend you're Linda, you broke a nail, and the beauty parlor's closed."

"Oh, that's a good one!" He flashed his perfect set of teeth. "Thanks for the assist." Pierce hurried off down the hall.

The man made no sense whatsoever.

Before I maneuvered my way outside, I took over a payphone in the hospital lobby. My first call was to the house rather than Shannon. After several rings, Dai's father answered. "Hello. May I ask who's calling, please?"

"Sir, it's Jacques." The other end went silent. "Everything is all right. I just wanted to phone to let you know we'll be running late. One of the cars broke down, and Dai offered to take the couple home. I wished to inform you so you wouldn't worry."

"Oh, yes. Thank you, Jacques." Tye sounded relieved. "That should be fine. I'll tell Lien." He hesitated a moment. "Is there anything else to report? Anything I should be concerned about?"

I felt terrible for him. "No, sir, nothing at all. All is well. We'll be home as soon as we can."

"Good. Good. I know you will look out for her."

"You may count on me, sir." I put as much confidence into my voice as I could. "There's nothing to worry about." As I hung up the receiver to fish more change from my pocket, I really hoped it was true.

I called the Jefferson Hotel and they sent someone to Shannon's apartment, but no one answered the door, which didn't surprise me. So I asked the operator to connect me to the Adolphus, and from there, the Bank Underground. Even though I said it was a dire emergency, they would only take a message rather than bringing Shannon to the phone. I left enough information for her to find us, and a promise to reimburse her for cab fare.

Now for the last item on my list: sneaking in a rascal where he wasn't meant to go.

This would not be the first time Prince had slipped into prohibited environs. Dai had long ago worked out the best way to get him into places he wasn't welcomed. She refused to look upon him as a mere dog. At times she relied more on his keen senses and uncomplicated understanding than she did mine.

He barked a greeting from inside the car when he noticed me approaching. I put a finger to my lips to signal him to be silent. He sat in the seat, his tail wagging madly as I moved on to the Ford's trunk rather than the driver's door. I was sure he sensed something was up.

Strapped beneath the trunk cover was an average looking dark brown travel case, one I'd modified at Dai's instruction several years prior. I'd carefully drilled air holes at the bottom of the case, and added small rubber stubs to the corners so that even if the suitcase were placed on the floor, the air holes would not be blocked.

Prince moved back as I opened the rear passenger door and set the suitcase on it, unlatching the lid. A quick glance at my surroundings verified no one was paying us any particular attention, so I let the lid fall to the seat, exposing the interior. I rearranged the small loose weave brown blanket inside to lie on the bottom. It made the inside more comfortable, allowed the air through from the breathing holes, and muffled any sound of hard nails against wood and leather if Prince moved around. As soon as I finished, he stepped in and curled up on it. Giving him a brief scratch behind his ears, I closed the case.

Making sure once again that no one was watching what we were up to, I re-latched the suitcase and gingerly removed it from the car. It weighed more than it had the last time we'd pulled this trick—someone needed to cut back on treats.

We returned to Asquith's room without incident, and I found Dai sitting in a chair tucked at the far corner, her hands folded neatly on her lap. Her head was angled toward the bed as if she could see William lying there.

"Welcome back, Jacques. Any problems?"

I closed the door behind me and set the suitcase down. "None. I left a message for Shannon with the Bank Underground. I also informed your father we'd be running late. Your second bodyguard has likewise arrived."

Unlatching the case, I let the lid fall so Prince could get out. He padded over to Dai and rubbed her leg so she'd realize he was there. She scratched him behind the ear. "Under the bed will be the best place for you. The room might soon get a little crowded."

He gave her palm a lick and then slipped beneath the hospital bed. He wouldn't be seen, but would still be at hand if needed. I tucked the suitcase into a corner.

"Are you sure this is how we want to do this? There are a lot of ways this could go wrong." With nothing to do but wait, the thought of the coming ordeal made my stomach roil.

"Our options are limited. Plus, this seems to work for Agatha Christie, so why not for us?"

I sighed. Never in a million years would I have imagined reading those books to her would lead us to this predicament. "As you well know, those novels are fiction. This is real life, with real consequences."

"Yes—consequences Laura's murderer must be made to face."

I sighed again, closely acquainted with that stubborn tone.

"If we don't do this, Jacques, who will?"

That was the crux of the matter. Without our intervention, no one would have known there'd been a murder committed in the first place. Even now, we didn't have sufficient evidence to point out the guilty party. She was right, but I didn't have to like it.

CHAPTER 41

Aiden returned in short order. She checked Asquith's vitals, then set herself in the corner to watch over him. "I was able to get hold of George. He should join us soon. As yet, there's been no response to his telegram. He left instructions for one of the deputies to send a messenger if it came in."

"I suppose it was a bit much to hope we'd have a quick answer, with it being the weekend," Dai said. "But we'll make do."

The Adolphus stood but a couple of miles from the hospital. It wouldn't take the popinjay long to get there, rile up those we needed, and herd them back here. Even so, the minutes seemed to stretch forever.

"They're here." Dai sat up in her chair, her head turning in the hallway's direction.

I stiffened beside her, not sure what would transpire. Her safety, however, would remain my principal concern, whether or not we caught a murderer.

"He's in here!" The door yanked open, and a frazzled-looking Pierce hurried inside. He shot me a wink as he moved further into the room so those behind him might enter.

His performance must have been quite convincing. The

grave looks on the faces of Mrs. Grey, Lizzie, and Domberry showed as much. Their expressions quickly turned to surprise at seeing Dr. Campbell, Dai, and myself there.

"Why are *you* here?" The nanny appeared more surprised than upset.

The popinjay answered for us. I had no idea what tale he'd woven for them to get them here, so I let him take the lead.

"We were all together when William collapsed. Did I not mention that?" The ham was still milking his previous performance of an overly-distraught friend.

Domberry sent him a disgusted look. "No. As a matter of fact, you've told us very little about what happened."

Lizzie moved to the foot of the bed. "He looks so pale." Her complexion was pallid as well. "Is he going to be all right? What's wrong with him?"

Mrs. Grey put her arm around her. "Calm yourself, my dear. Give them a chance to speak."

Though she sounded in control of herself and was a soothing influence on the distraught Lizzie, the nanny appeared years older than when we'd last seen her.

"It was the box." Dai's words snapped everyone to attention, and they turned to look at her as if they were puppets on a string.

"Box?" Domberry stared in confusion at the others. "What box?"

Dai continued as if he'd never interrupted. "The one with the old-fashioned ball gown. Well, the one that *had* contained the ball gown." She slowly shook her head. "William was looking for the dress to take back with him. Something to remind him of Laura. But it had gone missing."

"What drivel are you on about?" Domberry demanded. "You're not making any sense."

"Paul, she's talking about Mother's dress," Lizzie said. "The one William asked us to bring when he first told us about the engagement."

"That antiquated thing?" He snorted. "I'm sure the American gold-digger sold it the instant her 'friend' died.

Though I doubt she got much for that ugly dress. Ouch!"

Domberry rubbed at the back of his head where a well-aimed pack of Malboros had struck him.

"British asshole! How *dare* you? I never did any such thing!"

Framed in the room's entrance was Shannon. Her cheeks were flushed and she seemed out of breath. It looked like she'd gotten my message and hoofed it over immediately. She hadn't even taken the time to change—she was still wearing the short frilled skirt and round cap, the uniform for the Adolphus' cigarette girls.

"Violent commoner!"

Aiden suddenly loomed behind him. "This is a hospital. You will keep your voice *down*." She sent a glare in Shannon's direction. "Both of you."

Domberry looked like he might argue until he caught a glimpse of her wintry expression. Lizzie grabbed his sleeve and pulled him closer. Shannon ignored him and stepped into the room, allowing Aiden to close the door. The last thing we needed was someone complaining about the noise before our business was finished.

"What do you mean the dress has gone missing?" Lizzie asked. "It wasn't in Laura's apartment?"

Shannon was the one who answered. "No. I looked for it when I packed up her things, but I couldn't find it. I don't know what happened to it. But *she* took the box it came in." She stabbed a finger in Dai's direction.

I raised a brow, noticing how Shannon had conveniently used the word 'took' instead of 'bought.'

Dai picked up where she left off, making no mention of the edited facts. "William asked if he might have it. So we arranged to meet him this evening to say goodbye and give him the box.

"It seemed a harmless enough request at the time..." As her voice trailed off, you could feel the pressure build in the room.

"Harmless enough at the time?" Lizzie's eyes had gone round.

Dai's expression grew sad. "Jacques, tell them what you

saw."

I fidgeted inside, hoping I could do my part as well as the others had. "Asquith had some trouble opening the box, so it was jostled about a bit before he managed to get the lid to come off. But when he did, a… a cloud of powder wafted into his face. A few seconds later, he collapsed. When he wouldn't wake up, we brought him to the hospital."

"Powder? You mean like talcum powder?" Domberry sneered. "Since when does that make people collapse?"

"When it's not talcum powder, but something else entirely." Dai's words plunged the room into silence.

"Oh, my word." Mrs. Grey turned even paler than before.

Now it was Lizzie's turn to hold the older woman upright. "Nanny, are you all right?"

"She's just realized what the rest of us have." Dai's voice was low, but each word seemed to punch the air. "William's been poisoned, and if we don't figure out what it is so we can counter it, he will die."

CHAPTER 42

"What utter rubbish is this?" Domberry glowered at each of us. "Is this some tasteless American joke? Why in the world would anyone want to poison William? He's not anybody of import. Why would they bother?"

"Paul!" Lizzie stared at her husband as if he'd turned into an ogre. "How can you say that?"

"You stupid *snob*. You're not listening to what they're saying." Though her words were sharp as daggers, Shannon's expression was horrified. "They're saying that the one who was really poisoned was Laura! William is just—just an *accident*."

"Laura was poisoned? That can't be right. Can it?" Lizzie looked stricken.

Mrs. Grey appeared to gather her composure and disentangled herself from Lizzie's arms. "Can they save him? Surely there must be something that can be done."

Dai shook her head. "They don't know what the poison is. If they attempt to give him any medication without knowing what it is, it might make matters worse."

It was a little chilling how good she was at steering all this.

"What utter poppycock! There's no way William's been poisoned. If there's no reason to kill him, going through the trouble of murdering Laura is even *more* preposterous." Domberry distractedly searched his pockets. He must have left his whiskey flask at the hotel.

"Even if she wasn't *good enough* for him?" Dai had finally thrown the biggest word grenade.

"All of you need to stop!" Lizzie made a cutting motion as if that might somehow hold back the discussion. "He's not poisoned. He's… he's got a cold. Will hasn't been eating as he should and just pushed himself too far. He simply needs some rest, that's all."

"Like Laura did?" Dai interjected. "Rest and sleep didn't do much for her, did they? She's dead."

Asquith moaned. Everyone but Dai turned to look at him, but all for different reasons. His waking up now might very well make solving the mystery far more difficult.

"William?" Mrs. Grey was holding onto the railing at the foot of the bed in a white-knuckled grip.

"Oh, if we only knew what the poison was so we might help him." Dai hung her head as if witnessing a tragedy that could not be unmade. "If only…"

"Tests, aren't there tests for this sort of thing?" The nanny could barely get the words out. Her eyes pooled with unshed tears.

Aiden answered her. "Once the person has passed, yes. But trying to determine what it is from the symptoms—it would depend on the poison, the concentration, and other factors. We don't possess enough information to know what to rule out, let alone treat it. Assuming it isn't too late already."

She delivered all this with just the right touch of helplessness and regret. Dr. Campbell had more talents than I expected; I was quite impressed.

"Mother and Father will be devastated," Lizzie sobbed. "How can this be *happening*?"

"A-ar-arsenic. You should treat him for arsenic poisoning," Mrs. Grey declared. "The dress was green. I-I heard years ago that green dye was made with it, and it sometimes poisoned people."

"That can't be it," Domberry announced, as if he were an expert. "They said William breathed in a cloud of *powder*, not green dye." His tone proclaimed what he thought of the opinion and intelligence of the help.

"You shouldn't dismiss what Nanny says like that, Paul. She knows a lot!" Lizzie dabbed at her eyes, rallying to support the older woman.

"Come on, Lizzie. Powder, dye? *Not the same.*"

It seemed that, without his liquid support, Domberry became more boorish than usual.

"He isn't wrong. Though there is such a thing as powdered arsenic," Dai interjected.

Shannon's face scrunched up as if she'd tasted something bitter. "So, you think someone added even more arsenic to the green dress? To make sure Laura would die?"

"*None of that matters!*" Mrs. Grey's shriek brought everyone up short. "You need to help William! You must treat him for arsenic poisoning, *right now!*"

Dai may have already known, but until that moment, I'd not been positive. But now, the manic look on the woman's face, the desperation in her words—we'd found our murderer.

"Why did you do it?" I couldn't help asking. "Why did you kill Laura Cooper, Mrs. Grey?"

"Why? *Why*? How could I *not*?" Her cheeks were flushed, eyes flashing. "She was going to destroy him! Take away all his family had accomplished. He would not listen to reason, would not dissolve the engagement. What other choice did I have?"

"Nanny?"

William was awake and by the shattered and befuddled look on his face, it seemed he'd heard the last bits of the conversation.

"My sweet boy, how are you feeling?" Gone was the expression of mingled loathing and hatred we'd just glimpsed, replaced by one of concern and love. But it was too late.

"You're the person who killed Laura?" He half sat up, his face a mixture of disbelief and horror.

She tried reaching for him, but he jerked back so she

couldn't touch him. Lizzie swooned on her feet as if about to faint. Amazingly, Paul noticed and pulled her back to support her.

"She was an innocent," Asquith protested. "She welcomed you with open arms. How could you do this to her? Do this to *me*?"

"My dearest baby boy, I did it *for* you!" Mrs. Grey once more tried to reach for him and was again rejected. "She would have ruined you, ruined your family name. I had to protect you. Protect the family."

He shook his head in utter denial. "You're insane. She would have done no such thing!"

"But she would, whether she meant to or not." The nanny didn't reach for him a third time, though she seemed desperate to do so. "It was bad enough she was American, but she was also an orphan—less than a commoner. The scandal alone…"

William's face filled with disgust. "Scandal? What scandal? I'm the fifth son. And this is America, the land of the free. It's 1930, for Pete's sake! We need to push such antiquated thinking away; we ought to move forward!"

"Your naïveté is such an endearing quality. It's why I love you best out of all the children, but it's also the reason I had to do what I did." Mrs. Grey wrung her hands, her whole posture begging him to understand. "It's only been two generations since your family was raised to the peerage. Many would like nothing more than to strike the family back down to being commoners rather than acknowledge your right to be among them. We've all worked hard, *too* hard, to throw it all away for some no-name *American*."

William's face contorted in deep pain and ever increasing befuddlement. "I've known you my whole life, Nanny. Where… where is all this coming from? You never cared about such things before. Why would you destroy my happiness over something so *meaningless*?"

Mrs. Grey moved a step back as if he'd slapped her. "You—you can't mean that! It isn't meaningless. Do you not realize the doors your elevated status opens for you? How high you might reach if you applied yourself and took advantage of them?"

William's expression crumbled. "What difference would any of it make to me now? When you've robbed me of the one person who brought me the greatest happiness? Who do you think I would have worked so hard *for*?"

"You can still be happy," she admonished. "With a proper English girl. One who will bring you added advantage, who knows how to comport herself in society. Someone who would enhance your reputation rather than be an embarrassment to your family."

Each word seemed to add a layer of support to her frame, helping her stand taller and more confident.

Asquith stared, stunned.

"Having a murderer in the household sounds like a much bigger source of embarrassment than a young, loving, American wife," Dai said.

Mrs. Grey spun around to glare at her. "*You*. You are the one responsible for taking William away from me."

"I'm sorry, but you did that all on your own. You did it the moment you conceived your nasty plan. You calculated how to kill Laura before you ever met her, before you even left England."

CHAPTER 43

"No! Surely not." Lizzie's stricken face begged for this latest revelation to be untrue. "Nanny couldn't have. Not that far back."

"Most definitely," Dai told her. "Adding the extra arsenic in case the dye was insufficient. Purchasing it in England, then using it here, where it was unlikely it could be tracked back to her. Getting rid of the dress in such a way that any additional evidence would be washed away even if the gown was found. Having the body cremated.

"That was your idea, wasn't it, Mrs. Grey? Every single step thought out and calculated. Nothing left to chance except chance itself. Feeding her more arsenic as she lay dying, just to be sure."

Gasps rang out all around. The cold-bloodedness of the deed left me shaken.

"But the box. You forgot about the box. That was sloppy."

The woman bristled, but she had control of herself now. She didn't rise to Dai's bait. "I've listened to more than enough of this rubbish. I'll be taking my leave now."

"You will not!" William yanked the covers off himself, swaying, and swung his feet out from the bed. "You're a cold-blooded murderer. You don't get to go free, not after what you've done. No matter what you may have once meant to me."

"I'm afraid I have to agree with him." Pierce moved to block her way to the door. "We might be mere Americans, but even we don't allow killers to run amok."

A heavy leather handbag swung around from behind her and smacked him in the side of the face, knocking Pierce down. She swung it again, forcing me to step backward or become the next casualty.

Before Pierce could recover or I could rush back in, she unlatched the purse and withdrew a pair of scissors. She sliced at me with them. Her eyes were hard, a determined look on her face, like a general making a last stand. She forced me to take another step back, then dropped her purse. She grabbed Dai, yanking her from the chair.

Terror cut through me as I realized she meant to use her as a hostage, possibly even to kill her for having exposed her plot. My heart pounded in my chest, my worst nightmare realizing itself before me.

"Razor, to me!" Dai's command rang with imperious authority.

Launching from his hiding place beneath the bed, Prince switched to attack mode. He chomped down hard on Mrs. Grey's ankle, then yanked. Her pained scream filled the room as she lost her balance and fell, taking Dai with her. Lizzie, Shannon, and Paul all yelled or screamed in various levels of panic and distress.

I rushed forward and snatched the scissors from Mrs. Grey's hand before she could try to use them on Dai or Prince. Pierce grabbed her discarded purse and slid it beneath the bed, one hand clamped against the side of his bashed face. Dai scooted away from her, Prince staying between them and growling at the fallen woman.

"Good boy, Prince. Good boy," Dai whispered to her guardian. She looked disheveled but unhurt. I slipped the scissors into my pocket, out of everyone's reach. Then I helped

Dai back to her vacated chair.

"Are you all right?"

"I'm startled more than anything." Her cheeks were flushed. "Truman may have gotten the worst of it."

The door to the room opened, surprising all of us. Sheepishly, the constable we'd met at the courthouse peeked into the chaos. "I guess this is the spot where I should let y'all know I'm here, isn't it?"

"George, you made it!" Aiden was struggling to move past William, Lizzie, and Paul to examine Mrs. Grey, whose ankle was bleeding. The older woman stayed on the floor, her face a grimace of pain. Truman had a hand clamped on her arm, not about to give her a chance to get away or try to hit him again.

The constable's cheeks reddened slightly. "Been here a while, actually. Didn't want to disturb the goings-on. Was getting quite an interesting earful, to tell the truth. I paid special attention to the confession. Got all the other fascinating bits in here, too." He tapped the notebook that rested in his vest pocket. "I still have a load of questions that'll need answering, but for now, I think I'm good."

He pulled out a pair of heavy handcuffs. "Ma'am, I am placing you under arrest for the murder of Laura Cooper."

"Wha-what are you talking about? I did no such thing! If anything, you ought to arrest this woman. Her dog attacked me! In a *hospital*!"

George Higgins shook his head. "Ma'am, a dog bite is the least of your problems. Like I mentioned before, I heard everything." He threw a glance in Dai's direction, then gave me a quick smile. "I even have an entire room of witnesses."

"What the hell is going on here? Who *are* you people?"

I recognized the offended voice from our previous encounter: It was the bully, the hospital's chief of staff. His washed-out gray eyes were bugging out of his head, struggling to make sense of what lay before him. A cigarette girl, an old woman on the floor with a bloody ankle, a young lady sitting primly in the corner, and more people than the room had ever been meant to hold. Luckily, Prince had heard him coming and dashed under the bed, where he wouldn't be seen.

His gaze sharpened, his long face showing displeasure as he spotted Aiden. "*Campbell*, what is the meaning of this?"

Still wrapping a bandage around Mrs. Grey's ankle, Aiden said nothing, but her shoulders hunched as if waiting for a blow. I hadn't liked the fellow before, and seeing her reaction, I liked him even less now.

I was about to try to intercede somehow, but luckily for Dr. Stewart, Constable Higgins beat me to it.

"Sir, thank you for your cooperation in this serious police matter. Without your aid, we wouldn't have been able to bring a murderer to justice." The constable finished placing the handcuffs on Mrs. Grey, then got up. "You should be commended, sir. I will mention your contribution to the justice."

"What? Um, why, yes—yes, of course." Stewart stood taller and ran his fingers through his thick head of hair as if primping for an unexpected photograph. "We're always happy to lend a hand. If you could just hold the noise down? It's disturbing some of our prominent patients."

"We're about done here, sir. Sorry for the trouble."

"Yes, quite. Carry on then." With a curt nod, Stewart strutted away.

"Nicely handled, Constable." Dai sounded impressed.

"Aw, it weren't nothing." He blushed. "Little trick I learned about just recently." He gave her a slight nod in acknowledgment.

Dai smiled as if she'd seen it.

Higgins helped Mrs. Grey to her feet. The woman stared forlornly at the floor, all the fight she'd had in her gone.

"She probably shouldn't walk on that foot," Aiden said. "Let me get a wheelchair and a blanket." Her cheeks reddened. "Best not to parade what she is through the hospital by letting people see the handcuffs, or we'll hear from Stewart again."

"Good idea," the constable said. "Much obliged."

"You might also want to keep her from her purse. I swear she has a brick in the thing. There were scissors—who knows what else she's got hidden in there." Pierce straightened his clothing, a purple bruise already forming on the right side of his face.

"I will need to talk to each of you," Higgins said. "If you have any travel plans, you'd best to put them on hold."

Paul puffed up. "What? We're leaving for New York on Monday to catch a ship back to England. We had nothing to do with any of this."

"You can do what you like," Higgins said. "But don't blame me when you find Scotland Yard waiting for you when you get off the boat. There'd also be an arrest warrant waiting for y'all if you come back to the States. Either way, I think staying will cause y'all the least amount of hassle." The twinkle in the constable's eye promised more aggravation than Paul would ever want to deal with.

"Oh, I see." Paul deflated. "I guess we've no choice then."

While we waited for Aiden to return, Higgins quickly collected everyone's contact information. Truman took pity on William and offered his details when the constable moved to ask. Asquith sat back on the bed, his face hidden by his hands. In a way, he'd just lost a second loved one. I did not envy him his pain and crushing disappointment.

When Aiden returned, Higgins helped the subdued Mrs. Grey to the wheelchair, then covered her cuffed hands and her legs with a blanket. The room was silent as he wheeled her away, with Dr. Campbell following in case of any difficulties.

"What… what will happen to her now?" Lizzie's voice trembled as she asked the question.

"She'll be taken to the Dallas County Criminal Courts building and placed in one of the jail cells in the top five floors," Dai told her in a quiet tone. "She'll be charged and held there until her trial. I believe you can request to visit her there, if you wish."

Shannon propped herself against the wall and lit a cigarette, a sour look on her face. "If she's found guilty, they'll ship her off to Huntsville and make her dance in the electric chair." She took a long puff. "It's what the bitch deserves. Laura wasn't all that, but she was my friend. She shouldn't have died that way. Especially for such a stupid reason."

As if suddenly finding the cigarette distasteful, she dropped it to the floor and ground it out with the toe of her bright red shoe. She walked out without a backward glance. It seemed she'd had her fill of aristocracy.

"For once, I agree with the gold-digger," Paul said. "I never liked the woman. She never knew her place." As haughty as the words were, their tone didn't have much bite—but that didn't stop Lizzie from turning on him as if he'd burned her.

"Shut your filthy mouth!" She pushed Domberry from her as if he were a leper. "That woman *raised* us! She was like a second mother to us. Nanny was our teacher, our friend. What she did was despicable, but I won't bloody let you slander her anymore. You're not worth *half* of what she is, low birth or not!" Lizzie ran crying from the room.

Flabbergasted, Paul could only stare after her.

"Mr. Domberry, if you care at all for your wife or your marriage, you might want to chase after her and apologize." I wasn't sure what motivated me, but the family had suffered so much from Mrs. Grey's foul act, I hated for it to cause even more damage. "She needs you. And whether or not you like it, you need her as well."

He shot me a venomous look for my trouble, but headed off after her anyway.

CHAPTER 44

The popinjay jabbed me with an elbow, his voice close to my ear. "I would have never taken you for a romantic, Jackie old boy." Pierce grinned from ear to ear.

I rolled my eyes, not willing to give him the satisfaction of a comment.

In a slightly louder, though still soft, tone, he added, "Leave William to me. I'll get him back to the hotel and keep an eye on him. The two of you should head on home."

"Thank you, Truman," Dai said. "You're a good friend."

I frowned, hoping she meant this with regard to Asquith rather than herself. With any luck, this would be the last we'd see of him. Life might even return to normal shortly.

Pierce shrugged, "Perhaps. Still, it's been a pleasure, China Doll." He took her hand and bent over it. Prince's warning growl came from under the bed, overriding my own. He released her hand, chuckling softly to himself. "May we meet again soon."

Not if I had anything to say about it. The cad.

While he spoke to William, I retrieved our suitcase and set it down so Prince could climb aboard. I slipped in a well-deserved treat for doing double duty. "Well done." I added a scratch behind the ear before closing the case.

Dai was already standing, waiting for us.

"Mr. Asquith, I'm truly sorry for all you've been through, and the part we played in it." She turned in his direction as I took her arm. "It is not much of a consolation, but at least you know the truth of what happened. It will not bring Laura back to you, but now her killer won't go free."

A heavy sigh filled the room. "I think you miss the point, Miss Wu," William said, his voice full of pain. "If I hadn't been so set on marrying her, she never would have been a target in the first place."

"Sir, that's like saying I'm responsible for my blindness because I was stubborn enough to be born." Dai's disdain for his comment laced her words. "You were happy, and from all I've been told, she was happy. It was another's selfish actions that robbed you of your future, not yours. Giving up and taking the blame is the easy path, the *coward's* path. You would honor her more by living. Try to get past this and to enjoy the rest of your life—for the both of you."

Truman had better do as he said and monitor the man, I thought. If he decided to check out of this world and it could have been prevented, there would be hell to pay. The hard grip of Dai's hand where she hung to my elbow told me so.

I sent the popinjay a meaningful glance. I was glad to see him nod back.

We departed, the sounds of sobbing echoing behind us.

Aiden found us waiting for the elevator. Of Lizzie and Paul, we'd seen no sign.

"George and Mrs. Grey have left." She looked exhausted. The whole evening had been emotionally draining for everyone. "He said the sooner we could meet with him to go over everything, the better. He wants all the details before doing formal interviews with everyone else."

"Sunday morning might be problematic," I said. "But we should be able to sneak away for an hour or two in the afternoon, especially if he'd be willing to join us at the laundry." As a business, White Laundry would be closed because of the Blue Law, but it didn't stop us from using it as a meeting place. It also wouldn't attract any attention for us to go there—Dai preferred to blend most of the company's cleaning solutions on Sundays, the better not to offend the workers, and also for the peace and quiet. And since the vats were not running, the temperature was kept down a bit.

Aiden nodded. "I believe he and his family attend early Sunday service, so the afternoon should work." She handed us a note with two telephone numbers.

"Thank you again for all your help with this." Dai gave her a smile. "We couldn't have achieved it without you."

"If not for you, we would never have known a murder was committed, and the perpetrator would have gotten away with it." Her ice-blue eyes shone.

"Will you have problems with Stewart because of us?" The last thing I wanted was to cause her any trouble, after all she'd done on our behalf.

She didn't quite meet my gaze as she responded. "It'll be fine."

I didn't like it. "If he does, you call me, and I'll pay him a visit. I know how to deal with his kind."

Aiden looked up in surprise at the vehemence in my voice. I tried to ignore the dimpled grin growing on Dai's face.

Luckily, I was saved from further opportunities to embarrass myself by the elevator, which signaled its arrival with a loud ding.

Aiden stayed behind as we climbed aboard, her gaze on the floor and her cheeks lightly colored. From the burning sensation in my neck and ears, I was sure I looked much the same.

"No comment from the gallery, if you please."

Dai said nothing as requested, but I could feel her smugness anyway.

Soon we were piled in the Ford and headed toward home. We had one more hurdle to overcome before the evening was over.

Dealing with murder seemed the easier chore.

They'd left the back light on for us. Prince rushed off to do his nightly business as I helped Dai out of the car. Upon opening the door, the soft sounds of classical music made their way to us from the living room. Glancing at the kitchen clock, I saw it was just past eleven, which sent a slight shock through me; the evening's ordeal had felt much longer. We might survive this after all.

Without hesitation, Dai made her way through the kitchen toward the front of the house. I followed not far behind, after removing and hanging my hat and coat.

"We're home."

Glancing into the living room from the shadows of the foyer, I spied Mr. and Mrs. Wu sitting at their usual places, yet there was a sense of tension hovering in the air. Their disagreement about Dai's marriage prospects looked to still be a point of contention between them. With the case almost over, it was my hope this disruption of the household's energies would soon disappear.

"Welcome back," Lien said, closing the book she'd been reading. The dragon swished just below the surface. "Did you have a good time?"

The light glinted off Tye's glasses as he sent a furtive glance their way, as if fearing what he might see.

"It was interesting but rather tiring," Dai told them. "If you don't mind, I'd like to turn in for the night."

Tye's expression brightened, even as the dragon's dimmed. What had they been expecting to happen? Dai had only known Pierce for a handful of days. Especially after the rude treatment at Pierce's home, it puzzled me why Lien would wish her daughter to associate with them.

"Do you want me to help you undress?"

"No, thank you, *Mǔqīn*, I can manage. Good night."

"Good night, Daiyu."

As she turned away, I slunk back toward the kitchen. While I wouldn't be able to escape if either parent requested a detailed accounting of the evening, I didn't intend to tempt them by remaining within view. The bruise I had received from

Asquith was most likely in full bloom, so it would be best to avoid them as much as possible.

I watched Dai go upstairs, each step bringing my own exhaustion more and more to my awareness. Prince trailed behind her. I happily sought my bed after filching a few ice cubes for my jaw, glad this was almost over. I couldn't stop thinking of the jolt of horror that had run through me when Mrs. Grey grabbed Dai. I never wanted to feel anything like it ever again.

CHAPTER 45

"Do you plan to sleep the day away, Jacques?"

I sat bolt upright, startled. Dai was sitting primly at the edge of my bed. Prince lay on the floor, his tongue hanging out as if amused.

"Dai," I hissed, "you shouldn't be in here!" Though she had snuck into my room at all hours during our youth, the dragon had put her foot down a couple of years before and had promised dire consequences if we were ever caught.

I would never take advantage. Dai knew this, but convincing the dragon was another matter. It wasn't that she didn't trust me, exactly, but she preferred to keep temptation out of reach. After having to deal with Pierce, I understood her point of view a little better than before.

So why had she risked coming in here? I glanced at my clock.

It looked like I'd forgotten to set my alarm. It was half past eight. Luckily for me, the family slept in on Sundays since they did not attend church. Rosa would be up early, attending mass at the Church of the Blessed Sacrament before joining us later. Dallas had a healthy Catholic base, though most churches were Baptist. The lack of Buddhist temples—or even any knowledge of Confucianism or Taoism—kept the Wus' worship centered around the home.

Dai grinned. "Then I guess you better get up in a hurry then."

"I will, as soon as you get out."

She placed a hand over her heart and batted her lashes at me. "I'm blind, you know; it's not like I'd see anything I wasn't supposed to."

"That won't mean much to either of your parents, as you well know. So shoo."

Soft laughter trailed after her as she took pity on me and left.

Prince still sat before me, tongue lolling.

"Get out, you mutt." I waved him toward the door. "I'll serve your breakfast soon enough." He could have gotten here ahead of Dai and woken me, something of which we were both aware. Whatever impish impulses were driving Dai this morning, they looked to be contagious.

I locked my door just in case. It wouldn't do to take unnecessary chances. Dai's mood seemed lighter than I had anticipated. With the adventure almost over, I would have expected a more lethargic atmosphere.

Rushing through my shower and toilette, I got dressed. I found Dai at the kitchen table, nibbling on a cookie, Prince beside her lapping up any escaping crumbs.

"Eager to get going, are we?" I grabbed a frying pan, thinking eggs, toast, and fruit might best serve for today as they'd be quick to fix. Our congee reserves were low, so I'd start a batch for tomorrow's breakfast later in the day, saving what we had for the older Wus when they rose. With Dai rising so early, I had a feeling we wouldn't be here by the time the others woke.

"I do have work to do," she said. "I'd like to get it out of the way before we meet with the constable. Calling from father's office at the laundry will also keep our business from possibly being overheard and derailed."

Yes, that definitely sounded like the prudent course.

In short order, I served Dai her breakfast before going outside to pick up the milk delivery and feeding Prince. Then I had my own. I prepared a note for the Wus, telling them where we could be found as well as mentioning the covered dishes so they could help themselves to breakfast when they woke.

Dai dressed, and I packed away something more appropriate for her to change into once her work at the laundry was done.

I considered us quite fortunate at our undisturbed escape.

I picked up a newspaper on the way, but didn't see any headlines about the arrest. One nice point about meeting the constable at the laundry was that it would help keep our involvement a secret. The last thing the Wu family needed was to have any attention drawn to them over a murder.

After grabbing all the items she would need, Dai mixed the batches for the week. I sat down to entertain myself with the paper, though I didn't get far. I couldn't concentrate, and kept checking my watch and the clock on the wall. There was no reason for it, but I still felt jittery and nervous.

Dai seemed unfazed by the coming meeting, her hands as steady as ever. Prince also appeared unconcerned, napping at her feet.

Around eleven, I headed to the office upstairs to try to finalize the meeting time. Aiden picked up right away, as if she'd been waiting for our call. "Campbell residence."

"Good morning. This is Jacques."

"Good morning!" While the original greeting had been stiff, this one was much more relaxed and warmer.

"We're at the laundry, so whenever it's convenient for you and the constable to come over, we'll be ready."

"That's great. Should we come in from the back?" she asked.

"Yes, please. The door will be unlocked."

The silence lingered for a moment before she spoke again. "Is it strange that I feel nervous about this? I've written plenty of reports for George and the judge before."

I smiled, glad I wasn't the only one. "It's probably because you've never been on this side of things before. To be honest, I've been feeling a little nervous myself."

"Really?" She sounded truly surprised. It was rather amusing.

"Yes, really. I've done nothing close to this before."

"You'll do fine," she said. "I've no doubts about that."

The tips of my ears felt hot. "Thank you, Aiden. I'm sure we'll get through it together."

They were still warm when I made my way back downstairs.

"All is well?" Dai was placing the lid on the last batch of laundry cleaning chemicals.

"Yes. Aiden is going to round up the constable for us and bring him here. You should have time enough to change and eat something before they get here." I'd brought some sandwiches and fruit with us from the house; they were in the refrigerator upstairs.

About an hour later, our visitors arrived. I'd brewed some iced tea and already had the pitcher and glasses at the table.

"Good afternoon, constable," Dai said. "Did you have any problems finding the place?"

"No, ma'am. Dr. Campbell helped me find the right building."

Higgins was wearing a nice suit, more than likely the same he'd worn to Sunday service. Aiden was in her preferred slacks, shirt, and vest.

"I hope this isn't too inconvenient for you," Dai said. "I hate to take you away from your family on your day off."

"With the judge out of town, they kind of expect it." Higgins scratched behind his ear. "I promised to make it up to them this evening with some ice cream." He grinned. "My Gretchen forgives a lot of sins for a scoop of good vanilla with caramel sauce."

I served everyone tea, then sat down with my own glass.

The constable pulled a pencil and notebook from the inside of his jacket. "I heard back from Scotland Yard. They not only found the place she bought the arsenic but dug up some information on Mrs. Grey."

Dai sat forward. "Do tell."

He flipped through his pad for a moment. "Amelia Grey, married at eighteen, widowed at twenty, no children of her own. She's served the Asquith family since she was an adolescent girl, and they took her in when her husband died. Raised all the Asquith offspring. Their father was prime minister during the war, and the family moved up in the world about five years ago when he was elevated to an earl, which made them nobility or something. The inspector seemed to think this was quite an enormous deal. Said it would increase not only the family's status but also that of those working for them. Sounded rather strange to me, to be honest."

"Which part, constable?" Dai asked.

He tapped the pencil on the table. "Well, if you're a nanny for a family, how does one of them becoming an earl make you any more than what you were already? A nanny is still a nanny, right?"

"I would normally agree with you, Constable Higgins, but recently I've learned that some people enjoy thinking they are above others. While we don't have a monarchy here, such things seem incredibly important overseas."

I didn't say it out loud, but people living abroad weren't the only ones who seemed to consider themselves better than those around them. I had yet to see any evidence proving they actually were.

"As you say, Miss. Mrs. Grey has never been in any trouble, though she's been known to shore up the family's interests with some zeal. Sometimes a bit too much of it, from what they said."

"What else did they tell you?" Dai asked.

"Purchases of arsenic are written down at drug dispensaries because a lot of folks buy it for rat poison and some for monkey business. Though not in Chinatown, where it's sold for medicinal purposes. But they still make a note of who's buying it. That's where they found an entry for Mrs. Grey."

Dai nodded as if having expected nothing else.

"Now, if you wouldn't mind, Miss, walk me through the crime."

She nodded again, hesitating for a moment as if putting her mental documents in order. "I imagine it began innocently enough: Asquith sent a telegram home to give them the news of the engagement. The more the group found out about Laura, the more 'inappropriate' she seemed. I'm sure Mrs. Grey was not the only one who was less than excited about welcoming an orphan—and an American one, at that—into their family. Direct and indirect means would have been used to get him to either postpone or cancel the betrothal.

"When that didn't work, Mrs. Grey might have approached the busy parents and suggested coming to meet the interloper. That would have set things in motion. She was quite capable of manipulating the more malleable Mr. and Mrs. Domberry, and I'm sure her coming along would have appeared to be someone else's suggestion. All the better for meeting the upstart American and breaking her hold on Mrs. Grey's dear charge."

Despite knowing most of the same facts, I was as spellbound as the others while Dai laid out the awful plot of Laura Cooper's demise.

She took a sip of her iced tea. "Upon learning that some of his family were coming to visit, William made a request. He asked them to bring one of the ballgowns his mother no longer used, so he could give it to Laura as a present. He'd surely been lavishing her with stories about being an earl's son, and I am certain she'd been fascinated with the pomp and circumstance of British royalty, something a Texas orphan had never dreamed she might experience. Sadly, this gave Mrs. Grey the very means for removing her."

"I don't quite follow what you mean." Higgins tapped the pencil on the table again, a confused look on his face. "Why would a dress make a difference?"

Dai's brow rose. "If it came to it, deniability. You see, while those of the younger generation wouldn't necessarily know of it, Mrs. Grey is old enough to remember that arsenic was, in the past, used to create the color green for dyeing clothes and wallpapers. This caused workers and consumers to get sick when the concentrations were too high. There were even documented cases where people died from it."

"Whoa, hold on!" The constable leaned back in a hurry, staring down at his green tie. "I never heard of such a thing!"

"It's nothing to worry about now," Dai assured him. "Other means for creating the color were eventually found and there are more laws in place now regulating how things are done. But this knowledge of the past problems gave her the idea of using the dress as a weapon. She couldn't guarantee it would cause Laura to be sick, however, so she took steps to make sure. So she went to Chinatown to buy what she needed."

"The Yard said proper ladies rarely visited the place, it being near the docks. It's considered slums." The constable's eyes glittered as he waited to see what Dai would make of that.

If he meant to trip her up, he would be sorely disappointed. Her dimpled grin told as much.

"Mr. Domberry frequents the area. As Mrs. Domberry's childhood nanny and continued confidant, and the fact that Paul Domberry is something of a boisterous character, she would have had plenty of opportunities to hear about the place."

The constable made some quick notations in his notebook.

"Mrs. Grey would have taken the responsibility of packaging the gown. This would give her ample opportunity to dissolve the arsenic in water and paint it on the inside and outside of the dress. The dissolved poison would be colorless and odorless, making it hard to detect. She most likely made sure no one else came in contact with it. And no one would have questioned her taking charge of this—she was not only a servant of the household who would naturally take care of such things for her charges; she was a fixture in their lives, trusted and by some even revered.

"We learned from Shannon Daugherty that Laura immediately fell in love with the dress, dancing around their apartment with it on at every opportunity, unknowingly contaminating herself each time. William would hear nothing of calling off the engagement, too besotted to care about their objections. So despite the fact Mrs. Grey could have halted the poisoning, she did nothing."

Aiden visibly shivered, her expression troubled. I felt much the same. It was hard to imagine how a human being could begin such a thing and watch it unfold, yet do nothing to stop it because it served her selfish ends and feelings of superiority.

"Laura's constitution was known not to be the best, so when she first started getting ill, no one thought much of it. That she was suffering from the effects of poison wouldn't have occurred to any of them. As we learned from Aiden's research into the matter, when Laura finally sought medical care, the clinic she visited missed the signs of what was actually happening to her. Which was a grave pity—they might have been able to save her.

"Constable, this next bit is pure conjecture, but can be verified by asking the right questions of the others involved."

Dai paused to drink again, as if to give us time to reinforce ourselves for what would follow.

"Mrs. Grey may have volunteered—or, as William's nanny, been asked by Asquith—to help watch over Laura. Entrusting the woman who'd been a surrogate mother with his most prized possession, William would never have suspected her of any evil intent. Then more arsenic—soluble, tasteless, and odorless unless heated—was introduced into Laura's system under the guise of tender care, until she finally passed."

It was my turn to shiver, though Dai had mentioned something similar at the hospital. I just couldn't grasp how someone could start such suffering and knowingly make it worse until it ended in death. A love so strong and singular that, to protect its object, others turned from people into mere obstacles to be dealt with. I slipped a glance in Dai's direction. While I understood only too well the first part, I hoped I would never be so blinded as to fall into the trap of the second.

"Dang, these British have ice in their veins." The constable rubbed at his arms as if chilled.

"Sadly, we all hold the capacity to commit horrid acts," Dai said. "We are all selfish creatures in our own way. If we forget that others are as important as ourselves and turn our backs on empathy and mercy, we are lost."

Silence reigned for a moment as we all contemplated what had been revealed.

"God smiled on us when she chose to drop the dress at your laundry, Miss." The constable shook his head. "If not for that marvelous nose of yours and our Texas heat, we might have never known someone murdered one of our own—let alone been able to bring them to justice."

"I wonder if Mrs. Grey realizes what she's truly done." Aiden's voice was small, a sorrowful look on her face.

"What do you mean?" I asked.

"By killing Laura, she stole William's happiness—a happiness he might never find again. But she did more than that. Mrs. Grey also destroyed his childhood, and Lizzie's. She betrayed their love and their trust. All their memories will be tainted by the evil she has done. She has tarnished their souls forever."

The constable stood up, putting away his notepad and pencil. "I've got a feeling she'll get plenty of time to realize what pain she's caused to those she loves. All we can do for her victims is to pray for them, and make sure justice is served."

CHAPTER 46

The meeting broke up after that, leaving us all with much to think about.

Dai and I remained at the laundry, while the constable offered Aiden a ride back before returning to his family. I tidied up the break room and washed the glasses we used, my thoughts heavy. While I was glad we had been able to bring Laura's murderer to justice, the collateral damage established the victory as a rather bitter one.

"I suppose we should head on home once you're finished, Jacques." Dai reached down to pet Prince, who rolled onto his back and made sure his furred belly was within her reach.

Though I had expected it, it still made me a little sad to hear the touch of despondency in her voice now that the case was over. She had experienced more in the last few days than in the last five years put together.

"You were magnificent, Dai. No one else could have pulled this off like you did." I would need to find a way to distract her. Perhaps inviting Aiden for a visit in a few days would do the trick. Meeting her had been the bright spot in this ugly business. I would be more than happy for Dai to forget this—and the fact Pierce existed. "Though I must admit, even with your bodyguard in place, my heart almost stopped when Mrs. Grey grabbed you."

Her fearless guardian was currently wriggling in pleasure at his mistress' ministrations.

"I doubt we'll ever have a situation like that come up again." The wistful tone lacing her words contrasted with my relief at hearing them.

While I was glad she'd made new friends and solved the prickly mystery, I could have done without the dangers she had encountered, both socially and physically. I would be more than thrilled to never run such risks again.

But even as I thought that, I felt the nape of my neck prickle, as if it knew something I did not.

The End?

Thank you for reading **Black Jade**! I hope you found it as much fun to read as it was to write it. Please take a moment to leave a one or two sentence review at your favorite online retailer. It makes a BIG difference!

Send me a link to the review, and I will send you a FREE Daiyu Wu prequel short story called "Jacques."

Also, get "Elixir of Life" an urban fantasy short story as a gift, if you subscribe to my Newsletter.

Contact form and subscribe page are at www.gloriaoliver.com

THANK YOU!

OTHER WORKS BY GLORIA OLIVER

SCIENCE FICTION

Alien Redemption - What if the savior was the one who needed saving?

https://www.gloriaoliver.com/alien-redemption/

FANTASY

Inner Demons - It took everything from her, except revenge!

https://www.gloriaoliver.com/inner-demons

Vassal of El - Torn between two worlds, will he be able to save either of them?

https://www.gloriaoliver.com/vassal-of-el/

The Price of Mercy - Which is worse…the monster within or without?

https://www.gloriaoliver.com/the-price-of-mercy

Jewel of the Gods - Long Live the King! But will he?

https://www.gloriaoliver.com/jewel-of-the-gods

YOUNG ADULT

In the Service of Samurai - The choice: Serve the undead or become one of them.

https://www.gloriaoliver.com/in-the-service-of-samurai

Cross-eyed Dragon Troubles - Talia didn't want to be apprenticed, not even to the prestigious Dragon Knight's Guild.

https://www.gloriaoliver.com/cross-eyed-dragon-troubles/

Willing Sacrifice - To save the world, she must die! Or must she?

https://www.gloriaoliver.com/willing-sacrifice

HORROR/ALTERNATE HISTORY

Charity and Sacrifice (Novelette) - Trapped in a loveless marriage, will Elizabeth's sacrifice to regain Robert's attention be in vain?

https://www.gloriaoliver.com/charity-and-sacrifice/

www.gloriaoliver.com

ABOUT THE AUTHOR

Gloria Oliver lives in Texas making sure to stay away from rolling tumbleweeds while bowing to the never-ending wishes of her feline and canine masters. She works full time shoveling numbers around for an oil & gas company and squeezes in some writing time when she can.

"Black Jade" is Gloria's first cozy historical mystery novel. This is also her ninth book to see publication. Her previous works have been fantasy, urban fantasy, science fiction, and young adult fantasy novels. Several contain romantic and mystery elements. Her short stories of speculative fiction can be found in all manner of anthologies, covering things from the fantastic and strange to a Bubba Apocalypse.

Gloria is a member in good standing of BroadUniverse though she has yet to make the list for Cat Slaves R Us.

For some free reads, novel related short stories, sample chapters, appearance schedules and more information on her and her works, please drop by and visit her at www.gloriaoliver.com

Made in the USA
Coppell, TX
19 January 2022

71923425R00146